Erik's

SALVATION

BEAUTIFUL PIECES 💔 BOOK ONE

NYSSA KATHRYN

ERIK'S SALVATION
Copyright © 2023 Nyssa Kathryn Sitarenos

An NW Partners Book
Cover by Deranged Doctor Design
Developmentally and Copy Edited by Kelli Collins
Line Edited by Jessica Snyder
Proofread by Amanda Cuff and Jen Katemi
Cover Photography by Andrey Bahia at Wander Book Club

She'll mend his broken heart. He'll shatter anew to protect her.

Hannah Jacobs is intimately familiar with pain. Growing up in foster care, she experienced all of its varying shades, in ways that still impact her as an adult. But she makes a daily conscious effort to overcome her past, to bear the heartache of losing her only source of care and support, and to live her life with purpose…

Purpose like her new neighbor.

Hannah recognizes another broken soul when she sees one. Erik isn't open to healing, but she's never shied away from a challenge. Even if she did…something won't let her stop chipping away at the man's nearly impenetrable exterior.

Life as he knew it shattered for Erik Hunter in the space of a single phone call, leaving pieces so small and jagged, he fears they'll never be put back together. He's a different person now. Largely estranged from his family and doing dangerous work for the government, when he moves back to his hometown, he's seeking peace and solitude.

He didn't count on his neighbor. Her determination, her indomitable will, her beauty. She makes him want something he hasn't had in years. More terrifyingly…she gives him something to lose.

Turns out that fear is well founded. When a faceless enemy emerges, Erik must risk everything to protect Hannah—or see his world shatter again.

Acknowledgments

I have so many people to thank on this one.

Savannah, you read my messy first draft to check that Hannah's Type 1 Diabetes was authentic and accurate. Your insight and willingness to help made such a difference. Thank you.

Kelli, you always put so much time and effort into making sure my plot is solid. I appreciate your honesty and dedication and the way you answer my countless questions.

Jessica, thank you for your seamless line edits. You ensure I don't reuse the same word a dozen times and that my sentences read well.

To my proofreaders, Amanda and Jen, thank you for being that last line of defence. You give me confidence to release my book baby into the world.

To every member of my ARC team, thank you. I so appreciate the time it takes to not only read but also review my work. I read every one of your reviews, and they are everything.

Thank you to my readers. If you picked up this book, you are the reason the next gets written.

And, finally, thank you to my beautiful husband, Will, for steering this ship, and making sure I have the capacity to do what I do. You are the most beautiful husband and father anyone could ask for.

And thank you to my daughter, Sophia. My work takes time away from us, but I hope that in watching me do what I love and support our family, you can see how powerful women can be.

Prologue

Some people find art in broken pieces. Beauty in fragile things.

Those people know that broken doesn't mean the end. Rather, it could be the beginning. Of something new. Something that's been fixed and made whole again.

The cracks will still be visible, the tears and frays like little fractures of a story. But they're supposed to be visible. Evidence of strength and a will to survive. A history that wouldn't have been known otherwise.

It's only when something breaks that one can realize it wasn't the art that was beautiful, it's the pieces.

Chapter One

"Mr. Bonetti! Hi."

Hannah Jacobs fumbled the cell phone against her ear as she tried to balance the box of lingerie in her left arm. It was awkward, especially when she also had a grocery bag filled with cereal in that hand.

The cereal? Totally worth keeping. The box of lingerie her best friend Brigid had asked her to pick up from the post office? Debatable.

"Miss Jacobs. Have I caught you at a bad time?"

Uh, yeah. It was five o'clock on a Friday afternoon, and after she delivered this box, she had a night of the new season of *Survivor* and a tub of bubbles waiting. But man, was she desperate to sell one of this guy's mega-mansions. She'd probably talk to him in a pool of snakes if she had to.

"No, not a bad time at all. Have you put any more thought into who you'd like to sell your home?"

Please say me. Please say me.

She wasn't above begging. Not when she was about a day and a bill away from selling her right kidney.

Yeah, times were tough when the new real estate agency in town was getting all the business.

Mr. Bonetti cleared his throat. "I have some questions, if that's okay?"

The box slipped down her hip. She stopped and leaned against a wall in an attempt to shuffle it up. "Of course. Ask me anything. I'm an open book, Mr. Bonetti."

She was also a step away from teetering off balance and landing on her butt. *Jesus, Brigid, you owe me for this one.*

"Please, call me Angelo. How long have you been selling in the area?"

"Four years. I'm very familiar with homes in the Redwood and Leavenworth area. And before moving here, I was selling in Seattle."

She'd been selling in Redwood, Washington, and the neighboring Leavenworth as long as she'd been living here. And to say she loved this small town was an understatement. The place had felt like home within the first day. Good coffee. Good people. What else could a girl need?

She started moving again, her gaze shifting to the end of the street. A man stood on the sidewalk. One look at him made her steps falter. He was tall, maybe six and a half feet? Certainly a lot taller than her five foot seven. His hands were shoved into his pockets, and the black material of his shirt pulled across his muscles. And his shoulders... God, how were they so broad?

The box started to slip again, and she quickly jostled it to gain a better hold.

"Miss Jacobs?"

Crap. She'd been so busy ogling Broad Shoulders that she'd missed what Angelo had said. "Hannah, please, and sorry, could you repeat the question?"

"Do you have references?"

She passed the giant hulk of a man, stepping into the road,

attempting to play it cool with a small straightening of her spine and the click of her heels against the asphalt.

"I do have references. I can email them over to you if you'd like?"

Thud.

Crap! The box landed right in the middle of the damn road. Great.

"I'm so sorry, Angelo, I'm going to need to call you back. I have a…situation."

A box of lingerie falling from her grasp in the middle of a street counted as a situation, didn't it? Thank God there wasn't any traffic.

"Of course, Miss Jacobs. I'll call on Monday."

She cringed, hating to end the call like this. *Damn you, Brigid.*

Once the phone was in her pocket, she started to bend when a loud, deep voice shouted from behind, causing her to jump.

"Watch out!"

A body suddenly collided with hers, then she was flying, the whip of the air brushing across her face as a car sped past. The world was a blur as she gritted her teeth, preparing for impact with the ground—but the person turned so they landed on the pavement, and she landed on top of them.

For a moment, there was stillness, not even the whistle of the wind. Once the shock passed, she pushed against a very hard chest to look into the most intensely beautiful set of hazel eyes she'd ever seen.

Man, he was gorgeous. And that short, thick brown hair had her fingers twitching to run through the strands.

Her breath stalled as his crisp pine scent filled her lungs. She opened her mouth to say hi, to maybe slip in a marriage proposal, but he spoke first.

"What the hell were you thinking?"

Her lips snapped shut, the heated air turning cold.

Well, he sounded far from the Prince Charming she'd pegged him for in her mind.

He stood, pulling her to her feet as he went. Then he towered over her. "What were you thinking?" he repeated. "Crossing a street on the phone while carrying so much shit? Were you trying to get yourself killed?"

Okay, so Mr. Tall, Dark and Handsome wasn't going to be her softly spoken knight in shining armor. Fantasy officially dead. "A lot of people talk on the phone while carrying stuff."

"You shouldn't. It's dangerous." His gaze shifted behind her. "Also, there are panties all over the road."

For a single heartbeat, she was distracted by the way he'd said panties in that deep, erotic, raspy voice. Then his words computed in her brain, and she spun around to see, yep, there were women's panties everywhere. Dozens of red lace panties. Black thongs. Hell, there were even purple pairs with little black love hearts.

Heat blasted her cheeks, and she made a silent vow to murder her best friend.

She turned back to Mr. Tall, Dark and Grumpy—yeah, his nickname continued to change—and worked hard to keep her embarrassment at a normal face-isn't-a-complete-tomato level. "It's for a friend. She runs a lingerie shop."

He didn't seem to care about her explanation. "You need to be more careful."

Some of the earlier heat returned to her cheeks, her heart thumping that this man would care about her safe—

"I don't need to spend my Friday nights saving women I don't know."

Her jaw dropped. Was he trying to be an ass, or did it just come naturally?

She cleared her throat. "Well, lucky for you, we'll probably never see each other again." She straightened, trying to regain just an ounce of dignity and control. "Thank you for saving me. I'm going to go now."

He shoved a hand into his pocket. "Need help getting your stuff off the road?" His tone told her he'd rather bathe in lava.

"No. Thank you. I'll text my friend to come down and help me." Then she'd kill her and hide the evidence. "I'll need her to bring a new box anyway," she muttered to herself, gaze moving to the sad-looking broken box sitting off to one side. The guy who'd hit it hadn't even stopped.

And her poor cereal. Frosted Flakes. Cocoa Krispies. Honey Nut Cheerios. The boxes were crushed.

Farewell, dinner.

"Are you sure?"

She switched her attention to the grump of a man. He seemed reluctant to leave her on the sidewalk alone. Maybe he wasn't such an ass. "Yes, I'm sure. But thank you."

A beat passed as his intense hazel eyes bore into hers. Then he nodded. "Okay."

He started to turn, but she touched his arm and, when he looked at her again, she said quietly, "Again, thank you."

He may be an ass, but he was an ass who'd just saved her from a trip to the emergency room. If she wasn't going to give him a marriage proposal, she may as well give him her gratitude.

His jaw ticked. "Don't do it again."

⊂⊃

ERIK HUNTER STEPPED inside the large old house. An eerie quiet surrounded him, the only noise the creaking of the wooden floorboards beneath his feet. Musky pine scented the air and just a hint of whiskey and mint.

That almost had Erik's lips twitching. The old man had been gone for months, yet the place still smelled like him. He shouldn't be surprised. Fifty years in a house meant it wasn't just a home, it was part of the fabric of a person.

The late-afternoon sun cast a dim glow over the large living area. Memories tried to slip into his head. Memories of the person he was the last time he'd been here. The uncomplicated life he'd led. It was only eight years ago, but it felt like a lifetime. Because that man had been another fucking person.

He ran a finger over his brown leather couch. Movers had been here earlier in the day, getting his shit loaded into the place. The house still didn't feel like his. Why his grandfather had left it to him, he had no fucking clue. Maybe to get him back here? Back in Redwood. Back with his family.

Family...the word felt heavy. Like a rock on his chest that pressed and weighed him down until he couldn't suck in a single full breath.

He dropped his bag, the thud whipping through the silent room like a bullet.

Every corner of this house held a memory. Holidays with family. Playing with his brother and sister. Eating around the large table.

A collection of moments, each running into the other and painting a picture of his childhood.

He lifted a framed photo from the fireplace, one of the few belongings of his grandfather's that remained. He stared at his fourteen-year-old self, standing between his younger brother and sister. The teenager who smiled back was happy. Had dreams of becoming a Marine, joining the special operations community.

He had no idea of the evil in the world. The fucking torture that was to come.

The ringing of his phone cut through his thoughts. He pulled it from his pocket, not surprised to see Chandler's name on the screen. Chandler wasn't just the tech guy who helped him with jobs. He'd also become a friend. A right-hand man. Barely a day passed when they didn't talk.

"Was wondering how long it would take for you to call," Erik said quietly, running his finger over the dusty mantel.

"Well, when I saw you were in Redwood, I almost fell off my fucking chair. You're not supposed to get there until Friday."

His lips twitched. He wasn't surprised by Chandler's tone. The guy wasn't just his eyes and ears, the person who found the information no one else could find, he also dealt with home security—security Erik didn't have yet.

"I decided to come early."

"You just decided? Is there even fucking power in the house?"

"I think you need a vacation."

Chandler let out a slew of curses, which made Erik's impulsive decision to come up early feel worth it.

"In your line of work, you can't just up and go whenever you want," Chandler barked. "You need a security system in place. We need to vet the neighbors."

"I'm on four acres," he said, moving toward the window at the side of the house. "The only house within sight is an old piece of shit that no one would ever—"

What the fuck?

What had always been a falling-down shack that resembled a pile of rotting wood was now a house.

"I have a neighbor." For as long as he'd been alive, that house had been deserted. Hell, he and his siblings used to pretend it was a fort and play in it.

"See," Chandler barked, laptop keys dinging in the background. "Should have given me some damn time to look into things."

"I want a full background check on whoever lives there."

Fuck. He thought he'd be alone out here. It was part of the

lure of coming home. To see his family but still have his space. His land. Windows looking out onto nothing.

"I'll have the information within the hour."

And Chandler would. If there was information to find, he'd dig it up. He could hack any system. Find any information, even if it was supposed to be buried. Dead. Gone.

"And Hunter…" Chandler paused. "Welcome home."

Erik's gut clenched. Home. This was his goddamn home now.

"Thanks." He hung up, his gaze moving to the dark kitchen before returning to that framed photo, memories once again trying to prick at his mind. Good memories, but also heavy.

He blew out a breath and focused on a chipped corner of the fireplace. This house needed work, and that work would take a while because this place was huge. But that was fine. He'd already decided to take a couple months off work to get everything fixed.

He was about to get more of his shit out of the garage when a car sounded outside. His hand twitched to reach for the Glock in its holster. Both his house and the one next door were shielded from traffic noise by long driveways, so the car must be his neighbor's. He could only hope they didn't have people over often.

Beyond the window, a small red Honda was pulling in. It stopped in front of the house on the gravel drive. When a woman stepped out, his eyes narrowed.

Average height, long, flowing blonde hair. But it was the clothes that caught his attention. A tight skirt that hit her knees and a blazer. Clothes he'd seen earlier that day.

Because he'd seen *her*.

No fucking way. The woman with the box of underwear, who'd almost gotten herself killed, was his neighbor? The one with piercing blue eyes and a body so damn soft he'd had to force himself to release her?

He watched as she grabbed some bags from the back and disappeared into the house.

Every part of him already rebelled against having a neighbor. But her? A woman who looked so fucking innocent she just needed a damn halo to complete the image?

He grabbed his bag with too much force and went upstairs, shoving thoughts of the woman out of his head. He hadn't planned to sleep in his grandfather's old room, but this was where his shit had been placed by the movers, so it looked like the decision was made.

It only took a few minutes to unpack what he needed for the night, then he pulled the curtain back from the window. The entire front part of his land was visible from here and just a hint of the neighboring house.

He was about to turn when he saw movement from the other side of the fence.

Erik stared at the woman. She'd changed into a large, oversized sweatshirt and the shortest denim shorts he'd ever seen. Fuck, he could almost see her ass.

It was damn cold outside. What the hell was she thinking?

The sun hit her hair, making it glow. Making her look even more like a damn angel.

An angel who was opening the side gate separating their properties and stepping onto his land.

Chapter Two

Cereal. It was the food of the gods. The nourishment that kept all the had-a-long-day-and-can't-even-turn-on-the-burner type people alive. Today, it kept *her* type of people alive.

It was also the one food Hannah refused to give up for her type 1 diabetes. Technically, she could eat whatever she wanted, she just had to give herself the right amount of insulin. But, as a fully functioning adult, she tried to eat a balanced diet.

Not tonight. Because tonight, all she could think about was her near-death experience. Oh, and those beautiful hazel eyes and that big, strong back... God, who was she kidding? It wasn't just his back that was perfectly sculpted. It was all of him. Every. Beautiful. Inch.

She lifted the spoon to her mouth, trying her best to ignore the pile of bills to her left. Her stomach sank anyway. The pile was big, and it was expanding every month.

It was officially time for her to start applying for second jobs. Goodbye spare time. It would be hard, but she was used to hard. She'd had it hard her whole life and had always come out the other side stronger.

She spooned another heap of cereal into her mouth, turning toward the view outside the kitchen window, and almost sighed.

Spectacular. And it made every hard moment of her life worth it. She still had to pinch herself to prove that she wasn't dreaming. That she owned this land.

The house was small, only one bedroom, and when she'd bought it, it hadn't been even close to habitable. But her friends had pitched in to help renovate, and she'd spent close to a year making it livable, including completely gutting the old bathroom and combining it with the previous second bedroom to create a walk-in closet and new primary bath.

The home wasn't anything spectacular, but it was hers. And that was more than she'd ever had before. Now she had peace and quiet. Empty land.

Well, empty bar Mr. Hunter's home, which wasn't so much a home as it was a two-story mansion. She had a view of the side of his house and part of the backyard from her kitchen window.

Her heart gave a sad little turn at the memory of Mr. Hunter. God, she missed him. His smiles as he watered his plants. The low hum of his voice as he sang under his breath. The man had loved nature and music.

At least he was with his wife now.

She scooped up some more cereal, almost groaning when the honeyed goodness hit her tongue.

Her phone vibrated on the counter. She smiled when she saw it was a text from Brigid, regaling Henry with their tale of picking up the panties from the road. The three of them had a group chat that never silenced for long. What did they send, two, maybe three hundred messages a day?

Brigid: Norman passed us and offered to help. I thought the poor old man was going to have a heart attack when he picked up a lace thong.

Hannah laughed. It was true. Norman was sixty and ran

the local coffee shop, Black Bean, with his wife. When he'd seen the chaos, he'd offered to help, but she was almost certain he'd regretted his decision when he'd had to actually touch the sexy lingerie.

Henry: Ladies, let's not give Norman a heart attack. I rely on his coffee to survive.

Hannah: Um…what about poor Hannah? I almost got hit by a car…

Brigid: You were saved by a hot guy, Hannah. I do not feel sorry for you.

Henry: Oh. Tell me more about the hot guy.

Hannah: No. He may have been good-looking, but he wasn't very nice.

Brigid: They're always the best in bed, Han. And you could use some good sex.

She'd had plenty of sex. Maybe not recently. But she was not so desperate that she'd consider Mr. Grump.

Henry: She's right, Han. You've been stressed.

Brigid: James said if you're feeling overworked, he'll take some of your houses.

Over her dead body! James was another agent who worked at Reuben's Real Estate. And just like her, he was struggling with the competing business in town. It was seriously slim pickings.

Hannah: I don't think so.

Henry: Tell James to get his own damn houses. Our girl works hard and needs her commissions.

Brigid: I did tell him that. But he's been stressed, so I'm not getting enough sexy time.

Hannah grinned. Brigid was not shy about her sex life. At the start of their friendship, the amount of information she'd disclosed about her sex life with James had been kind of awkward. But four years later, Hannah was used to it…kind of.

Henry: Tell the man to get it up! His woman has needs.

Brigid: Oh, don't worry…I have been. What are you having for dinner?

Hannah: Cereal.

Brigid: Again?

Henry: Didn't you have that last night?

Dammit. She had. Tomorrow, she was making a chicken salad. She'd send a picture to her friends just to keep herself accountable.

Henry was a construction worker, but he didn't fit the stereotype. He was too clean-cut and easy to talk to. Brigid had introduced them shortly after Hannah had moved to Redwood, and she'd never looked back.

Hannah: Maybe.

She ate another mouthful of cereal, her gaze catching on the flower beds at the back of Mr. Hunter's house.

Crap, she'd almost forgotten about the flowers.

Her phone kept dinging, but she left it beside her half-empty bowl. The two of them would keep going. She'd probably return to a stream of fifty unread messages she'd have no hope of catching up on.

The old wooden floorboards creaked beneath her feet as she donned her boots, and the second she stepped outside, a gust of wind blasted her skin, causing her flesh to pebble.

Holy cow, it was cold! Unseasonably cold for the start of October in Redwood. Were they really out of sunshine already? God, winter would be long.

For a moment, she considered going back inside and changing into sweats, or at least a piece of clothing that would cover her legs, but she quickly shoved that idea away. She'd be quick.

She pulled the door closed and crossed the yard to the gate between the properties. The flowers had been Mr. Hunter's pride and joy. Every morning and night, she'd watched him go out there, water them, weed. Sometimes, just stand by the little garden and admire the buds. There was often a sadness to him when he did so. Like he was remembering his wife.

Sometimes she'd go over and talk to him. Bring him some coffee or food. It was just a week before he passed that he'd asked her to water the flowers when he couldn't anymore. Like he'd known he wasn't going to be there much longer.

There'd been so much emotion in his voice…his eyes. So she'd said yes. She'd promised the older man that she would keep them alive.

Keeping her head down to protect her neck from the wind, she slipped through the gate and beelined for the bed of flowers against the back of the house. There were golden asters and coneflowers. Hibiscus and lavender. She didn't regret for a second that she'd promised to look after them. They deserved to be kept alive.

When she reached the bed, she grabbed the watering can and filled it from the wall spigot, wondering again who was paying the bills for this house. Mr. Hunter had passed away at least three months ago, and it had sat empty for just as long, but the water was still on.

Did whoever had inherited it intend to sell?

At first she'd been hopeful that his family would ask *her* to sell it. She'd never met them, though she'd seen a few people regularly coming and going from his place while he'd been alive. But the weeks had turned into months, and the place had never been listed.

Once the watering can was full, she started with the hibiscus. She wasn't a gardener by any means. A person just had to look at her yard to know that. But over the last few months, she'd found peace in this. Also pride in seeing a plant live and grow because of the water she fed it. She'd even started weeding the garden.

She lowered to her haunches, giving the delicate lavender a bit of extra love.

Once every plant had been watered, she smiled as she rose —and almost ran smack into a tall, dark figure.

She screamed and swung the watering can like a machete. The figure dodged the hit easily, but her arm kept swinging and she lost her balance. She would have fallen if long fingers hadn't wrapped around her upper arm, tugging her up.

The second she looked into those hazel eyes, everything stopped. Her movement. The rise and fall of her chest.

"You!" she gasped. "Did you…did you follow me home?"

Oh, Jesus, was this man some woman-stalking crazy person? Was he here to kill her? Could such a beautiful man even *be* a killer?

Of course he could. Ted Bundy hadn't been terrible looking, and he'd turned out to be one of the worst serial killers in history.

She was just spiraling down a Ted-Bundy-followed-me-home well when the guy spoke.

"No, I didn't. Why are you on my land?"

Her mouth dropped open. Did he just… He'd said *his* land, right? Or was that fear-induced psychosis making her hear things? Okay, not all fear. There was a bit of something else. Something hotter that she would not, under any circumstances, be owning up to.

"I…" She shook her head, trying to make her brain process the situation. "Your land?"

"Yeah, honey. You're trespassing."

He stepped away, his fingers finally releasing her, and she almost wanted to tug his hand back and curl those fingers around her arm again.

God, she needed to get her head checked. "No, this was Stanley Hunter's house."

"I'm his grandson."

His grandson? Stanley Hunter had been five feet tall, small-framed and sweet. This man was not any of those things.

17

Granted, he was a good fifty years younger…but still, she hadn't seen him visit Mr. Hunter once.

She fiddled with the little charm on her bracelet—a nervous habit, and this man definitely made her nervous.

"So you didn't follow me here with plans to kill me? You live here?"

His brow lifted. "I didn't follow you here. I don't plan to kill you. And yes, I live here."

She let that information sink in. The ass of a man who'd saved her life was her new neighbor. So they'd be seeing a bit of each other. Meaning, she had to try to be nice to him.

Once the shock had passed, she forced her lips into a smile. "I think we started off on the wrong foot. I'm Hannah Jacobs. I live next door."

She gestured her head over his shoulder toward her place, but his gaze didn't move. It just stuck to her like that Gorilla Glue that was so strong you could glue your fingers together and never get them apart.

"Erik Hunter," he finally said.

Erik…it suited him. Masculine and sexy and—

Argh, what was she thinking? She gave herself a mental shake. The man wasn't sexy—he was dangerous. One look at him and she knew that. "So, you're…living here now?"

"Yes."

"I didn't see you move in."

"Movers were here all day."

She wanted to slap herself. Of course they were. She was at work all day. The man could have been parading around the property naked and she would have had no idea.

When he just kept standing there, looking at her with those intense hazel eyes, she wanted to squirm. It wasn't just his eyes that were intense. All of him was. A big, beautiful, intense—

Shit. Stop it, Hannah.

"Why are you watering the garden?" He tilted his head

toward the bed as if she'd forgotten about its very existence. Which was a fair assumption. He did make her forget about most other things.

"Stanley asked me to before he...passed. I'm sorry, by the way." She swallowed, still hating that he was gone.

"You don't need to do that anymore."

His response came so quickly, she pulled back a bit. "Oh, I don't mind. I promised him I'd keep them alive, and I've actually been enjoying it."

He shoved his hands into his pockets, and when his biceps rippled, she almost swayed toward him. "I'd prefer you didn't. It was nice to meet you, Hannah."

He turned and started walking away. She was just left standing there, mouth open. When he disappeared around the side of the house, she kicked her ass into gear and ran after him.

"Um, sorry," she said when she finally caught up, struggling to match his strides, "but you heard the part where he asked me to, right?"

So where was the thank you? The look of gratitude?

"I did."

Two words...that was it. "Are *you* going to keep them alive now?"

She followed him around the corner to the front of the house and almost crashed into his chest when he suddenly stopped and turned.

Jesus.

"Hannah." A tingle sparked in her lower belly at her name on his lips. "I'm not a flower guy. But I *am* a private guy. So please don't trespass again."

Spark officially extinguished.

Chapter Three

"Well, hello there. You're a bit sexy. And a bit scary."

Hannah's lips quirked at Brigid's words. She and Henry stood at the kitchen window, ogling Erik like he was a piece of meat as he did pull-ups on the tall bar he'd cemented into the ground beside his house.

She shoved a piece of celery into the juicer with a bit more force than she should have. "He's out there every morning."

Every. Freaking. Morning. And always shirtless despite the cold, sweat dripping down his chest as if he'd just been dunked in oil.

It was torture. It was like a piece of cake being put in front of a starving victim. Yes, she was the starving victim. She hadn't dated in an entire year, and now this gorgeous jerk of a man had moved in next door.

She looked out the window for what had to be the third time that morning. *Jesus.* His abdomen rippled on every pull-up.

"Oh. My. Lord." Henry started to fan himself like he was moments from passing out, while Brigid seemed to be salivating.

For a second, Hannah paused on the celery and watched his six-pack glisten with beads of sweat. Something fluttered in her lady parts.

God, get a grip, Hannah. He's just a man.

She'd tried talking to him a couple of times since that fun little *don't trespass* conversation. And, nope, he did not warm up. There had been no smiles. No laughs at her funny little jokes. In fact, he'd looked like he couldn't wait to get away from her.

"Shame the man's about as cheery as a snake." She pushed in another piece of celery, the machine chewing it away to liquid. "I miss Stanley."

Liar. Watching this man go for his shirtless morning run and finish with a series of pull-ups and sit-ups had become an obsession. One she absolutely would not be telling anyone about, especially her nosy, loudmouthed best friends.

"Moody men aren't that bad," Brigid said quietly, eyes stuck to the kitchen window like there was a three-part play happening. "As long as they're good in bed, the man can talk or not talk."

Typical. "James still holding out?"

"No, we did it six ways to Sunday last night."

Hannah pulled a face, trying to delete that little image from her long-term memory.

"But James's body doesn't look like *that*," Henry cut in.

Now Henry was salivating.

Another stick of celery into the juicer.

Hannah shook her head. She loved her friends, she really did, but they were not helping.

She'd met Brigid through James, and after the woman had introduced her to Henry, the three of them had been inseparable. Brigid was the pretty one. Huge brown eyes. Thick red hair that ran down her back, with breasts and hips men fantasized about.

Basically, she was gorgeous, and she knew it. And even

though she joked about Erik, Hannah knew she was completely devoted to James.

Henry was cute, with his hard jaw and short brown hair. He had a nice tan from working as a building contractor and the muscles to go with it.

When the last piece of celery was liquified by the machine, she lifted the jug and split the juice between three cups before handing two of them to her friends. She literally had to jam the glasses into their hands because their entire attention remained outside.

Before drinking hers, she opened a drawer and pulled out her glucose monitor and test strips. After pricking her finger, she placed a drop of blood onto the strip. Her friends had seen her test her glucose so many times they didn't bat an eye. Not that they were looking at her right now.

The number came up and she put away her kit before a quick glance over their heads told her Erik was up to the hanging sit-ups—simultaneously her favorite and most hated part.

"You know," Brigid said suggestively, "he could have set up his little workout area on the other side of the house. It's almost like he *wants* you to watch him."

Henry smirked. "Thank you, Mr. Hunter."

"Don't call him that," Hannah said quickly. "Mr. Hunter is Stanley. That guy is…something else. And no, he probably couldn't cement it into the ground on the other side or something."

That sounded reasonable, right?

"No, he could have put it on the other side." Henry sipped his drink, then spat it back out. "What in the ever-loving hell is this?"

Hannah frowned. "It's celery juice."

Brigid tasted hers and cringed. "It tastes like feet."

"It's worse than feet," Henry said, shaking his head like he was trying to get rid of the very memory of it. "It's like the juicy sweat that comes out of feet."

Brigid pulled a face. "Ew."

"You're so dramatic." Hannah lifted her glass and took a sip. Oh, shit…it *was* like feet juice. "Maybe it's an acquired taste. Some people drink this every morning."

"What people?" Henry asked, eyeing the cup like it held Satan's poison.

Brigid tilted her head. "Why are we drinking this again?"

Hannah tried another sip. If possible, it got worse. "I'm trying to be healthier."

"Because of your diabetes?" Brigid asked.

"No. Celery has literally no carbs in it, so it would do nothing for my blood sugar." Another sip. Yep, still awful. "I'm just trying to be healthier overall."

"This is not the way to do it." Henry tipped his juice down the sink.

"Hey—"

"We'll finish watching this sexy-as-sin man sculpt his body," he said, not caring about her protest. "Then we'll go to Black Bean and get you real nourishment for this little endeavor of yours."

"We can at least finish the juice. It's not that—" Brigid took another sip, and this time, her body did an every-limb shudder. "It *is* that bad. We need Norman and Rita."

Nothing at their coffee shop tasted like this. They made the best pastries and coffee in Washington…according to Hannah, anyway. They'd even started stocking lavender syrup so she could have her favorite lavender oat milk lattes.

"Fine," Hannah grumbled. "But don't let me order anything that's going to spike my blood sugar."

Henry nodded. "No cherry strudel, got it."

"Oh, and no sitting next to Mr. Tallon from the grocery

store," Brigid added, pouring her juice down the drain next. "I'm not emotionally equipped to listen to his loud chewing."

"Sigh, sexy neighbor's going inside." Henry tilted his head and squinted. "Hey…are there cameras on his house?"

"Yep," Hannah said, swirling the green juice and trying to get up the courage to finish it. "The man has been adding so much security the last few days, you'd think he was building another Fort Knox."

Excitement lit Brigid's face. "Oh, he's dangerous, too!"

"Yeah, well, he'd better not bring that danger to my doorstep."

"Maybe you should bake him cookies," Henry offered, finally turning away from the glass. "As a 'hey, I'm your sexy single neighbor' peace offering."

Brigid scoffed. "That man doesn't eat cookies. There wasn't an ounce of fat on him."

"That man does not *deserve* my cookies," Hannah said quickly. "He didn't even say thank you for watering his plants."

"He was probably too taken by your cute ass," Brigid said, turning away from the window. "You said you were wearing your denim shorts, right? You look hot in those."

She shook her head. The only place he'd been looking was toward the gate, encouraging her to get the hell off his property.

She started taking apart the juicer. Stupid waste of time that endeavor was. "Do you know he drives a Corvette? He lives in a mansion and drives a Corvette."

Way out of her league.

"Money and brawn." Henry smiled. "You are one lucky woman, Hannah Jacobs."

She filled the sink with water and put all the pieces of the machine in to wash.

"Hey, is this your résumé?"

Hannah turned at Brigid's question and cringed. "Yeah."

She frowned and looked up. "Because you're leaving Reuben's, or…"

"I'm applying for a second job."

Her friends knew she wasn't exactly thriving at the moment. Heck, neither was Brigid's boyfriend. "When I sunk all my savings into this house, things were going well at Reuben's. Now, with this competing agency…it's tough. I've held out for as long as I can."

Sympathy darkened Brigid's eyes. "I didn't know it was *that* tough. I'd offer you hours at the shop, but business has been slow lately."

She shook her head. "No. I wouldn't ask you to do that anyway. I'll find something around town."

She had to.

Hannah turned off the tap, but the thing kept leaking, reminding her she needed a damn plumber. *Good timing, God.*

She deserted the juicer and crossed the room to take the résumé out of her friend's hand. Maybe she'd drop a few off before they ate. "Breakfast?"

Chapter Four

Twenty-nine, thirty.

Erik felt the eyes on him as he did his pull-ups, all coming from one window in the house next door. And it hadn't just been today. He'd felt them all week, but usually from just one person. Today, it was more than just Hannah. He'd seen her friends arrive an hour ago. Hell, he'd heard them.

He didn't care that they were watching. If he did, he'd work out inside. But he preferred the bite of the cold on his skin, the air on his face, and the whistle of wind in the trees.

He'd spent the last week organizing the house. Getting security and cameras installed. Making sure all of his shit was where he wanted it and fixing and updating the parts of the house that needed work. He still had plenty to do. Fixing the rotting deck out back. Some plumbing and internal issues.

Forty-nine. Fifty.

He dropped to his feet. He hadn't ventured out of his house much since returning to Redwood. Hell, he hadn't even seen his family. Because he was a fucking coward.

He scrubbed a hand over his face. He needed to just do it. Problem was, he knew what they'd see. The same thing he saw in the damn mirror. The new darkness inside him. The ripped, frayed edges of the man he'd become.

He let the cool air soothe his lungs as memories of his last mission as a special operations Marine pinged in his mind. It should have been a simple raid to rescue some US citizens who'd been taken from a university. But it had ended in death and devastation.

And then that phone call…the one he'd made when he'd switched his phone on just before boarding the military aircraft to return home…the one that had changed his very existence.

His heart rattled against his ribs, sweat beading his forehead.

He forced the memories away, fucking running from the torture of his past. Something he'd become good at.

He stepped into the house that still didn't feel like his. In the office to the left, a small sheaf of papers sat on the desk. Information Chandler had pulled on his new neighbor.

He headed up the stairs and into his bedroom, then the connecting bathroom, still thinking about his neighbor.

Foster care from the age of two after both parents had died in a car crash. No siblings.

Some may have been surprised that there was such darkness in her past, especially when she looked so happy. He wasn't. Nothing surprised Erik anymore. People didn't always wear their pasts on their sleeves for the world to see. He knew that better than anyone.

He stripped off and stepped into the shower, making the water as cold as possible in an attempt to rid his damn mind of his neighbor. Yesterday, he'd seen her on the side of her house, planting flowers. Every so often, she'd turn to look at his grandfather's flower bed, and her expression would turn sad.

It was clearly killing her that he'd told her not to water them. If he wasn't who he was, he'd let her do whatever the hell she wanted.

He closed his eyes and let the water hit his shoulders, those memories of his past biting at him again. Tormenting him.

Erik couldn't breathe. Twelve hours had passed since the fucking devastation that was his mission. Four of his seven teammates were dead. Dead! All because of one fucking new recruit who hadn't listened.

He wanted to hit something, but he knew it wouldn't be enough.

He swallowed, trying to calm his breathing as he made his way to the military aircraft. He had to calm the hell down before he got home. Vicky couldn't see him like this, not in her current condition. He had to be okay for her.

At the thought of Vicky, he pulled his phone from his pocket and turned it on for the first time since arriving in Syria. He was about to step onto the plane—but he stopped at the sight of so many missed calls. Text messages asking him to get in contact. Some from family. Some from numbers he didn't know.

He stepped away to click on the number that had called the most—his mother's.

His chest tightened, fear catapulting his heart into a faster rhythm. Was it his father? Someone else in the family? Had something happened?

His mother answered on the second ring. "Erik…"

The second he heard her voice, that fear twisted into something worse. Something uglier. Her voice wasn't itself. It was pained. Heavy. "What is it, Mom?"

There was a pause, and in that time, the dread spiraled throughout his chest, weaving and poisoning, burning like acid. "Tell me."

"Honey…it's Vicky."

Erik turned off the water and stepped out of the stall, every muscle in his body suddenly unbearably tight.

When his phone vibrated on the counter, he picked it up to see his sister's name.

Andi: See you in twenty minutes. If you're not at the coffee shop, I will hunt your ass down and find you. And I won't be held responsible for my actions.

He dropped the phone and went into the bedroom to

throw on clothes. He'd already canceled on her twice in the last week. He wasn't getting out of this one.

He threw on some jeans and a T-shirt, then shoved his phone into his pocket.

The phone rang again when he was behind the wheel of his Corvette, pulling out of the garage. He thought it would be Andi, already asking where the hell he was. It was Chandler.

He used the car's Bluetooth to answer. "What do you want? I'm off work for two months."

"Well, hello to you too, sunshine."

"Chandler."

"They're pushing for you to come back early."

"No." The word was out before Chandler had finished speaking. "I'm on break."

He turned left when he reached the road, letting his fingers glide over the smooth leather steering wheel.

"That's what I told them. Meanwhile, Marco's having all the fun."

Marco was another contractor. Erik wouldn't go so far as to call the guy a friend, but he was as close as it got in the industry. "Let him."

Chandler sighed. "Fine. But if you change your mind, you know where to—"

"I won't. But thanks."

Chandler laughed. "Okay. Everything else going all right?"

"Yeah, slowly getting there. Some of the house has been kept in great condition, other parts, not so much." Like the damn deck. He'd been working on it bit by bit this week and was still nowhere near finished.

"You know, you could always hire someone. You have the money."

"Where's the fun in that?"

"Right. Well, call if you need anything from me."

"You know I will." He ended the call, his mind on his job.

It was dangerous, and usually he needed dangerous. The rush of knowing every breath could be his last. The high of ridding this world of scumbags.

But right now, he needed to sort out his shit. He also needed to spend time with his family.

When he pulled into the parking lot of Black Bean, he spotted his sister's car immediately. Of course, Andi hadn't gone in. She'd waited in her car, foot probably on the gas, ready to go find him. His sister was nothing if not a woman of her word.

Not only was Andi the best at riding his ass, she was also a doctor, which meant she had eyes like a hawk and observed everything. A hell of a lot more than he wanted her to.

The second he was out of his car, so was she, and when she was close enough, she pounced on him like a five-and-a-half-foot bear. Erik caught her easily, and the second she was in his arms, he breathed her in.

God, she smelled like home.

He tightened his hold, not realizing how fucking much he'd missed his family until this moment. "I missed you, A."

She dug her face into his shoulder. "You have no idea." When she pulled back, her eyes glistened. "You doing okay?"

No. The voice was a loud shout in his head. A shout he didn't dare say out loud to his sister. "Yeah."

The slight narrowing of her eyes told him she didn't believe him. Hell, if he were her, he wouldn't have believed it either. "You?"

She sniffed and nodded. "Better now. But don't ever disappear on us again. You're home, and you need to stay home. Got it?"

"Or you'll hunt me down and beat my ass?"

"Worse. I'll lock you in my house and make you eat endless supplies of Dad's cooking."

His lips twitched. His dad was a terrible cook, and

everyone in the family knew it. They hadn't been exposed to it much growing up since their mother had prepared most of the meals, but there had been the odd occasion when she was sick or away, and their father had insisted on inflicting his culinary torture on them.

When they stepped into the café, he was hit yet again by that old nostalgia. He got it every time he came here. "I can't believe they haven't changed this place at all." Not one bit in eight damn years.

The old wooden tables were still mismatched and painted in different colors. The brown wooden counter still had the same hanging rattan pendant lights above. He'd been here a handful of times since getting to town, mostly for coffee, and it still shocked the hell out of him.

"I know," Andi said softly. "It's exactly the same. Norman and Rita are nothing if not creatures of habit."

She pulled him to a table near the window. He took the seat opposite her, his back to the wall so he could see his surroundings. Andi didn't blink. She had two special operations siblings—their brother, Nate, was a Navy SEAL, stationed at Coronado. She got it.

"Tell me how you've been. The real story, not the made-up bullshit."

He lifted a brow. "You think I'd give you made-up bullshit?"

"I know you would. It's why you've been avoiding the family since you stepped foot in this town."

His jaw clicked. So fucking true. "I'm doing as well as I can be."

She nodded. It was a slow movement that told him she was far from done dissecting him. "I know I've said this many times over the phone, but I'm sorry about…everything."

His gut twisted, pain ricocheting off all his vital organs.

Not at what she'd said, but because of what she *hadn't* said. Sorry about his team. Sorry about Vick and—

He shut the thought down before it was complete.

She tilted her head. "Do you miss the military or boxing?"

He'd done a stint in the professional boxing world after leaving the Marines, and he still boxed regularly. Getting into the ring was like a dose of life-giving air to his lungs. It loosened the band that was always so fucking tight around his chest. Exactly why he'd already turned his basement into an indoor workout room with a heavy bag. "No. It was time."

He already knew what the next question would be.

"So, what are you doing now?"

Despite expecting it, he hated when people asked him that. His job was classified—a secret government office he didn't talk about. Giving other people bullshit answers was easy. His family? Not so much.

"You know I can't talk about that, Andi."

That was the best he could give his sister. And by the disappointed twist of her lips, she didn't like it.

"I'm gonna go order our drinks," he said, before she could get another question in. "You still drinking mochas?"

She laughed. "Brother, I've grown up since then. Latte, please. One sugar."

He smiled and headed toward the counter.

Rita approached on the other side. She was a short woman in her mid-sixties, and as motherly as they came. She had a few gray hairs woven throughout the brown and a wide smile.

"Hi, dear. Black coffee for you and latte one sugar for your sister?"

He should have known…the woman knew everyone's order. A chime sounded behind him, indicating the door to the café opening, but he ignored it. "Yes, thanks."

Someone came to a stop beside him at the counter, and he smelled the sweet scents of citrus and flowers. The muscles in his forearms tightened, and he took a beat longer than he normally would have to turn his head.

Hannah. She looked up, her crystal-blue eyes colliding with his gaze. Immediately, blood pounded between his ears.

Fuck, what was that?

Shut it down, Erik. Even if you weren't too fucking dangerous, she's too young. Her twenty-three didn't come close to his thirty-six.

"Hey, Erik." Her soft voice rolled over his skin like silk.

"Hey."

He didn't say her name, because the last time he'd done that, parts of him had hardened that had no fucking business hardening. At least she wasn't wearing those shorts today. She wore them too damn often while she was home.

Her redheaded friend came into view as she leaned against the counter from behind Hannah. "Hi. My name's Brigid. I'm the best friend."

"As am I," a tall, toned guy behind them added. "Henry."

Rita turned her head from the coffee machine. "Hello, usuals for you guys, too? Cappuccino, latte, and lavender oat milk latte?"

What was the bet Hannah's order was the lavender one? It fucking suited her…floral and feminine.

"Thanks, Rita," Hannah said. She turned back to Erik. "So, how are you settling in?"

She played with a charm on her bracelet, and it took every scrap of his restraint to not look down at her delicate wrists, the way her slender fingers grazed over the bead.

He cleared his throat. "Fine."

The small smile dropped from her face, and he knew he was being an ass, but there was something about this woman, about her sweetness and beauty and fucking light, that made him want to run. Put as much distance between them as possible.

Her friend Brigid put a finger to her chin. "You're not a man of many words, are you?"

Henry snorted. "Don't need to be good with your words when you're good with—"

Hannah elbowed Henry in the gut.

The man grunted. "Hey, watch it. You'll bruise me before my date with Jake."

Rita set Erik's coffees onto the counter, and he paid her and turned, giving Hannah and her friends a small nod as he went. He was almost back to his table when a soft hand touched his elbow. His mouth tightened, and he wanted to ignore her and keep on walking.

But he didn't. He turned and, yep, there she was, standing too damn close.

"Hey." Hannah smiled. "I've been thinking. I really hope that since we're neighbors, we could try to get along. We could even be friends."

He bit back a sigh. He wasn't going to be friends with this woman. Not only because he couldn't, what with his hands twitching to touch her every time she was near, but because if she knew even the CliffsNotes version of the fucking shitstorm that was his life, she'd run as far from him as possible.

"You don't want to be my friend, Hannah."

Her lips parted. "Why not?"

He lowered his voice. "Because you're good, Angel...and I'm not."

Chapter Five

We appreciate your interest in selling our property. In this instance, we have decided to go with someone else.

For a moment Hannah was tempted to throw her laptop to the floor of her office and stomp on it. She'd been so sure she had that contract. What was going on? The last three properties she'd been approached to sell, the owners had gone with someone else just before the contracts were signed. Her only current saving grace was that Angelo hadn't made his decision, so it wasn't a no...yet.

Oh man. She needed more work. How was she going to pay her bills or her damn mortgage? Or buy her insulin?

She dropped her head, thudding it against the solid wood of the desk.

Screwed. She was screwed. And what was more, every evening job prospect she'd approached had told her they weren't hiring. So unless by some miracle she found a handful of properties to sell, or managed to sell the few she still had listed, those bills on her kitchen counter would turn into living, breathing debt collectors.

"I take it you didn't get the Wilfred account?"

She peeled her forehead off the desk, unable to muster even the smallest smile for James, who stood at her door. He was cute in a clean-cut kind of way, with his perfect sandy-blond hair and button-up shirt.

"Nope. And no reason was given." None. Squat.

"Maybe you're losing your touch."

She knew he was joking, but it still stung. She was a people person. She *always* got the listing after the meeting stage, but lately that wasn't the case. "Maybe I have. Maybe people have realized I'm a grouchy diabetic who barely has her life together."

Taylor stopped beside James. "Hey." When her eyes fell on Hannah, they softened. "No luck on the Wilfred account?"

Taylor was the third realtor at Reuben's Real Estate. She was in her mid-thirties and a single mother, which made her a great agent because she was motivated to sell. They were all feeling the pinch right now.

"No."

Her voice gentled. "Competition is tough with that new office in town taking all the houses. Did you ask why they went with someone else?"

"I ask *everyone* who goes with someone else, but I only seem to get wishy-washy, polite responses that tell me nothing." She blew out a frustrated breath. "How are both your sales going?"

"Not great," Taylor said.

A crease formed in James's brow. "Terrible. But I'm confident they'll pick up soon."

Well, at least one of them was.

"I've got to go pick up Elliot," Taylor said. "I'll see you both later."

James tapped the doorframe. "Try to have a good night, Hannah."

With a heavy sigh, she turned back to her laptop and quickly typed out a reply to the email, then packed her stuff and left the office. The second she slid behind the wheel of her car, she turned her key in the ignition.

The thing didn't start.

She tried again. Nothing.

No! What was this, Hate on Hannah Day? She already had the damn tap in the kitchen that wouldn't stop leaking—she couldn't afford this problem too. Oh, she'd tried to fix the water issue herself. Even pulled up a ton of YouTube clips and followed them step by step. She was pretty sure she'd made the leaking worse.

Three more times the car refused to start. It was on the last turn of the key that the engine finally turned over. Thank God. Still, on the way home, her chest felt heavy. Her car was on its last leg, something she'd been aware of for a while.

It wasn't just the lack of commissions and mounting bills that were stressing her out. Her boss, Reuben, had let people go for long-term low sales. Even though James and Taylor were struggling too, they were still doing better than she was.

The idea of being jobless had her breaking out into a cold sweat. She needed her job for the health insurance. The insurance wasn't great—hell, it didn't even cover a continuous glucose monitor or a pump. But it covered her insulin. The stuff she was dependent on to, you know, *live*.

She knew how lucky she was to work for an agency that offered benefits. Most didn't. It was one of the reasons she stayed at Reuben's.

Her fingers tightened on the wheel. It was fine. She'd be fine. She'd get more houses to list, then she'd sell the shit out of them.

Unless she didn't…

Her debt and her sink and her car all swirled through her mind during the drive. By the time she reached her house, she'd well and truly spiraled. So much so that she was a breath away from hyperventilating.

She climbed out of the car, her gaze brushing over the house next door as she walked, her mind flicking to her conversation with Erik at Black Bean a few days ago. At the dismissive way he'd barely answered her questions. Even Henry had agreed he was an ass, and Henry usually had a mountain of leeway for hot men.

In the kitchen, she dropped her bag onto the table with a loud thud before moving to the cabinet and grabbing a cup. She filled it with water, but when she turned the tap off, it kept going. It was just a steady trickle, but those drops were fuel on the fire of her frustration.

She sucked in a deep breath as she glanced out the window, trying to find peace. What she actually found was her neighbor's bed of flowers...dying.

They were freaking *dying* because that broody, angry jerk of a man wasn't taking care of them. How much trouble was it to throw some water on a few plants?

That was it. She was done with this. They were goddamn *flowers*, and she'd made a promise to keep them alive.

Hannah marched outside and grabbed her watering can. A normal, sane person might have tried to avoid the cameras skirting his property. Not her. She was fearless. Either that or stupid. She looked straight into the lens, chin lifted in an I'm-watering-the-goddamn-flowers-and-I-dare-you-to-stop-me kind of way.

She reached the backyard and filled the can, then she started watering the poor flowers.

Yeah, take that, Mr. Erik Hunter. I'm on your damn land, watering your grandfather's flowers, and there's nothing you can do about—

"What are you doing?"

She yelped and spun, tipping the watering can so half the contents fell onto the lawn. "Jesus Christ, man. Wear a bell or something!" She grabbed her heart, swearing it was about to leap out of her chest.

Once her pulse returned to normal, she looked up at him. Way up. God, he was tall. "What I'm doing is obvious. I'm watering the flowers."

"I asked you not to do that."

She laughed, and the sound was almost manic. "No. You *told* me not to."

"So why are you here?"

"Because you"—she stepped forward and jabbed a finger into his rock-solid chest—"are letting them die like some heartless, flower-killing psychopath!"

She poked him again, almost straining a muscle in her finger as she let loose every pent-up frustration inside her. "You move into this house, you don't even want to get to know your only neighbor. I don't know why—I'm a freaking *awesome* neighbor. You're rude. You give me one-word answers like you can't even be bothered with a sentence. You say stupid things about me being *good* when you don't even know me. And now you just stand there like…like…"

"A heartless, flower-killing psychopath?"

"Yes!"

———

ERIK'S LIPS TWITCHED. This woman was something else. She'd stepped onto his property, glared at his camera as if daring him to stop her, and was shouting at him while trying to break her finger on his chest.

"You seem very attached to these flowers." It was clearly the wrong thing to say, if the narrowing of her eyes was anything to go by.

"What I'm *attached* to," she yelled, "is the memory of your grandfather, standing out here every morning and night, tending to the flowers with a smile on his face. What I'm *attached* to is keeping my promise to him. He cared about them. Doesn't that make *you* care about them?"

"No."

Another wrong answer. A vein in her neck popped and that finger once again shot into him. If it were a knife, he'd have a hole in his chest by now, and he had a feeling this woman would still be stabbing and yelling.

"You know, I've met men like you before."

He doubted that. "What kind of men would that be?"

"Men who think the world revolves around them. You think the goddamn sun only shines when you wake."

"I get up before the sun."

"But you know what?" she asked, ignoring him. "It doesn't. In fact, the sun wouldn't care if you didn't get out of bed all damn day!"

It had been a while since a woman had spoken to him like this. He kind of liked it. "You having a bad day, Angel?"

"Don't call me that! But if you want to know, yes. I've had the day from hell. No one will let me sell their house, my tap keeps leaking, my car took half a dozen tries to start, and *now* Stanley's flowers are dying."

He looked from her house to her beat-up old Honda, then back to her. "Would you like me to look at your water and car?"

Her mouth opened, ready to dish out another series of insults, then snapped shut, as if she'd just heard what he was saying.

She was cute when she was angry. A little unapproachable, but cute.

"I...*what?*" She shook her head. "No. Don't get all nice guy on me now."

"I can be a nice guy and still not want people I don't know on my land." He wasn't saying he *was* a nice guy, just that he *could* be.

40

She swallowed, and he could almost see the effort she put into speaking with less edge to her voice. "I need to keep my promise to Stanley. Let just *one* aspect of my life go right today."

"You did keep your promise. You kept them alive until I moved in. Now you don't need to worry about them. I think you should go home, Hannah. It's getting late."

Fire bloomed in her eyes. "Argh! I could just—"

She stopped abruptly, the color bleeding from her face as her hand dropped.

Then she rocked on her feet.

Alarm replaced any humor, and he grabbed her arm. "Hey. You okay?"

She pressed both hands to his chest and lowered her head. Three beats of silence passed while she used him to steady herself. Her warmth bled into his skin, changing the rhythm of his heart to something fast and uneven.

Finally, she lifted her head and nodded. "Sorry. I'm okay. I haven't eaten for a while and my blood sugar's probably low."

Type 1 diabetic. It was something he'd read in the information Chandler had dug up. "You need food?"

"I have food. I've just been a mess this afternoon and rushed over here without thinking."

She tried to step away, but he didn't release her. She was still too pale.

"I'm okay," she repeated. "I just need to get home and eat something."

"Let me help you get home."

She shook her head before he'd even finished. "No."

His jaw clenched, and reluctantly, he released her arm. He may not like people on his property, but he also didn't like letting people who were a stone's throw away from passing out just walk away by themselves.

Her knuckles were white around the watering can as she stepped around him.

He scrubbed a hand over his face, shouting in his goddamn head not to do it, but…

"How often do they need watering?"

She stopped and turned, eyes widening. "They could probably get away with every three days. And that's only when there's been no rain."

Don't fucking do it, Erik. Don't—

"Fine. You can water them."

The smile on her face was so fucking wide, it was radiant. Then she did something he didn't expect. She dropped the can and threw her arms around his shoulders.

Her sweet scent surrounded him, suffocating him. And all that softness against his hard, her damn hair tickling his face… it made every inch of his skin burn.

She whispered into his ear, her breath brushing against his cool skin. "Thank you, Erik Hunter. Your grandfather's smiling right now."

No. The old man wasn't smiling. He was laughing so goddamn hard that he was probably falling off his cloud. Because *now* Erik understood why his grandfather had left him the house.

Chapter Six

"One cup of flour. In. One tablespoon of baking soda. Done. One cup of sugar, aka, the good part. In the bowl."

Hannah peeked over Brigid's shoulder as her friend threw together the ingredients for the muffins. If there was ever a woman who shouldn't be baking, it was Brigid. Heck, she was pretty sure her friend had once given her food poisoning in an endeavor to bake her a birthday cake.

Hannah wasn't the best baker, but she was better than Brigid.

She cleared her throat. "Brigid, the recipe says half a cup of sugar."

"Shit." Her friend started scooping tablespoons of sugar from the bowl. She got about three scoops in before leaning back and staring at the bowl like her eyes could measure it. "That looks like half a cup, right?"

Hannah laughed and lifted a shoulder. "If it's not, it will just be a bit sweet. Might even make it better."

"This is why I came here to bake. I need your words of confidence."

Was that it? Or was her friend scared of burning down her own kitchen, so she'd chosen Hannah's?

Hannah went to the fridge and grabbed the wet ingredients. "Tell me again why you need to bake muffins?"

"Because James has an important meeting with Mrs. Cullen, and I know she has a sweet tooth, so if anything can tip her over the edge and get her to give James the contract to sell her house, it's baked goods."

Ah, yes. Mrs. Cullen. The woman had been talking about downsizing for years. She would be offended that the woman was going to James and not her, but everyone knew she had a thing for young men.

"And now that you have Angelo's home to sell, he feels like he's on the back burner."

Her heart thumped at the reminder. That call yesterday to tell her the house was hers...God, it had been everything. A weight off her shoulders. Now she just had to sell it.

As Brigid cracked the eggs, Hannah's gaze flickered to the kitchen window, a smile stretching her lips when she saw Stanley's flowerbed. Alive and thriving...thanks to her. And thanks to Erik granting her visitation rights.

"How are things going with you and your new neighbor?" Brigid asked as she poured in some milk.

"We've come to somewhat of a truce these last couple of weeks. I water the flowers as needed, and he doesn't yell at me. Win-win."

Every so often, they smiled at each other. Okay, she smiled at *him* and received a tiny chin dip in response. But there was kind of a ghost of a smile on his face. And at least the man wasn't glaring, or worse, sending her away.

Brigid looked up, a grin on her face. "I think this might be the start of a beautiful love story."

Hannah rolled her eyes, then frowned at the amount of milk going into the mixture. "Ah, Brigid..."

Her friend looked down. "Shit." She plonked the carton of milk back onto the counter, then grimaced. "Should I try scooping it out?"

"It's kind of submerged with the other liquids."

"Should be fine...right?"

Hannah debated telling her friend that, no, it would not be fine, but instead went with a nod. "Would you like me to take over?" She'd already offered half a dozen times, but Brigid seemed determined to do this on her own.

"Nah, I'm almost done."

Brigid grabbed the block of butter and sliced some off before putting it into a pan.

Hannah's brows slashed together once again. "Aren't you going to measure it?"

"I don't need to. I need four tablespoons. That's about a quarter of this block."

At least Brigid was confident.

She glanced back at Erik's house, where an expensive-looking Ferrari sat in his drive. He had a visitor...one who wore a black tailored suit.

"You spying on your neighbor again?" Brigid asked.

"I'm not spying."

"Really? So you weren't also watching when his visitor pulled up ten minutes ago?"

Okay. Maybe there'd been a little bit of watching out of her window. Was that spying, though? "I just find it interesting that not only does Erik obviously have money, his friends are well off too."

"I wonder what he does for work."

Oh, she'd been wondering that herself. "Something dangerous that pays a lot, I think."

The man had edgy vibes coming off him in waves. But that wasn't all. There was something else about him too. Hurt of some kind, perhaps. A darkness. It reminded her of the darkness in her own past.

She fiddled with the cloud charm on her bracelet.

The bracelet and charm were the most precious things she owned, because they were the only remaining items from the people she'd loved most in the world. The bracelet had been her mother's, and the charm a gift from her foster brother.

Her heart gave a big thud at the memory of her brother. She'd been two and he'd been three when they'd first met. She'd had other foster siblings after him, but none like Nico. He'd made her feel safe. They'd lived together for several years with their foster mother, Janet. She hadn't been the best foster mom, often drinking and gambling too much, but she hadn't been the worst. And she'd looked after them until she died.

A shudder rocked Hannah's spine at the memory of her life *after* Janet. Not only being separated from Nico, but the horrible homes they'd both experienced.

She clenched her jaw, hating that the one person in the world who truly understood her, the only family member she'd had left, Nico, was now gone.

When she looked back to Brigid, it was to see her friend's eyes had softened. "You thinking about Nico?"

Hannah swallowed. Her friend knew her too well. "I miss him."

"I know, honey. I'm sorry."

Brigid and Henry had been by her side for months after he'd passed away. They'd gotten her through the worst of her days, just another reason she was grateful for them.

She ran her finger over the cloud charm. That's what he'd called her—Cloud. Because he'd often caught her gazing up at the sky.

He hadn't chosen the best path, often getting into trouble, but he'd had a good heart. He'd proved that to her more times than she could count and was her rock during her hardest times.

Hannah had seen darkness. She'd seen many shades of it, in fact, while tossed around the foster care system as a teenager. Especially that one home…

Her skin chilled, but she pushed the memory to the back of her mind.

Now, she made a conscious decision every day to not only see the light, but to let it in. Though she still recognized darkness in others…like Erik.

She blew out a breath and looked out the window again—until the smell of burnt butter had her gaze shifting to the pan.

"Brigid! The butter!"

"Shit, shit, shit!" Brigid pulled the saucepan off the heat and grimaced. "Is melted butter supposed to be a bubbly brown?"

Hannah shook her head and took the pan from her friend. "No." She tipped the butter into the trash before cutting off more. But unlike her friend, she measured it carefully. "I'll do this. Why don't you start whisking the wet ingredients together?"

That would be safe for her, right?

When the butter was melted, she added it to the wet ingredients and mixed them together before combining them with the dry.

When it was done, the mixture was a bit thin thanks to the extra milk, but Brigid didn't seem to care as she added a ton of chocolate chips.

Hannah laughed as her friend just kept heaping them in. "Uh, I think that's enough, Brig."

"Is there such a thing as enough chocolate?"

Hannah would argue yes. "Did James ask you to bake these muffins?"

"No. It was my idea. He's been stressed lately, so I'm trying to be the supportive girlfriend."

She nodded. He didn't show his stress at work. Other than the occasional remarks about sales being down, he tried to remain positive. "Well, I think he'll be very grateful."

Carefully, Hannah helped Brigid spoon the mixture into the baking cups, which were bright pink and blue with little hearts. *That* definitely screamed Mrs. Cullen.

Brigid lifted the tray, and Hannah opened the door for her friend to slot them into the preheated oven.

Brigid straightened and grinned. "See! I can bake. I almost want to give myself a pat on the back."

Hannah's gaze shifted to the unopened vanilla extract on the counter.

Brigid followed her gaze. "Oh, crap."

⸻

"YOU WANT me to take a private mercenary job?" Erik asked, brows slashed together as he watched Marco across his kitchen.

"Yes. They approached me, and when I found out who the target was, I knew I needed to do this."

Erik was shaking his head before he'd finished speaking. "You know I can't—"

"He's the reason my brother's *dead*, Hunter." A vein throbbed in Marco's neck.

Erik's muscles tensed at his lethal tone.

"He lured my brother into his organization, then murdered him. I may not have the proof, but I *know* it was him. And now, thanks to this job, I have the chance to end him."

Erik ran a hand over his face. "I can't do it. I'm sorry."

"Just tell me you'll think about it, at least," Marco argued.

He sucked in a breath. At this point, he just wanted the man out of his house. "Fine."

It would still be a no. There was no part of him that was okay with taking private contracts. He worked for the government. Everything he did was sanctioned.

Marco shoved his hands into his pockets. "Thank you. That's all I ask. There's no rush, we've been given time. But remember, I'm not the only one who'll benefit. It's not just revenge. The money is good."

His friend knew he didn't need the money. Neither of them did. Their work paid well. "They said they want both of us or neither?"

"Yes." Marco lifted a shoulder, his Italian accent thick. "If you won't take the job, they'll go with other contractors." His lips quirked up then. Even though the guy was dangerous as hell, he was good at hiding that part of himself when he wanted to. "You know I generally get what I want, right?"

Erik shook his head. *Not this time.* The words were a whisper in his head that never reached the air. Nothing about the job sounded right.

The smirk disappeared from Marco's face, and he pushed off the counter. "Think about what it would mean to me, Hunter. As a friend."

They weren't exactly friends. But this man wasn't someone he wanted to make an enemy of, either.

They stepped outside and headed toward Marco's Ferrari. When a flicker of movement caught his attention from next door, his muscles pulled tight. He turned his head to see Hannah with her friend Brigid, who was carrying a container. They were walking toward a blue sedan.

When Brigid saw them, she smiled and tugged Hannah's arm. She tried to pull back, but her friend just tugged harder.

Marco stopped and stared, his brows lifting in interest. "Friends of yours?"

"No." The word came out too quickly.

Fuck. There was no part of him that wanted Hannah to

meet Marco fucking Salvatore. The guy was dangerous. Hannah shouldn't be anywhere near him.

The women crossed the expanse of yard and stopped by Marco's car, the redhead smiling.

"Hi, Erik." She turned to glance at Marco. "Hello, I'm Brigid. And this is Hannah. We just baked some muffins and thought we'd offer one to each of you."

As Brigid talked, Hannah mouthed, "Sorry," to Erik.

His gaze focused on her intense blue eyes. On the way the sunlight hit her hair, casting a glow around her head like a halo. When he turned to Marco, it was to see him carefully watching the short exchange between him and Hannah. *Fuck.*

Realizing Erik wasn't going to introduce them, Marco stepped forward. "Hi. I'm Marco Salvatore."

When Salvatore held out a hand, Erik wanted to rip the thing off.

Brigid placed her hand in his first, then Hannah. The second he touched her, Erik didn't just want to tear his arm off, he wanted to shove it down his fucking throat.

"Marco was just going," Erik said through gritted teeth, unable to keep the bite out of his tone.

Brigid's brows flickered, then she opened the container and handed a muffin to Marco. "Here. Take this for the ride."

The thing was so dark brown, he was sure it was burnt, and the center looked to be sinking. They were the saddest muffins he'd ever seen.

Marco smiled and slid it from her fingers. "Thank you, *cara.*" Then he gave Erik a look. "I'll leave you to it." He got into his car and took off down the drive.

Brigid took another muffin out and placed it in Hannah's hand. "I have to go. I'll see you both later." Then her friend went back toward Hannah's drive and drove away also.

Hannah wet her lips nervously. "Sorry about Brigid."

"What the hell are you doing here, Hannah?" The words

were rough and angry, but he felt like he had no damn control over his emotions.

She cringed. "I know. Brigid gets a bit excited sometimes. I tried to pull her back, but—"

"You know I don't like you on my goddamn property." The second the words were out, he regretted them. God, he fucking hated the hurt that slashed across her face. But he was instantly on edge from seeing her so close to Marco. The guy was a serious threat. And he'd *touched* her.

She visibly shifted from hurt to angry. "Sorry. Next time I'll just drop to the ground and force her to drag me." She spun, but before she could get more than a few steps, he grabbed her arm.

The shot of awareness that ran through his body was like a damn bolt of electricity. "I'm sorry."

It was a moment before she turned. The look she gave him bordered on suspicion. "You're sorry," she said flatly.

"Yeah. I know she pulled you over here." He'd grown used to this woman living next door, but he still needed her to keep her distance. Marco Salvatore, rocking up out of nowhere, was a perfect damn reason why. "Is that muffin for me?"

Her brows shot up. "You want it?"

"Yes."

She looked down like she was considering denying him, then with a sigh, she handed it over. When she looked at him expectantly, it took him a beat to realize she wanted him to taste it now.

He peeled back the liner and took a bite. *Shit.* It looked bad, but it tasted worse. Like sweetened cardboard that had been soaked in liquid.

"It's really good," he said, once he'd forced the overly sweet batter down his throat. God, how could a muffin taste both burnt and undercooked at the same time?

Hannah lifted a brow, humor dancing in her eyes. "Really?"

The batter turned to sludge in his gut. "Yeah. Thanks."

Her smile widened. "You're welcome. And, again, I'm sorry we came over unannounced. I'll talk to Brigid about not doing that again." She whipped her phone from her pocket. "And if you're willing to give me your number, I'll text ahead if I need to come over for any reason."

He hesitated. Why did it feel dangerous for this woman to have his number?

Her smile started to slip at his hesitation, so he quickly rattled it off, not feeling emotionally equipped to see her face fall again.

"Great." She slipped her phone back into her pocket. "Enjoy the rest of the muffin."

He watched as she crossed back to her yard, trying to work out why the fuck he was so drawn to her.

Chapter Seven

"I love him so much, I just wish he would up his romantic game. Some flowers here, a Magic Mike dance there."

Hannah turned right, driving so slow a bicycle could have passed her. Fat raindrops came down hard and fast on the windshield, the wipers barely able to clear them before another deluge came.

Damn her idea to stay late at work, following up on some leads.

She cleared her throat before responding to Brigid, who was on speaker. "I'm sure he's trying."

"Trying? He hasn't given me a good fuck in... God, I can't even remember."

Hannah's lips twitched. Brigid had sent her an SOS message, then called the second she'd climbed into her car. If her friend ever spoke at normal-person decibels, Hannah was sure she'd barely be able to hear her over the storm. But Brigid being Brigid, she knew how to speak over any weather phenomenon.

"Brigid, there is more to a relationship than a good..."

Nope. She couldn't say that. Her inner child was too modest. "Than good sex."

"I know, but I'm craving fireworks, Hannah! And we used to *have* fireworks. We used to—"

Her words cut out, and Hannah shot a look at her phone in the console. Crap, she'd run out of battery. She'd known it was coming. Usually, she charged it at work, but she'd gotten so consumed in what she was doing, she'd forgotten.

At least she was almost home, then she could read the dozen messages Brigid would no doubt send between then and now, explaining all the things she needed from James.

She took the next right, spotting the entrance to her long drive halfway down the road. She was nearly there—and already picturing a long, hot Epsom salt bath—when a loud bang sounded from under the hood, quickly followed by clouds of smoke.

She'd just managed to pull the car to the side of the road when the engine switched off. It just…died.

No!

She tried turning it back on, hoping it might start and run just long enough to get her the remaining small distance home. Nope. Not even a jingle.

She threw the keys against the passenger door in anger, fully ready to go to battle with this hunk of metal. She stopped herself…just.

It's fine. The positive is, I'm almost home. Yes, it's raining, but once I'm inside, I can sink into the tub and forget all about the storm and my stupid car.

The raindrops on the windshield looked even heavier than seconds before, and anticipation of the cold already had her skin pebbling as she grabbed her work bag, then wrapped her fingers around the door handle.

Okay, quick race down the street and driveway, Hannah. Then a nice warm bath.

The image of the bath in her head was the only thing that lured her out of the car and into the rain. A strong gust of wind slapped her in the face, water hitting her head and shoulders so hard she was drenched in seconds.

She tucked her head low and ran.

Her feet sank into the wet grass beside the road, her skin completely chilled by the time she reached the driveway. She cursed the distance from the road to her house throughout the entire run.

Had she actually thought living so far from the road would be *nice?* Peaceful even? Well, this run wasn't peaceful. She wouldn't wish it on her worst enemy. Well, maybe Erik when he was scolding her, but that was a special case.

By the time she reached her front porch, her teeth were chattering and she was pretty sure she looked like a drowned rat.

She rummaged through her bag with a wet hand, searching for three whole heartbeats before remembering...

No.

Her keys. She'd thrown them in the car during her little fit and never picked them back up.

She allowed herself one second for her heart to drop and frustrated tears to prick at her eyes, then she shook her head and straightened.

This was fine. Aggravating, but fine.

She ducked her head once more and ran back into the rain. If possible, it felt like it was falling harder, and when lightning flashed through the night sky, rumbling thunder was quick to follow.

When she finally reached her car, she was almost contemplating just sliding inside and sleeping there—until she tried the handle.

It didn't open.

Oh God! She'd clicked the lock. It had just been instinctual. Muscle memory. She hadn't even thought about it.

This was it. The final nail in her coffin. No keys. Dead phone, so no way to call a locksmith. And, just to top it off, her sugars were low and she'd eaten her last snack while leaving work.

Panic bubbled inside her, almost drowning out the sound of the rain. Then her gaze caught on her driveway again.

Was Erik home? Please let him be home.

With gritted teeth, she ran back down her drive, water drowning her as she went. She'd just stepped into his yard when her foot slipped, and she fell flat into a puddle of mud.

Okay, she'd been wrong. Locking her key in the car wasn't the last nail in the coffin, *this* was.

She wasn't usually a crier. She couldn't even remember the last time she'd shed a tear. But right now, she could shed a bucket load.

"What the hell?"

The deep growl had her head shooting up and her gaze colliding with a very wet, very handsome-looking Erik as he stepped outside. The rain soaked into his crisp white shirt immediately, making it stick to his chest like a second skin. She could see every one of his dozen abs while he power-walked across the yard. Big. Sexy. Dangerous.

The second he was by her side, his strong fingers wrapped around her upper arms and pulled her to her feet like she weighed nothing. His touch was warm, and she wanted to sink into it.

"Are you okay?"

Even though he'd shouted, his words barely crossed the inches separating them, the storm almost washing them out.

She nodded, her teeth now chattering so fiercely she could barely get a word out. "My c-car stopped down the s-street. Then I locked my house k-key inside."

He cursed, and before she realized what he was doing, he whipped her up into his arms and carried her to his door.

Hannah stopped breathing. Her lungs literally wouldn't let a single breath through, but that had nothing to do with the cold or the rain and everything to do with the hard chest pressed to her side. The powerful arms wrapped around her back and legs. Hell, the storm around them almost ceased to exist.

She didn't manage a single breath until she was in Erik's living room and he was lowering her to the leather couch.

Once she was down, she gasped and tried to get back up. "No, I'll g-get it wet."

He grabbed her arm, keeping her in place. Her mouth opened to fight him on it, but then snapped shut at his stony glare. "Stay here."

The moment he disappeared into the hall, the shudders returned with a vengeance. Rocking her spine. Shaking every limb of her body. But there was also something else there…a yearning in her belly. To have Erik touch her again. His arms around her, shielding her from the storm that now only existed in her body.

When he returned, he had a pile of big, fluffy white towels in his arms, and the second he wrapped one around her shoulders and covered her lap with another, she sighed. Heaven. Complete and utter heaven.

He crouched in front of her and cupped her cheek, cursing for what had to be the fifth time in as many minutes. "You're ice cold."

But that hand on her cheek was warm. Without even thinking, she leaned into it.

"I'm sorry, but do you have food? Maybe juice or candy?" She knew she was low; how low exactly, she wasn't sure. She had her kit in her bag but knew sugar was more important right now.

Concern flickered in his eyes before he got up and disappeared. The fire roared beside her, and she wanted to draw closer. Drop in front of it and let the flames heat her skin.

She didn't, but only because she wasn't sure her legs would carry her.

When Erik returned, he had his fist closed around something. He opened it to reveal M&M's.

He passed her a handful of the candy, and she tipped the entire lot into her mouth at once.

One side of his mouth twitched, but she couldn't even feel self-conscious. When she was low, there was urgency to get sugar into her blood.

He rose and moved to the kitchen again, this time returning with the entire bag of M&M's. He pulled one out and touched it to her lips. She opened, and the candy hit her tongue. She barely had time to process what the feel of his fingers on her lips did to her before another was there.

The man fed her half a dozen before his hand once again went to her cheek. "We need to get you out of those wet clothes."

She shuddered again.

His jaw clenched. "I'm going to carry you to the guest bathroom so you can have a warm shower. Do you think you'll be okay in there by yourself?"

Before she could answer, or hell, even consider what would happen if she said no, he touched another M&M to her lips. She opened, again feeling the strangely intoxicating mix of sugar and calloused finger.

"Yes. I'll be okay showering." At least she wasn't stuttering anymore.

"Good. When the storm dies down, I'll go get your keys from the car."

She nodded, not bothering to ask how he'd do that. If

anyone could break into a car, this guy seemed a likely candidate.

For a moment, neither of them moved, and every second that passed had her more conscious of his closeness. Of the way his heat seeped into her without them even touching. She noticed the specks of honey in his eyes. The small, faded scar near his hairline. Even the tiny hole at his eyebrow from what she could only assume used to be an eyebrow ring.

She carved every little fact into her memory. The little parts of Erik she wouldn't have seen if it wasn't for this moment.

Then he moved, the eye contact broke, and her exhale was more of a shudder. Again, he swiftly scooped her up against his chest and began moving toward the stairs.

She gasped, grabbing onto his damp chest. Her mouth opened to tell him she could walk, but then she felt his heart racing beneath her palm and the words just…didn't make it out. Maybe because that heartbeat felt like it was racing for *her*. Maybe it indicated a connection Erik refused to acknowledge.

He took the stairs quickly. She was still focusing on the thumping of his heart, the warmth of his chest, when he stepped into what could only be described as the most extravagant bathroom she'd ever seen.

Holy shit…the space was beautiful. So beautiful, she didn't even complain when he set her on her feet.

"Erik, this bathroom is…"

"Over the top?"

"No. It's gorgeous!" A beautiful mix of modern and Victorian. The vanity was a rich dark wood with a marble top and deep basin. The art deco wall paneling was stunning, and the arched ceilings made everything feel bigger and grander. Then there was the free-standing claw-foot tub with the open pipework… God, she'd die to have one of those in her house.

She stepped forward and ran a still-shaky finger over the

porcelain. "I lived in a lot of old houses growing up, and quite a few had claw-foot tubs. But none like this."

This was in pristine condition. And the details…

"You're welcome to use it." He said the words with ease, but she didn't miss the slight tensing of his jaw.

Excitement lit her chest at the prospect of taking a bath, but she shook her head. No. Bathing in her gorgeous neighbor's beautiful tub was *not* appropriate. "That's okay. A shower will warm me up just fine."

He almost looked relieved. Like a bath would have taken too long, and he wanted her out of his place quickly.

He ran a hand through his hair. "I'll get you a dry towel and something to wear."

The second he disappeared, another cold shudder rocked her spine…because he'd been providing warmth even from across the room?

No. That was crazy…wasn't it?

A few seconds later, he returned with a towel and a pile of clothes. "They'll be too big for you but hopefully will tide you over until you can get back to your place."

The words were spoken quickly. Then he walked out just as fast, closing the door after him like he couldn't bear to look at her in his space any longer.

Chapter Eight

Erik stepped out of the garage and back into his house. He moved to the hall and dropped Hannah's keys onto the side table. He'd planned to stay here while she showered, but it had been torture. All he'd been able to think about was her upstairs, in his shower, water cascading over her naked body...

So he'd chosen the storm.

He pulled his wet sweatshirt over his head before entering the kitchen and reaching for the leftover tub of soup in his fridge. There was no way he was letting the woman leave his home unfed, not with her diabetes.

He put the soup on the stove, then pulled out his phone and made a call.

"Jared speaking."

"Jared. It's Erik Hunter."

There was a short pause before the guy spoke. "You're shitting me, right? Erik fucking Hunter? Are you back in town?"

Erik placed two bowls on the table. "Yeah. Have been for a month. I need a favor."

Jared laughed. "Let me get this straight, you fuck off for

almost a decade and the first call I get when you return is to ask a favor?"

"Yeah. Is that a problem?"

"Nope. Just clarifying. What's the favor?"

He grabbed two spoons from the drawer. "My neighbor's car broke down about a hundred yards from my place. I need you to fix it and return it to her."

"You got it. Send me the address."

"Thanks. And Jared, send me the bill, not her."

There was a short pause. "Is this a lady-friend neighbor?"

"None of your fucking business." He opened a bag of sourdough bread and put a few slices into the toaster.

Jared chuckled. "All right. Send through the address and I'll go out there as soon as this storm eases."

"Thanks."

Erik shoved his phone into his pocket just as the soup began to simmer. He lifted the pan and spooned the liquid into the bowls. He and Jared had gone to high school together, and while Erik had gone to the military, Jared had become a mechanic. Even from the start, he'd been the best damn mechanic Erik had ever used, and he was betting nothing had changed.

He'd just set the buttered toast onto a plate when footsteps sounded on the stairs. When Hannah stepped into the doorway, Erik felt like he'd been sucker punched. The sensation was so real, he wanted to keel over to catch his breath and allow his lungs to work again.

She wore his hooded sweatshirt, which almost hit her knees, but her legs were completely bare. Her hair was wet and hung around her shoulders, making her look even younger than her twenty-three years.

Fuck. Again, he was reminded just how young she was.

His cock didn't care. It hardened at the damn sight of her.

"The pants didn't fit," she said softly, moving further into the room. "But the sweatshirt's like a dress, so…"

He tried to clear his throat, but it felt fucking impossible. Hell, even moving felt like too damn much, unless it was moving toward her.

She cleared her throat, her gaze shifting to the table, brows rising. "You made food."

Finally, he forced his voice to work. "I had some leftover soup, so I heated it up."

"That was thoughtful. Thank you." She lowered her head and sniffed the bowl. "It smells amazing. What is it?"

"Chicken tortilla."

"I should lock myself out more often." Her lips spread into a smile, causing his heart to thump. "I'll just take my insulin."

She grabbed her bag and pulled out a small pouch before sitting at the table. First, she pricked her finger, then placed the drop of blood onto the test strip. She waited for the number, and once it came up, she took out an insulin pen, attached the needle, and dialed in the amount of insulin.

His muscles tightened when she lifted the sweatshirt to reveal more of her creamy thigh. Her brows pulled together as she gave herself the shot.

She looked up at him. "You'd think after sixteen years, I'd be used to stabbing myself. I don't suppose you have a sharps container? Or an empty plastic bottle I can use as a makeshift container? And maybe some tape and a Sharpie?"

He disappeared into the hall, almost grateful for the moment away from her to breathe, and returned a minute later with an empty detergent bottle, tape, and a Sharpie.

"Thanks." She set the pen in the detergent bottle, then taped it up and marked it.

"Can it go in the trash now?"

She shook her head. "It needs to be set beside the garbage

can. There's a special way it has to be broken down." She rose and set it to the side of the room.

He waited until they were at the table to ask, "You do that at every meal?"

"Yep. Unfortunately, I have to act as my own functioning human pancreas or I die."

He was sure she'd been trying to inject some humor, but he didn't so much as smile. "I'm sorry."

She lifted a shoulder. "I was diagnosed at seven, so I've had a long time to come to terms with having an incurable autoimmune disease."

Still…it would be a lot some days. "Aren't there machines that can monitor your levels and give you insulin now?"

Her slight smile slipped, and he almost wanted to pull his words back. "There are. Continuous glucose monitors and insulin pumps. But they're expensive and the insurance I have at Reuben's Real Estate wouldn't cover enough for me to be able to afford the difference. Not right now, anyway." She lifted a shoulder. "My endocrinologist always pushes me to get one, regardless of whether I can afford it or not. But I've never had one before, so I don't really know what I'm missing, do I?"

Her words said one thing, but her tone another. She was upset she couldn't afford one. And, fuck, Erik was pissed as hell that machines that would make health easier to maintain weren't accessible to her. They should be accessible for everyone.

"It must have taken a lot of money to fix the house next door."

Her eyes lit. "Actually, it wasn't too bad. The property came up, and Henry said he'd help me fix it. It took over a year, and now I pay less than when I was renting."

"He sounds like a good friend."

She laughed and the sound punctured his chest. "I owe

that man beers for the rest of my life. He's the only reason I own my own home right now."

She lowered her head and breathed in the soup for a second time. Then she groaned, and he ground his teeth so hard he damn near broke one of them.

"My God. I wasn't lying when I said this smells amazing. Did you make it?"

He lifted a shoulder. "Like I said, it's just chicken tortilla soup. Nothing fancy."

She scoffed. "I'm not a bad cook, but I doubt I'd be able to pull this off."

He swallowed a mouthful of soup, even though his appetite was nonexistent. Appetite for food, that was. "I got your keys while you were in the shower."

"You went out there?"

"Yes. It wasn't that bad. My car handles the weather well."

She grinned. "Trying to get rid of me?"

Actually, his head battled with his body between wanting to stay as close as fucking possible and running far and fast.

"No." A half lie. "I want you to know, I may not be a builder, but I'm happy to help with any small issues that arise."

"Thank you." She tilted her head. "What *do* you do?"

He paused, spoon halfway to his mouth. Shit, he should have seen that coming. "I'm a government contractor."

Her brows rose. "Doing what?"

"That's classified." He fucking hated saying that to people, but he wasn't a damn liar so it was the best he could do.

Intrigue shaded her eyes a deeper blue. "Why do I feel like I live next door to James Bond?"

"I'm no James Bond." The guy may be fictional, but he was still a better man than Erik.

She tilted her head. "How old are you?"

"Thirty-six."

Too. Damn. Old. Something he clearly needed to keep reminding himself.

"Interesting. And what did you do before you became a secret government contractor, Erik?"

"I joined the Marines after high school. After that, I entered the professional boxing world for a few years."

Her eyes widened. "Wow. You really *are* dangerous. You probably know a hundred and one ways to kill me."

And then some.

Hannah continued to ask questions throughout the meal, and when she wasn't asking questions, she was still talking. He learned about a relationship between her friend Brigid and coworker James, about Henry's love for fitness models, her coworker Taylor's strong work ethic, and her boss Reuben's love for waffles. All things he cared nothing about. But for some fucking reason, he could listen to this woman talk all night. Her voice was melodic and soothing and calm…everything he wasn't.

Once their bowls were empty, he grabbed them and took them to the sink. Hannah stood too, and the second she did, he got an eyeful of those legs again.

She lifted the bread plate.

"You don't need to help," he said in a voice that was too deep and raspy.

"I want to."

She moved beside him. Even though she'd showered in his home, she still smelled like herself. That sweet fruit and flowers scent.

She touched his arm, and he couldn't stop the muscles beneath her fingers from tensing. "Thank you. You've been such a huge help tonight."

He turned, and she was right fucking there. So close he could reach out and—

He shoved away from the counter and headed to the door. "You should go."

"What?"

He grabbed an umbrella and her keys from beside the door. "The rain's slowed. You should be okay. I can walk you over if you need me to." Anything to get her and her scent away from him.

She frowned. "Oh. Um, okay. I'll just go grab my wet clothes."

It took every ounce of self-restraint he had to not stare at those thighs as she walked up the stairs. The second she was out of sight, he ran his hands through his hair, trying to get a damn hold of himself.

A text pulled him out of his turmoil.

Chandler: Marco just resigned.

Erik's brows flickered. What the *fuck*? So he could take on more private contract work?

He shoved the phone back into his pocket, still wondering about Marco's abrupt decision, as Hannah came back down the stairs, her blonde hair shining in the light. Because that's what she was. Light. Fucking radiance. He tried not to stare at the outline of her breasts against his sweatshirt as they moved with each step.

He *did* look though. And his body betrayed him.

"Got it. And thanks for the plastic bag you left outside the door." She was about to shove her feet into shoes that had to be soaked when he spoke up.

"I need to take back my offer to let you water the flowers." Shit, those words came out colder and gruffer than he'd intended.

Hurt skittered across her face. But both the fact that Marco was still on his case about that private job and had now terminated his government contract made unease stir in his gut.

"I can't tell if you're joking," she finally said.

"I'm not."

Her mouth opened and closed a few times before she spoke. "I don't understand you. One second you help me, the next you won't let me keep my promise to your grandfather. Why can't I water the flowers? Will you at least tell me that?"

"Because I don't want you here." Shit, he hated himself for that. He wanted to soften his damn words, but he needed her to stay away more. The combination of this woman in his sweatshirt and no pants, and having to worry about Marco? It was too fucking much. And how *else* could he keep her away? Tell her about who Marco was? What he could do?

The hurt clicked into anger. "You know what? Fine, I'll stop coming. I'll stop watering Stanley's flowers. Next time I'm stuck outside in the storm, I'll freeze my ass off. At least if I die, you won't have to see me when you look outside your window."

His silence seemed to enrage her more.

She reached for the door, and he followed. "I can't believe I was actually starting to think you were nice."

"I'm not a nice guy."

She spun. "Oh, but you pretend to be. Carrying me against your chest. Letting me use your million-dollar shower and feeding me." She stepped forward and jabbed that familiar finger against his chest. "*Why* do you do that if I repulse you so much?"

He had to clench his fists to stop from grabbing her. She was too damn close, and all he could smell was her sweet scent. The woman surrounded him. Choked and drowned him.

"Hannah." The single word was a warning. He only had so much self-restraint, and the little he had was about to snap.

"Is it because you like to toy with women's emotions? Playing hot and cold? Making me like you, making me *want* you, then switching back into an ass?" She stabbed him with that finger again, moving closer. "You are—"

He snapped. Grabbed her arms and crashed his mouth

onto hers. And *fuck*…those lips were as soft as he knew they would be.

For a moment, she was frozen, as shocked by his action as Erik, her finger still pushed into his chest. The second he swiped her lips with his tongue, there was the soft thud of the bag hitting the floor and she moaned. That moan twisted his insides. Gutted him. Changed him.

He pulled her closer. On her gasp, he slipped his tongue between her lips and tangled it with hers. Her groan competed with the raging storm outside. But that was nothing compared to the storm inside him. The one that writhed and howled and laid waste to his good intentions.

Having her in his arms, against him, almost made everything that had tormented him for so long go silent. Nothing else mattered but keeping her exactly where she was. Not the fragmented pieces that were his life. Not the age difference or the danger that was a constant threat in his world.

Her fingers smoothed up the planes of his chest, then tangled in his hair. For the first time in years, he felt like he could breathe without the oxygen being too thick for his lungs. Like he could touch someone without feeling his flesh recoil.

Her touch was soft and gentle, a complete contrast to his. Because *she* was a complete contrast. His opposite in every way.

She curved a leg around his own, and in one fluid movement, he lifted her. Immediately, her thighs hugged him, and that sweatshirt tangled at her waist. He pressed her to the door like he was trying to mesh them together. Forge them into one.

It was only that thought that had the dust of reality settling in the air around them.

They didn't fit. They would *never* fit. Because he wasn't capable of being what she needed. He wasn't capable of being what anyone needed.

Like her touch suddenly burned him, he lowered her to her feet and stepped away. "Jesus. I shouldn't have done that."

Fuck, there were *so many* reasons why he shouldn't have done that. What the hell was wrong with him?

At her silence, he forced himself to gather the strength to look at her. He regretted it instantly. Her lips were red, her hair ruffled, and her eyes hot and hooded.

"I—" She stopped, as if she didn't have words.

He wasn't sure if he expected more fight from her. Maybe anger tinged with hurt. He got none of those things.

Instead, she stepped back. "I'll go now."

She shoved her feet into her wet shoes, lifted the bag, her keys, and his umbrella, and left.

And he remained, standing there, forcing the chaos that was his mind to accept that he couldn't have her. That she'd never be his.

Chapter Nine

"Let me get this straight—the man gives you a kiss that almost has you orgasming there against the wall, then tells you not to come back?"

Hannah swirled the vodka soda in her glass, letting the truth in Brigid's summary sink in. "Yep."

Brigid's jaw dropped, while Henry just looked confused. She'd dragged her friends to the bar because she needed her drinking buddies and their sympathetic ears. Two days had passed since the kiss, and she was still struggling to comprehend how good it was.

"Oh, and that's not the only thing." Hannah held up a finger. The very same finger she'd jammed against Erik's chest. "I woke the next morning to a knock on my door. It was Erik's mechanic, telling me he'd fixed my car and returned it to my house. And he refused to bill me, saying it was 'taken care of.'"

On one side, it was a huge weight off her shoulders, knowing she had a working car and the bill had been paid—but, on the other, it wasn't Erik's responsibility. She'd pay him back. It may take her a while, but she would.

Henry sighed. "I need to get myself a sexy neighbor with money coming out his ears."

"No, you don't. The man's mood swings are giving me whiplash. He's nice one second, an asshole the next, then kissing me like it's our last day on Earth."

No man should be able to kiss like that. Like he was claiming her. God, she still trembled at the very thought of it.

She gulped down some more vodka soda. Alcohol tended to make blood sugar drop, so she needed to take it easy. That meant no overindulging while she felt sorry for herself.

Tatum's was a bar in Redwood that was attached to a hotel. There were other bars, but this one tended to be less busy and a bit more upper class, something she liked to pretend to be every so often.

"So you haven't seen him since?" Henry asked, sipping his martini, eyes wide like he was watching a movie unfold. It wasn't really a movie, more of a train wreck.

"Oh, I've seen him." Brief glimpses when he'd occasionally step outside his house. "Yesterday when he got home, he was all sweaty with a bag over his shoulder and some boxing gloves poking out."

It was the sexiest damn sight she'd ever seen. Her ovaries had gone into overdrive.

"And you said he's a government contractor, but the actual title of his job is classified?" Brigid asked.

"Yup."

"Maybe that's code for wife and kid elsewhere." Brigid cringed as the words left her mouth. "That would explain him being attracted to you but barely able to touch you."

Her heart thrashed against her ribs. Would he? "No. He can be an asshole, but he's not at dirty scumbag level."

At least, she was pretty sure he wasn't.

"I didn't think Peter Howser was at scumbag level," Henry sneered, lifting his beer to his mouth. "Yet there he was."

She reached across the table and squeezed his hand. "We're still sorry about Peter."

Henry had dated him for three months. They'd agreed their relationship was exclusive, except, for Peter, it actually hadn't been. He'd already been in a long-term relationship with someone else.

"Screw Peter." Brigid scowled. "You're too good for him, Henry. There are tons of better-looking, more successful men in this bar alone."

"All straight."

Hannah tilted her head. "How do you know?"

"Hannah, we've spoken about this. We just know." Henry rolled his eyes and turned to Brigid. "Talking about good-looking men, where's James?"

"He's meeting us later. I told him if he doesn't, I'll hold out on him for a month."

Henry scoffed. "You wouldn't last a week, let alone a month."

"Hey, give a woman something to be mad about and she's unstoppable."

Hannah laughed as a man stepped into the bar from the hotel foyer. She frowned when she realized she recognized him.

"Oh God," she whispered, even though there was no way he'd have heard her from over there. "That's Erik's friend. Italian Ferrari guy."

Brigid looked first. "Oh my God, it is."

Henry glanced over, and Hannah gasped. "Don't! He'll see you looking!"

Too late. The guy turned, and when his gaze hit hers, his lips stretched into a smile.

Henry turned back, his eyes far too wide. "He. Is. Hot!"

Hannah drained the last drop of her drink before Marco stopped beside her.

"Hannah, Brigid, what a lovely surprise." His Italian-accented voice slid over her skin like silk, then he bent and kissed both her cheeks before doing the same to Brigid. "And may I say, you both look beautiful."

Henry made a choking sound beside them.

Brigid dipped her head. "It's nice to see you too, Marco."

"Are you staying here?" Hannah asked.

"I am."

God, the guy's gaze was so intense. She almost wanted to squirm under the scrutiny.

Henry cleared his throat.

"Oh, sorry." Hannah turned to look at him. "Marco, this is our friend Henry. Henry, this is Erik's friend, Marco."

He reached across and shook Henry's hand. Then his gaze returned to Hannah. "May I have a drink with you? I don't know anyone in town except Erik."

"Yes," Henry said so quickly, Hannah didn't have time to answer. "Join us. Please. We're always looking to expand our friendship group."

They were? She distinctly remembered the man telling her on numerous occasions he didn't have time for new people.

Marco gave them that smooth smile again. "Great. I'll get us a round."

They each gave Marco their drink order, and the second he stepped away, Brigid grabbed her arm. "Okay, we don't need to cry about Erik anymore. Marco being here is clearly a sign that you have a new sexy man friend to fantasize about."

Hannah laughed. "He's not really my type."

Both friends looked at her like she'd just declared it would be raining hot dogs tomorrow.

"Rich isn't your type?" Henry asked.

"Tall isn't your type?" Brigid added.

"Muscular?"

"Friendly?"

"Gorgeous?"

"Okay, okay," Hannah cut in. "Yes, he's all those things. But for one, he's staying in a hotel, so clearly not local or sticking around. And two, he's too…clean-cut."

She liked men who were rough around the edges…like Erik. Groan.

"Who cares about local?" Henry gasped. "One night with that man and your world will obviously be rocked."

She frowned and was about to tell Henry he couldn't tell that just by looking at him, but Brigid got in first.

"And something tells me he's anything but clean-cut in the bedroom."

Hannah rolled her eyes. Her friends were too much. There was no part of her that wanted to hop into bed with the man, particularly not when another dark set of eyes filled her every waking thought.

Marco returned with their drinks, and when he handed her a new vodka soda, their fingers grazed. And that right there was her big tell. She felt nothing. No spark. No tingle.

Whereas when she touched Erik…she felt everything.

———

ERIK KEPT his feet shoulder-width apart and his body low, weight evenly distributed between his legs.

Some would say boxing was all about defense. Shielding the body. Protecting it. Others would say offense. Making sure you hit first, and you hit hard. Sending the opponent to the ground and making sure they didn't get up.

Both were true. But the biggest thing that could make or break the fighter was the stance.

His opponent swung, and Erik slipped to the right, narrowly missing the hit. One heartbeat later, another punch careened toward him. He slipped to the right again. Another miss.

It was on the third punch that Erik blocked and followed up with a jab, then an uppercut. Both landed, but his opponent barely grunted. Just danced back, arms raised, ready to block the next hit.

Erik never felt freedom like when he was in the ring. It was the only time his mind truly silenced, and he could almost convince himself he hadn't lost his entire fucking world eight years ago—and that it hadn't been his fault.

Right now, he needed to be in this ring like he needed air to breathe. His mind had been a fucking mess the last two days. All because of one kiss. One kiss that had both freed and annihilated him.

He blocked a hit and danced back.

There had been a time he'd been open to love. That time was gone. Hell, there wasn't a fucking shred of that man left.

He blocked another hit.

But despite that, in one kiss, he'd felt more with Hannah than he'd ever felt with anyone…even Vicky. And for a fleeting moment, he'd wanted more. He'd wanted *her*, all of her, and not just in bed. He'd wanted her to be *his*.

He blocked another hit, absorbing the force behind it, welcoming the ache to his limbs.

He had to stop. Stop thinking about her. Stop letting memories of that kiss wreak havoc on his system. He needed to stop the emotions that stirred inside him when he saw her. Spoke to her. *Touched* her.

He threw a hook at his opponent, catching him in the mouth.

Ryker stopped and swiped the blood from his lip.

"You okay?" Erik asked.

He nodded but pulled off his gloves. "Yeah. Are *you*?"

He wasn't even in the vicinity of okay, and for once, he couldn't lie. He tore his own gloves from his fists. "No."

Before he'd moved to Redwood, he'd boxed in this gym,

76

Mercy Ring, regularly. It was owned by four former Delta guys, men who had become friends. But since moving an hour away, he didn't make it back nearly as often as he liked.

Ryker dropped his mitts into a box before grabbing a towel and wiping the blood from his face. "Didn't think so. Usually it's me calling *you*, needing to get into the ring. Wanna talk about it?"

He could have laughed. The voices in his head had been loud these last couple days. Did that qualify as conversation? "I thought this house I moved into would be isolated from other people. It's not. I have a neighbor."

Ryker seemed to let that information sink in for a minute before responding. "A neighbor in the form of a woman?"

He threw his own gloves into the box. "Yep."

"Let me guess. Sexy with an attitude."

Ryker was good at this. "How'd you know?"

"Been there, man. So, what's the problem?"

He scrubbed a hand over his face, wondering how much to tell Ryker. He never spoke to anyone about this. "My life isn't a cookie-cutter, white-picket-fence, settle-down kind of life anymore. It's dangerous, and I don't want her anywhere near that."

"I've been there too. But trying to keep yourself away from someone to protect them isn't a good idea. Our path always finds us in the end."

Ryker had gone through a lot in the last year and a half. He'd tried staying away from his woman, but she'd found him. And so had a shit ton of danger.

Erik blew out his breath. "It's more than that. I was married once. And when I tell you that her death ruined me, that's just the tip of the iceberg."

Because her death had been his fault. It didn't matter that their marriage hadn't been great or healthy, she'd still died because of him. And she wasn't the only one who'd died that day.

The familiar darkness tried to close in on him, but he forced it away.

"Shit. I'm sorry, Erik."

He fisted his hands. "I can't do that again."

The man he'd been had died right along with Vicky. He couldn't die a second time. He might not come back again.

Ryker was just opening his mouth to respond when Erik's phone rang, an unknown number showing up on the screen.

"Who is this?" he answered.

Loud music blasted in the background, then a woman's voice. "Erik? It's Brigid, Hannah's friend. I'm calling from Hannah's phone."

Erik straightened. Why was she calling him? Was Hannah okay?

"Henry, stop it!" she said quietly over the muffled sound of movement. "She's not gonna kill me. I'm doing her a favor."

"Where's Hannah?" Erik growled, his feet already moving toward his bag.

"That's why I'm calling. I just thought you should know she's been having a very intimate conversation with your hot rich friend, and he's looking quite smitten. I think when she gets back from the bathroom, he might even ask her to his room."

"Oh, Jesus," someone scoffed in the background.

A muscle in Erik's temple began to pulse. "Friend?" He didn't have any fucking friends in Redwood. Unless—

"Oh, you know. That sexy Italian who drives a Ferrari and goes by the name of Marco."

Chapter Ten

It was rare that Hannah underestimated a person. Overestimated? Of course. She was constantly looking for the good in those around her, even when there were barely crumbs. On this occasion, though, she'd definitely underestimated Marco. Over the last hour, the man had proved he wasn't just a pretty face with a nice car. He had a sense of humor. Charm. And when she spoke, he looked at her like he was really listening.

She wasn't attracted to him, but it was nice to laugh and drink with a good-looking, charismatic man. Especially one who didn't go hot and cold on her all the time. And now, a warm hum had settled in her veins, thanks to the vodka sodas she'd consumed.

"You look deep in your thoughts, *cara*."

Her gaze flashed to the man beside her. He'd been calling her that a lot.

"A bad habit of mine."

"You've barely touched your drink."

She laughed. It was both too loud and completely out of

proportion to the question. "I've already had four. If I drink any more, you'll have to carry me out of here."

Fortunately, she'd downed a bunch of nuts and pretzels, and checked her blood sugar, so at least she didn't have to worry about that.

"Don't tease me, *cara*."

Was it the Italian in him that made him so unafraid to speak his mind?

She set her chin on her hand, the man almost blurring at the quick movement. Yeah, she'd definitely had enough to drink. "Do you always have a comeback designed to make women want you?"

"Not just women," Henry said under his breath, though she heard him clearly. It wasn't just Hannah who'd drunk too much.

Poor Henry. He was probably bored. James had arrived half an hour ago, shortly after Hannah returned from the restroom. Since then, Brigid had been distracted by him, leaving Marco's attention solely on Hannah.

Marco chuckled, and the sound was a deep baritone that rumbled over her skin. "No. I just speak the truth, and the idea of carrying a beautiful woman like you in my arms is almost too much."

So freaking smooth.

"Dance with me," Marco said quietly.

Oh boy. Dance with the Italian ladies' man? Her immediate inclination was to politely decline, mostly because she didn't want to give him the wrong impression. But then she gave herself a little shake. A dance wasn't a marriage proposal. And she should not be letting Erik dictate her night when he wasn't even here.

There was a small shove in the back from Henry before she replied, "A dance sounds nice."

Marco's eyes darkened, then he took her hand, his skin

surprisingly soft. She'd expected it to be rough and calloused like Erik's.

She grabbed her drink and quickly downed a big gulp, then let Marco lead her to the dance floor. When he tugged her into his arms, she sucked in a sharp breath. There was no space between them. None. Zip.

His mouth immediately went to her ear. "You really are beautiful, *dolcezza*."

She swallowed, trying to wet her suddenly dry throat. "I have a question."

"Ask away." There was humor in his voice. Probably not the response he was used to getting from women after he called them beautiful.

"Erik seemed tense when you left his home last week. Are you friends?"

The man chuckled. "We are work colleagues, and I like to think of him as a friend, yes."

Interesting wording. Did Erik not see it the same way?

"We work in the same…field. He probably saw me noticing his beautiful neighbor and got jealous." Marco's arm tightened around her. "Do you have something with him?"

How did she answer that? Did she tell him about the kiss? The way he'd pressed her to the wall, then iced her out? "No. He's just a neighbor."

The words tasted wrong on her tongue.

"Then he is blind. If I lived next door to a woman as beautiful as you"—he gently brushed some hair from her face—"I would treat her like a queen."

The way he said queen…the way his touch slipped over her skin so delicately…he was like the perfectly crafted bachelor. Almost *too* perfect. "You keep calling me beautiful."

"And I do not anticipate stopping."

Too. Freaking. Polished. "I think," she said slowly, her

words definitely giving away her alcohol-soaked state, "you're a bit of a ladies' man."

"I am just a lover of women."

Just? Ha. Yeah, right. The man had Casanova looking like an amateur.

She sucked in a long breath, the alcohol now making her tired. At least, in addition to the snacks, she'd had her dose of insulin before leaving her house, so she knew she was safe from any diabetic episodes.

"Well, I must thank you for sharing an evening with me and my friends and giving me this dance."

"*Stella*, the pleasure has been all mine."

Then he surprised her by cupping her cheek.

She stopped swaying. "Marco—"

"You have had me transfixed all night. And those lips…" He looked down at her mouth like it was the most fascinating part of her. "They have consumed my thoughts."

There was a beat of silence. He was possibly waiting for her to say something. Maybe shift closer or further away. She did nothing. Absolutely nothing. And when he lowered his head, she *still* stood there, like a damn statue.

Goddammit, Hannah, stop this!

She pressed her hands to his chest and opened her mouth to tell him she didn't feel the same—but a large body shoved Marco from the side, making him stumble. The force almost tipped her over in the process, but strong fingers wrapped around her arm and tugged her upright.

She looked up to see a very stony-faced, very angry-looking Erik.

———

RAGE. It pumped through Erik's blood, roaring between his ears, almost deafening him.

Marco had been holding Hannah in his arms. Was about to *kiss* her.

He wanted to kill him. Rip his damn tongue out and shove it down his throat.

Hannah touched his arm. "Erik, what are you—"

"Stay out of this, Hannah." He kept his gaze on Marco. "What the fuck are you doing?"

Marco lifted both hands. He was pretty sure the stance was supposed to imply innocence. It didn't. "I was just dancing with your neighbor, Erik."

He wanted to know how the hell this had come about. Had Marco sought her out?

He stepped closer. The move was threatening, and a normal man would have moved back, but Marco was just as fucking dangerous and didn't scare so easily. Erik's voice lowered. "We worked together for a long time. That's the only reason I'm not knocking you on your ass right now. Stay away from her."

Intrigue lit Marco's dark eyes. "Now that I know how much you care about her, I won't ask her to dance again."

Erik's jaw clenched, and it took every ounce of self-restraint to step back. To not pound his fist into the guy and send him to the fucking floor. He turned, ignoring the crowd they'd attracted, and grabbed Hannah's arm again to drag her toward the door.

"Hey! Let me go," she seethed.

Not a fucking chance.

He pushed through the door, ignoring Hannah's tugs and pulls. People were staring, a couple of guys even took a few steps toward them, but one glare from Erik and they stopped.

Smart. He was in a dark mood and had no ability to show mercy.

A fist hit his arm, followed by a foot to his leg. It barely penetrated his black fury. It wasn't until he reached his Corvette that he felt the sting at his side.

He turned. "Did you just pinch me?"

"Yes, and I'll do a hell of a lot more than that if you don't let me go!" Her cheeks were red, and her chest heaved.

"I'm taking you home."

"Excuse me? You're taking me home? What am I, your pet? I don't do what you say!"

He stepped closer, so close his chest almost touched hers. Her eyes widened. "I am barely holding on to my restraint right now, Angel. Push me, and I'll snap."

She laughed. "This is you showing restraint? You're basically a metropolitan Tarzan. Wouldn't want to see what the *unrestrained* Erik looks like."

"No. You wouldn't."

She crossed her arms, and it took too much strength to *not* look at the way the movement pushed her breasts up against the low-cut top. "You think I'm afraid of you? I'm not."

"Maybe you should be."

She lifted a brow. "Why? Because you're so big and scary?"

"Because I'm dangerous. And that guy you were just dancing with? He's *just* as fucking dangerous. Believe me when I tell you, you are *not* safe with him."

She swallowed, the first bit of understanding seeming to slip into her expression. "Am I safe with you?"

No. Hell fucking no. No safer than he was with her. Because something told him they could destroy each other.

"I would never hurt you." Not physically.

Her brows flickered.

He tried to soften his voice, not entirely sure it worked. "Let me take you home, Hannah. You're drunk and tired."

"I am neither of those things." On cue, she swayed, and he grabbed her arm. "Okay. Maybe I'm a little drunk, and a tiny bit tired, but I'm a single woman who's allowed to have a good time. And I know you don't want me around him, but I'm also capable of fighting my own battles. It just so happens, I didn't want his kiss, and I was fully willing to push him away myself."

"Didn't look that way to me." Marco had been an inch away from planting his mouth on hers.

Erik's focus lowered to her lips...lips he'd kissed just two days ago. Lips that had destroyed him with a single touch.

His gaze rose to find her eyes on him. His cock hardened. It was a damn effort not to kiss her a second time.

His muscles ached with tension as he stepped back and opened the passenger door. "Get in." When the heat left her eyes, and the stubborn tilt of her chin returned, he forced his voice to soften for a second time. "Please."

"Hannah." They both turned to see Henry striding toward them, Hannah's purse in his hand. His eyes were narrowed on Erik as he spoke to her. "Are you okay?"

Two beats of silence. Then she sighed. "Yes. I'm okay. Thank you for bringing my purse."

He handed it to her before finally looking her way. "You sure? I can take you home if you'd like."

Erik's body tensed. He was ready to argue with them both, when Hannah shook her head. "No. It's okay. You go back in and finish your night. We can chat tomorrow."

He nodded, then gave Erik one more glare of warning before turning back.

Hannah grabbed the door, but before sliding in, she looked up at Erik. "Do not mistake this for me being some pushover you can bully into doing things."

"Wouldn't dream of it." The words were muttered under his breath, but by the glare she gave him, she heard just fine.

The drive home consisted of a stony silence. It was only when they were a street away that she finally turned to him, almost cautiously. "Can I ask you a question?"

His fingers tightened on the wheel. He wanted to say no,

but he knew that would get the woman's back up after she finally seemed to have calmed down. "Depends on the question."

"Do you have some secret family somewhere else?"

The word family made his breath come out in a hiss. "No, Angel. I was married. I'm not anymore." When she was silent a beat too long, he shot her a look. "What?"

He could see questions in her eyes. He expected her to ask what happened to his wife. Most people did.

"You were different then, weren't you?"

He frowned. That was *not* what he expected. "Every part of me was different." The very foundation of his world was made from a different slab back then. A smooth, neat one that had all been in one piece.

"Now I have something to ask *you*," he said before she could respond.

Her brows rose. "If you ask me to move so I don't live next door to you, the answer's no."

He chuckled. It felt good to laugh. A bit unfamiliar, but good. "No. That's not what I want." Although it would make his life easier. "Stay away from Marco."

She seemed to think about it for a moment. "I thought you were friends."

"I've done jobs with him, so we get along. That's all." After tonight, though, things had changed. "But that doesn't mean I want you around him."

She tilted her head. "It was only a dance. It never would have become anything more."

That's what *she* thought. He knew with every fiber of his being that *Marco* had wanted more. "It's never just a dance when a man gets to hold a beautiful woman."

Her breath caught. Then she swallowed. "I've been called beautiful a lot tonight but coming from you…it's different."

Another tightening of his fingers on the wheel. He didn't like hearing about other men calling her beautiful.

"Okay," she finally said. "I'll stay away from him in exchange for one thing."

Shit. "What's that?"

"Cereal."

His head whipped around to look at her. "Cereal?"

Hannah lifted a shoulder. "I'm an addict."

Where had this woman come from? "You got a particular kind you prefer?"

"Frosted Flakes."

A ghost of a smile played on his lips. "Done."

"Good." She straightened in her seat. "And when I called you an ass tonight, I only meant sometimes. You're *sometimes* an ass."

"I didn't know you called me an ass."

She shrugged again. "Now you do."

He shook his head, trying to keep the fully formed smile from his lips.

The second he stopped his Corvette in front of her house, she was out of the car. He cursed when she instantly stumbled, falling to her knees.

"Crap," she grumbled.

Erik jogged around the car and tugged her to her feet. "Are you okay?"

"Yeah, your car tripped me."

Maybe this woman should steer clear of alcohol. "Come on."

He kept an arm around her waist as they moved to her door. Even when they got there, his hand remained on her. The woman was a hazard.

She wet her lips. "Well, thank you."

"You're thanking me for tonight?"

She rolled her eyes. "Just for the ride home." Her bottom

lip sucked between her teeth. "And I know we fight a lot because you're an ass sometimes...but it's also nice having someone living so close."

She almost sounded like she was lonely. "You don't get many visitors?"

"Just Henry and Brigid. No family. I did have...someone. He's gone now."

Erik's chest grew so fucking tight it felt like there was a band around his lungs, trying to squeeze the life out of him. Who was the guy? *Where* was he? "Who?"

"He..." She looked down at her wrist and touched her bracelet—then stiffened. "Oh my God, it's gone!"

Her alarm had him straightening. "What's gone?"

"My charm...the charm he gave me!" Panic coated her voice.

She took a step away from the porch, but he grabbed her arm. "Hey, it's dark. You can find it in the morning."

She was shaking her head before he'd finished speaking. "No! You don't understand. That charm means more to me than... God, I can't even explain it. I need to find it. Do you think it's in the yard? Or back at the bar? We need to—"

"Hannah." He cupped her cheek, and finally she looked at him. "I promise you, we'll find it tomorrow."

Her mouth opened and closed, her gaze moving to the drive again, then back to him. "Really?"

"Yes. We'll have light then. It'll be easier."

She seemed to let that sit for a moment before nodding, some of the panic dissipating. "Okay. Thank you."

"You're welcome."

She opened her door, but before stepping inside, she turned and wrapped her arms around his waist, her cheek pressing to his chest.

His breath got stuck in his lungs. This was the second time she'd hugged him...she was a definite hugger. And just like the first, it felt intimate and warm and so fucking comfortable, he wanted to lean into it.

When she pulled away, she smiled up at him before saying good night and disappearing into her house. She did it with so much ease, like her touch hadn't changed him. Twisted him up and made him into something different. Something better.

He ran a hand through his hair. He needed to get a fucking grip. This woman was not his. She was too young. Too good. And he wasn't even close to deserving her.

Chapter Eleven

Hannah groaned as she rolled from her belly to her back. Her head hurt. It wasn't a hard pounding, but it was dull and constant.

What had she been thinking last night, drinking every glass of vodka that was put in front of her?

Dumb. So dumb.

Without opening her eyes, she grabbed her small gold pouch on the bedside table, waited a few more minutes, then with a pained groan, sat up. She'd never been much of a drinker, one here or there was usually all she allowed herself. And this was exactly why. Alcohol kicked her ass.

She forced her eyes open, but it was more of a squint than a good look. After removing the glucose meter from the pouch, she turned it on and pushed a test strip into the small slot. When she was a kid, she'd cringe at the next step. Now, her fingers were so calloused from pricking her skin, it barely registered as pain in her brain.

After a quick wipe with an alcohol pad across her finger, she pressed the lancet device to her skin and pricked herself before putting her bloodied finger on the strip. She knew she was low, she just wanted to know *how* low.

The number popped up and she groaned. Seventy-three. Not the worst but definitely time for some breakfast. Then she'd retest and dose if necessary.

She snatched up her phone before going to the kitchen, where she grabbed some oatmeal, milk, peanut butter, and blueberries. Post-alcohol Hannah just wasn't feeling the cereal this morning.

Her phone vibrated on the counter, and she looked down to see a string of messages from Henry and Brigid. Her lips curved at the last one.

Henry: Of course, she's in bed with him. What else would she be doing after a night of screwing the guy?

Jesus. She could just imagine the messages that had come before that one. All about sex and Erik. Well, they were going to be sorely disappointed. No wild sex. Minimal touching. Not even a kiss.

Still, her heart beat a bit faster at the memory of him standing between her and Marco. She'd been angry, but there'd also been other emotions at play. Emotions she hadn't let the man see but had made her belly twist and tangle. He'd been protecting her. Hell, he'd stormed into the bar to do just that.

How long had it been since a man had defended her?

But God, he was confusing. What did he want? And why did she apparently like dangerous guys so much? She hadn't dated much in her twenty-three years, but the men she was attracted to were all rough edges, hard lines...and they almost always had something in their pasts that had hurt them.

Her phone continued to light up with message after message as she cooked her oats.

Brigid: Big biceps do not equate to small cocks. Just look at James.

Oh God. She did not need to know about the size of James's penis. She lifted the phone.

Hannah: Guys, there was no wild sex. He walked me to the door and said good night.

Henry: Boo! That's no fun.

Brigid: Noooo…I was so excited for the debrief.

She laughed. They probably would have rushed to her house with popcorn and wine if she'd given them the green light.

She shot a look at the time. Nine a.m. Her first open house at Angelo's place was in an hour. She needed to get ready. There were a couple more open houses tomorrow as well, which she was fine with. Everyone knew real estate agents didn't get weekends. Well, not if they wanted to sell homes.

She ate her oats quickly and had just shoved the last mouthful in when another message came through. Her heart thrashed against her ribs when she saw who it was from.

Erik: I hope you're feeling okay today, Angel. Drink plenty of water and look after your insulin levels. I left something for you at the front door.

Her head shot up. Almost on autopilot, she moved out of the kitchen, through the small living room, and tugged the door open.

She couldn't stop the small smile from crossing her face.

Frosted Flakes.

She lifted the box, biting her bottom lip to stop the smile from spreading. It wasn't until she was back in her kitchen that she realized it had been opened. She lifted her phone to text him back.

Hannah: I may not have said it explicitly, but the deal was for a full box of cereal, Mr. Hunter.

Erik: Open it.

She frowned but lowered the phone to the counter and did as he requested. Her breath caught at what she saw.

There, taped inside the top flap, was the charm Nico had given her.

She tugged the tape off and held the charm in her palm, tracing the curves of the cloud with her gaze. With the headache and the messages, she'd almost forgotten about this. God, how had she forgotten?

Hannah: Where was it?

Erik: In the dirt by the car.

How long had he searched for it? *When* had he searched? She wanted to ask those questions. Instead, she went with a simple response.

Hannah: Thank you.

Saying thank you didn't feel enough.

Erik: You're welcome, Angel.

⊏⊐

"I'M SO HAPPY! Erik's home, and soon Nate will be home too, and I'll have all my babies back!"

Erik smiled as his mother gushed. He'd seen his parents a few times now since returning to Redwood. The first visit had been emotional as hell. His mother had cried for nearly an hour, and even after that, she'd continued to wipe her eyes intermittently. Even his father's eyes had gotten a bit wet.

And he understood. He'd been away for a long time. His parents had probably started to wonder if he was ever coming home again. He hated to admit it, but if it wasn't for his grandfather leaving him the house, and his dad's heart issues, he probably wouldn't be here now.

"Jennifer, let's not get ahead of ourselves," his father said softly, patting her arm. "We don't know if Nate's leave will be approved."

"I know, but a woman can hope."

They sat at a table at Black Bean, coffees in front of them, and fuck but did he need the caffeine. He was used to getting little sleep. Hell, he'd barely slept in eight years. But last night, after being close to Hannah, he'd only gotten a couple hours. Thoughts of her had tormented him.

Andi bumped his shoulder. "So, Finley said she saw you at Tatum's last night."

His shoulders tensed. Finley and his sister had been inseparable since high school. The woman was basically family.

"She said she was going to go up to you and say hi," Andi continued, "but you seemed...busy."

He bit back a groan at the questioning glances he could feel across the table.

"Busy doing what?" his mother asked.

He was careful to keep his features clear. "Nothing. Just helping a neighbor get home safely."

His father nodded. "I was surprised when that house next door was renovated. But they did a good job."

His mother shook her head. "I didn't like it. That place was a knockdown."

"She's pretty," Andi piped in, and he wanted to shove a rag into her mouth. She'd only seen Hannah that one time, when they'd been here at Black Bean.

His mother's eyes lit up like his sister had said he was engaged to be fucking married.

"A bit young," Andi added, clearly not noticing how close she was to being physically silenced. "But very pretty."

"*How* young?" his father asked.

Jesus Christ. "It doesn't matter. She's just a neighbor. She needed a ride home from the bar last night, and I gave it to her."

Fortunately, if Andi knew about his interaction with Marco, she didn't say anything.

Over the next hour, his mother and Andi filled every

second of silence. His mother was throwing a fundraiser ball in a few weeks. She threw a lot of them—this one for the American Heart Association.

His gaze flicked to his dad. No one looking at him would think he had heart issues. He'd lost some weight and muscle over the years and his face was a bit thinner, but otherwise he looked healthy. Of course, if anyone could take care of him, it was his mother.

They were almost done with their coffees when the door opened, and Hannah stepped in.

His heart sped up, his muscles tightening. She wore a tight black skirt that ended midthigh, a crisp white shirt, and a blazer. She looked both formal and sexy. Her hair fell around her shoulders like a damn waterfall.

Her gaze found his immediately, and a small smile stretched her lips. She mouthed a "Hi" just before a man stepped in behind her and touched her shoulder, shifting her attention.

Erik's hands fisted. He vaguely recalled seeing the man the previous night with her friends, while Erik had searched for Hannah, but his attention had quickly zoned in on Marco and Hannah on the dance floor.

Erik kept his gaze on them as they moved to the counter.

"Well, look who's here," Andi said in a singsong voice.

He turned back to her. "Are you trying to get a rise out of me today?"

"Always, and I feel absolutely no remorse."

Suddenly, he was remembering other reasons he'd stayed away for so long. He tried to refocus on what his parents were talking about, but from the corner of his eye, he caught sight of the guy moving to the bathroom.

He told himself to stay in his damn seat, even as his legs twitched.

Fuck it.

"I'm getting another coffee."

He was up and across the room before anyone could respond, but he distinctly heard the sound of his sister's laughter.

He stopped at the counter beside Hannah, so close his shoulder almost touched hers. "Hey."

Her navy-blue eyes lightened. "Hey."

Damn, her voice did things to him. "You doing okay today?"

"Yeah, just a dull headache."

He told himself not to ask...hell, he just about yelled it in his head, but he clearly wasn't listening to his damn brain anymore. "Who's the guy?"

Her brows shot up. "James? We work together. He's another real estate agent."

They worked together. But did the asshole want to get into her—

"He's also been with Brigid for over four years."

The familiar band around his chest released, and he fucking hated that it had been there at all.

She turned to face him fully and wrapped her fingers around his forearm. That simple touch seared him. "Thank you for finding the charm. You have no idea how much that means to me."

"Who gave it to you?" She'd mentioned a guy last night.

Hannah swallowed and looked down, her finger brushing over it. "There was a guy who I spent several years with in foster care. I thought of him as a brother. He died a couple years ago, and now this and a couple photos are all I have to remember him by."

Grief filled her voice. So much that it pressed down on his shoulders, making him itch to reach out and touch her. Comfort her in some way. It was only James returning to the counter that brought Erik to his senses.

The guy stood beside Hannah…too close. "Hi. I'm James."

"Erik." His gaze shifted back to Hannah. "I'll see you around, Hannah. I'm glad I was able to help."

Then he forced himself to walk away, even though it felt so much harder than it should have.

Chapter Twelve

Cross, cross, jab.

The bag flew back with the violence of each hit. At the sheer fucking force of his emotions.

Erik's basement was dark, bar a dim light that centered the ceiling. He'd been down here for hours, beating the shit out of this bag in an attempt to chase away his demons. Because today, more than any other day, he had them in droves. They crawled along his skin, pricking his flesh like he was a fucking pin cushion.

Eight years to the day since he'd received the news. The news that had come when he'd thought he was already at rock bottom.

He hadn't been. He hadn't even known the depths that one could reach. That a few words could plunge a person into a hell so bottomless, few knew it existed. A hell he'd yet to climb out of.

Jab, jab, hook.

He'd gotten his revenge. But since that day, he hadn't been living, only surviving. Now he was back in Redwood, and suddenly he wanted things he shouldn't fucking want.

He'd slept with other women since the day his world had imploded, but none of them had meant anything. With Hannah, every touch meant something.

His phone beeped, and for the first time all afternoon, he dropped his fists, chest heaving with his panting breaths as he looked at the screen.

He narrowed his eyes. Someone was here.

He clicked into his cameras and shock smacked him when he saw it was his brother, Nate.

When did he get into town? He wasn't supposed to be here until the fundraising ball.

The doorbell rang, but instead of going upstairs, Erik used the phone app to unlock the door. Nate would find him. He turned back to the bag and began to pound it again.

It didn't take long. He felt his brother before he saw him. It didn't matter how long it had been since he'd last seen Nate; today would always be a day he didn't want company.

"What are you doing here?" he asked without stopping or turning away from the bag.

Nate came into view. He was five years younger than Erik but just as tall and broad. He also had the same hazel eyes. There was no mistaking him for anyone but his brother. "I knew you were home. I also knew this was a heavy day for you. So I took the weekend off to check on you."

"I'm fine." When Nate kicked off his shoes and tugged his shirt over his head, Erik stopped and glared at his brother. "What are you doing?"

Nate grabbed some gloves from a box. "I haven't had a round with you in years. I think it's time."

"I'm not fighting you, Nate." His brother could well and truly hold his own, but right now, Erik was in a dangerous mood. That was why he'd chosen the bag instead of driving to a boxing gym.

Nate punched his shoulder. It wasn't a light fucking tap, either.

Erik faced him. "Don't do that."

"Hit me."

"No."

The next punch came hard and fast, but Erik brought up his arm and blocked. "Stop."

"Fight me." Another punch.

This time, Erik slipped to the side. "Nate. I'm not in the mood."

"You are, though. You want to beat the shit out of *someone*. Why not me?"

"Because I don't want to hurt you." He knew how stupid that sounded. His brother was a damn SEAL.

Nate lifted a brow. "Still underestimating me, big brother."

This time, Erik didn't just block Nate's right cross, he followed it up with his own. Nate slipped away, narrowly missing the hit.

"You can do better than that," his brother cajoled. Nate was pushing his fucking buttons and he knew it. It was something he'd always been good at.

Erik swung again, this time catching Nate in the gut with a hook.

His brother barely reacted. In fact, he smiled. "Felt good, didn't it?"

Erik breathed through the anger in his chest as it bubbled to the surface. Not anger at his brother. Anger at the fucking world for turning his life into what it was. For taking people from him.

He lunged forward, throwing blow after blow but only landing half of them. Nate was as good as Erik now, returning each hit with a punch of equal force. Some landed, and Erik almost preferred when they did. Because the physical pain took away from the mental and emotional turmoil. It competed with the devastation that tried to desolate him.

His brother didn't say anything as they danced around each other, exchanging blows. How the man knew Erik needed silence while he got rid of this angst inside him, he had no fucking clue.

After what felt like a good hour, they finally stopped, and Nate broke the silence. "How are you feeling?"

He pulled his gloves from his hands, letting several deep breaths move through his chest. "Like I can breathe again."

There was a flicker of emotion in Nate's eyes. It came and went so quickly, Erik could almost convince himself it wasn't there. The entire family knew what Erik had lost. But Nate understood the extra weight of also losing team members. He'd lost one of his own team members while on a mission. A man who was as close as a brother.

Nate stepped forward and grasped his shoulder. "I didn't want you to be alone today, brother."

"I could be in a roomful of people and still feel alone." Fuck, that was more honesty than he'd meant to give.

"I understand. Doesn't mean you should be." There was a heavy pause, then one side of Nate's mouth lifted. "I hear you have a neighbor."

"Who the hell told you that?" But he already knew.

"Andi. Said you helped her out at a bar, then took her home."

Damn, his sister had a big mouth. "Her name's Hannah."

His brother raised a brow like he was waiting for more. He wouldn't get it.

Finally, Nate sighed. "You know it's okay for you to move on, right? Vicky would want you to be happy."

"Vicky would hate me for what I did to our family."

This time, Nate's brows pulled together. "You really believe that?"

"I killed them." Each word felt like a physical blow that landed heavier than the one before.

Nate's eyes narrowed, and an anger Erik rarely saw in his little brother burned to life. "No, you didn't. That asshole broke into your house and killed her."

"Because of *me*. Because I led the mission to capture and kill his crew and shut down his organization."

"That does *not* make what he did your fault."

So much damn conviction. Erik didn't have even a shred of it.

Nate's stare burned into him. "Tell me you understand what I'm saying."

His jaw clicked. "I understand, Nate." He just didn't believe it.

HANNAH PAUSED in putting the dishes away as she caught sight of Erik moving to the fence separating their properties. The man looked like he was on a mission. He slipped through the gate and crossed her yard. The look on his face was… God, she didn't even have words. It was like deep torment.

Only ten minutes ago, she'd seen a man leave his house. Someone who looked just like Erik. A brother, perhaps? Did he have something to do with Erik's mood?

She waited, expecting to hear her doorbell ring. When it never came, she lowered the towel to the counter and looked out the living room window to see Erik slipping into the woods on the other side of her house.

Where was he going?

Before she could think better of it, she grabbed her jacket, slipped on her shoes, and went outside.

She hadn't gone into the woods much, mostly because the Wenatchee River, which wound down from Lake Wenatchee, ran through town and her property. The widest parts of the river were actually right there in her woods. It had been the one downside of her purchase.

It didn't take her long to find him. Of course, he was standing right beside the fast-moving water.

She weaved through the last of the trees before stopping beside him. She made sure that she wasn't too close to the water's edge, planting her feet firmly into the ground.

He didn't say a word. He didn't even look at her. But despite that, she felt the heaviness of his mood. It was as if there was a thick pane of glass between them…and she instinctively knew if she hit too hard, it would shatter.

So instead of speaking right away, she bent down and lifted a handful of small rocks and threw them one at a time, watching as they sunk into the water.

"Nico and I used to have competitions on who could throw the rocks the furthest," she eventually said, quietly. "When I was eight, I almost drowned in a river because I'd never learned to swim. After that, I flat-out refused to be near the water. But he made it fun, always letting me win. He almost made the water feel safe."

The only hint that he heard her words was the small flex of his forearm. He wore a T-shirt, no jacket, but didn't look cold at all.

She let the quiet seep into both of them for a while, the rushing water the only sound around them. Then, finally, she asked, "Are you okay?"

His jaw tightened. "No."

At least he was honest. "Want to talk about it?"

He shook his head.

She nodded, then one side of her mouth lifted. "You know, I should really be riding your ass for being on my land."

There was the tiniest hint of a smile. "I know. I'm sorry. I used to come out here when I was a kid. There's something about the flowing water that I always found calming."

Found...past tense. Because he didn't anymore? Because nothing could calm him now?

"When I was nineteen," she started softly, sliding her thumb over the smooth curve of a rock, "I started seeing this therapist. I'd seen a few before her, but I always felt like they didn't really care about my problems. This one was different."

She turned the stone over, letting its coolness soothe her skin. "I told her about some of the stuff I went through in my foster homes."

Erik's eyes were on her now, heavy like a weight. Hot and questioning.

"Some of it was so heavy..." she continued. "Stuff I'd never told anyone but Nico."

She lifted her gaze to the water and threw the rock, watching the ripples it created when it hit the surface. "I'd just finished telling her the worst story of all, when she said something I'll never forget." Hannah swallowed, remembering the woman's words like she was speaking them in her ear now. "She looked at me and said, 'And you think you went through all that for *nothing*?'"

Her gaze caught on a leaf that drifted through the water. "She said that our darkest moments aren't meant to cripple us. They're meant to make us stronger. Teach us, then turn us into warriors."

Finally, she turned to look at Erik. He watched her as if he was trying to peel back her layers to see beneath the surface, the one he just now realized she showed the rest of the world.

"So you're a warrior," he said quietly. It wasn't a question.

Still, she answered it as if it was. "Yes. And so are you."

Anyone could see he'd been through some kind of hell. Something that had twisted his world in a way he still hadn't recovered from.

He noticed she was out of pebbles and reached down to lift another, handing it to her. Their fingers touched, and that familiar electricity ran down her arm. "I don't know about that, Angel."

"I do." Two words of which she was absolutely certain.

There was that familiar tilt of his lips again. "Thank you."

She wasn't sure if he was thanking her for her words, or her company, or for not kicking him off her property—it didn't matter. "You're welcome."

When she just kept rolling the small rock over and over in her hand, he asked, "Are you going to throw that?"

She shook her head. "I think I'll keep this one. I'll give you some space now."

She'd made it five steps away before he spoke, causing her to stop.

"You really can't swim?"

She turned her head. "I really can't swim. And being that close to the edge just now scared the shit out of me. Shows how much I like you."

Chapter Thirteen

"Did you get a sale?"

Hannah groaned as she swung an arm over her eyes. It was only five o'clock on a Friday night, but she was already lying in bed, sloth pajamas donned and face scrubbed clean.

"No," she groaned to Brigid. The woman was on speaker, so she couldn't see her end-of-the-world dramatics but could probably hear them. "Either I have become the shittiest real estate agent around, or I'm cursed."

She had to be, right? Barely anyone was contracting her to sell their homes, and the few she *did* have listed, she couldn't move.

"I'm sorry, Han. I wish there was something I could do to help."

She nibbled her bottom lip. "Do you know if Reuben's said anything to James?"

Her boss had to be close to letting her go, right? James and Taylor weren't doing much better, but they'd each closed two sales in the last few weeks.

"No, why? You think he'll let you go?"

"Remember Nancy? She didn't sell anything for three

consecutive months, and he booted her out like she was chopped liver."

"First of all, Nancy was a bitch who liked to steal other women's boyfriends."

Hannah cringed. The woman *had* come onto James. Pretty aggressively, in fact.

"Second, you've got an awesome track record. You've been Reuben's top seller since you took the job. I would know—I've heard James complain about it enough."

Hannah traced a wrinkle on her bed sheet. It was true. Before this long dry patch, she'd done really well. It was why she'd felt confident funneling all her savings into her home renovation.

Still, she wished she had her friend's faith. But then, Brigid wasn't the one who faced living in a house with no power if she couldn't pay her bills.

"All right, I should let you get ready for your date, Brig. Thanks for listening, and have fun at your sushi night."

Sushi was her and James's go-to date-night dinner. The woman made it sound so good that Hannah occasionally got jealous and forced Henry to come over for their own sushi night…just without all the kissing and sex. Though Henry was a great cuddler.

Erik flickered into her mind. She could have a sushi night with him…only she hadn't talked to or seen the guy in five days, since they'd spoken in the woods.

"Thanks, hon. Chat tomorrow."

The second Hannah hung up, she moved to the window and glanced outside, looking over her beautiful property. Land that hadn't cost her nearly as much as it could have. Land she needed to be able to pay the mortgage on.

With a sigh, she was about to turn around when a flicker of movement caught her attention. A long shadow at the back of the house.

Her brows tugged together. What was that? An animal? No. It was too big.

It looked like a person.

Her heart rate kicked up a notch, and she lifted her phone to text Erik.

Hannah: Hey. Are you home?

The three dots appeared instantly.

Erik: No. Why?

Something sounded near her back door. It was so quiet, most people wouldn't have heard it. She only did because she was paying attention. It was one of the boards on the porch just beyond the door…someone had stepped on it and caused a slight squeak.

Her breath became a rattle in her chest as she took a small step away from the window. Had she locked her back door? Probably not. She rarely did, because she felt so safe out here.

Erik: Is something wrong?

There was a slight shake in her fingers as she typed out a response.

Hannah: Someone's at my back door, maybe trying to get in, and I don't think I locked it.

The next sound was even quieter, and she almost *did* miss it this time. But it made every hair on her body stand on end.

It was the sound of her back door opening.

Oh God…

Without thinking, she quietly rushed forward and wrapped her fingers around the knob on her bedroom door. Carefully, she closed the door and locked it.

Erik: Hide. I'm calling the police and I'm five minutes away.

She didn't respond to tell him they were already inside. There wasn't time. Her house was small—hell, there was only one freaking bedroom. The locked door was the only thing that would buy her time.

Her gaze darted around the area. She could hide, but

there weren't many places to go, and if he got in here, it wouldn't take him long to find her. She needed to take the offense.

Quickly, she ran into the bathroom, closed the door, and turned on the shower. Thank God she'd done a walk-in shower. Then she quickly moved into the walk-in closet off the bathroom.

Lowering to her haunches, she opened the bottom dresser drawer and dug under the clothes to pull out her gun. It was something she'd always had for safety but never thought she'd actually have to use. Nico had taught her how to shoot, and she'd never been more grateful than in this moment.

With trembling fingers, she clicked off the safety. Then she waited in the closet, hiding behind the doorframe so the intruder wouldn't see her.

She heard the rattling of the door handle as the person broke the lock. It didn't take them nearly long enough. Then the soft thuds of steps sounded in her bedroom.

Her breath caught and her skin bloomed cold with fear. She closed her eyes, begging her breaths to remain silent. For her fear to not seem as loud in the room as it was inside her.

She waited for the small click of the bathroom door opening, paused a few more seconds, then she stepped out to find a man dressed in dark pants and a long-sleeved dark shirt, slowly approaching her shower on the other side of the bathroom, his back to Hannah—and a gun in his hand. He wasn't wearing a mask, which made her chest tighten further. People only chose not to wear a mask when they didn't plan for their victims to survive, right?

She forced her hands to remain steady as she aimed her weapon and stepped fully into the bathroom. "I've got a Beretta pointed at your head and I know how to shoot."

The man stilled.

"Lower the gun to the floor, kick it over, then turn," she

said quietly but firmly. "If you make any sudden moves, I shoot."

There was a moment of pause, and in that moment, she wondered if he was going to follow her instructions or just spin and fire. Then he slowly lowered the gun and turned.

She barely stifled a gasp.

The man had a huge scar running down almost the entire left side of his face. His blue eyes were sharp and screamed dangerous. The fear inside her splintered into a thousand tiny shards.

"What do you want?" she forced out.

"Isn't that obvious?"

She frowned. "Me? Why?"

"I want—"

A car engine roared outside.

Instinctively, she glanced toward the door. It was only a half second of distraction, but that was all the intruder needed to lunge forward and knock her back.

She cried out as she fell, her head hitting the hard tile of the bathroom floor. The guy lifted her wrists and smashed them to the tiles above her head. The impact, combined with his tight grip, had her crying out again—and the gun slipped from her grasp.

She tried to get a leg up to knee him, but there was no space. She twisted her body. Turned beneath him. But two strong hands wrapped around her throat.

Immediately, the fingers tightened, her air cut off.

Panic flared when she wasn't able to breathe. She scratched and clawed at the hands, but they didn't budge.

Darkness hedged her vision, shifting her world from vibrant shades to deep, dark grays.

She was almost out when a gunshot exploded through the room.

The man fell to the side, and she gasped in a jagged breath.

FURY BLASTED through Erik's system as he got out of his car and ran to Hannah's entrance, his Glock firmly in his grip as he tried the front door. Closed but unlocked.

Fuck.

He stepped inside and scanned the living room and kitchen.

The soft sounds of a scuffle came from the bedroom.

He took off. When he reached Hannah's room, the edges of his vision blackened at the scene in the bathroom.

He lifted his Glock and fired without hesitation, hitting the asshole in the side. It wasn't a kill shot. It wasn't meant to be.

Erik was across the room in a second, dropping on top of the guy and pressing the muzzle of the gun to his forehead. "Who the fuck are you and what do you want?"

The guy groaned in pain. "Get the hell off me!"

Not a damn chance. He pushed the muzzle harder to the man's skull. "Answer the question or die."

"Fuck…you!"

Erik saw the glint of the knife moments before the guy could plunge it into his side. He grabbed the asshole's wrist with his spare hand, but the motion allowed the intruder to roll them so he was on top. He threw an elbow into Erik's face.

He absorbed the pain, then he let it fuel him, driving the butt of his Glock across the guy's face. He followed it up with a hit to the side of his head.

The asshole fell back, lifting a pistol from the floor. He only got it halfway up before Erik fired, hitting him in the chest.

The gun dropped. The man's eyes remained open, his body still.

Fuck! He hadn't gotten any damn information. Who the hell was this guy?

His gaze shifted to Hannah. She sat on the floor, fingers

gingerly touching the skin of her neck. The image made every protective instinct inside him fire. It made him want to go to fucking battle for her all over again.

He rose and moved over to her before lowering to his haunches. He was scared to fucking touch her in case he hurt her.

"Are you okay?" He'd been going for soft, but there was too much anger inside him to gentle his tone.

Her eyes were unfocused, but she nodded. She was in shock.

When she swallowed, she cringed. He tugged her hand from her neck, growling at the red bruises already forming.

That fucker. Erik wanted to kill him a second time but draw it out and make sure he felt the pain. "You're safe," he said quietly, his voice dangerously low.

"Who was he?"

"I don't know. But I'll find out." That was a vow he was making here and now.

Sirens sounded.

"Police and paramedics will be here soon." He'd called both.

She opened and closed her mouth before nodding. "Thank you."

He couldn't stop himself. He lifted a hand and grazed her cheek. "I'm so fucking sorry you got hurt."

"But I'm okay...thanks to you."

The words were spoken so quietly they barely crossed the distance. He didn't have time to respond before police were rushing in.

The next hour went too fucking slowly, with police traipsing through her house and paramedics coming and going. He made sure to keep Hannah within his sight the entire damn time.

He'd also called Andi, who was working with the paramedics to look over Hannah.

"There doesn't appear to be any damage to the voice box or windpipe," Andi said, pulling off her gloves. "Just bruising to the neck and a small bump on the back of the head."

Erik's stomach clenched. Still more than it should have been. "So she doesn't need to go to the hospital?"

"No." Andi turned back to Hannah. "But I would encourage you to call someone to be with you tonight, to help with pain meds and just keep an eye on you."

He opened his mouth to say he'd stay with her, but Hannah spoke first.

"I'll call Brigid." She swallowed. "Thank you, Andi."

When Officers Leaton and Sanders headed toward them, Erik inched closer to Hannah, unable to stop himself from touching the small of her back. She leaned into him, as if she found the same sanctuary in him that he found in her.

"Who was he?" Erik asked, before they'd even reached them.

He'd already snapped a photo of the asshole and sent it to Chandler, but if these guys could give him any information, it would speed up the process.

"We need confirmation, but we suspect this guy is responsible for a string of break-ins in the area. He's been stealing and fleeing the scene." Leaton looked at Hannah. "You said you turned the shower on?"

She frowned and nodded.

Leaton nodded as well. "No one else has been home before. He probably heard the shower, realized someone was here, and decided to get rid of you, since he wasn't hiding his identity. Then he could rob you at his leisure."

Probably? Erik didn't want to work on a fucking *probably*. He wanted certainty that this guy was working alone.

A shudder raced down Hannah's spine, and he shifted his hand to her waist, tugging her closer.

"Do you have someone to stay with tonight?" Sanders asked.

"She can stay with me." The words were out in a decisive rush. He didn't regret them. He needed to have eyes on her, and she needed safety. It made sense.

She turned toward him, frowning. "No, you don't need to do that."

"I do." There was no other way he'd feel okay tonight.

Sanders nodded. "Great. We should be done within the hour, then you can grab whatever you need."

The officers headed away just as Hannah shook her head. "You've already done enough for me. You don't need to share your home. I can stay with Brigid or Henry."

The thought made acid coat his gut. "I want you to stay with me. I've got good security. It will make me feel better, knowing you're truly safe."

Her eyes softened, bottom lip disappearing between her teeth. Her gaze shifted to her front door, then back to him. "Okay. Thank you. For everything."

His hand twitched to cup her cheek. Tug her into him. Instead, he briefly squeezed her hip. The simple touch burned right through him. "I'm glad you're okay, Hannah."

So fucking glad that his chest ached.

Chapter Fourteen

"Tell me you have something," Erik growled across the line before Chandler could get a word in.

"I do. Travis Hardy. A low-level street thug. He's been charged previously for petty theft, holding up a gas station, and breaking and entering."

Erik leaned back in his office chair. Maybe the police were right, and it was just a theft gone wrong.

"So you can get off the 'it's because she lives next door to you' train of thought," Chandler said, just about reading Erik's damn mind.

"Can you blame me in my line of work?"

"No. Still doesn't make this your doing."

He scrubbed a hand over his face. A few hours had passed since the police had left. They'd taken her statement in her living room, and when Erik escorted Hannah back into the bedroom to pack an overnight bag, the little color that had returned to her face leached back out the second she'd stepped inside. The bathroom had been cleaned, but he knew she'd revisited the attack in her head.

Once they got to his place, he'd had to force her to eat.

Thank fuck he'd prepared the spare bedroom shortly after moving in. Actually, it hadn't been him. Andi had come over and basically overhauled the room, claiming it was hers if she ever needed to stay. He owed her, both for that and for coming over tonight.

Now Hannah was asleep, but he wasn't. Probably wouldn't sleep much at all tonight. It was fine. He was intimately familiar with insomnia. The darkest hours of the night had almost become his comfort.

"What's going on between you two?" Chandler asked, pulling Erik out of his head.

"Nothing." The word tasted sour on his tongue. Because it wasn't *nothing*. But that little fact scared the shit out of him and wasn't something he was even close to voicing out loud.

"If there *is* something going on, that's okay, you know."

He could have laughed. "No it's not, and you know it. Danger is always a step away from knocking on my fucking door."

"True. But maybe she's not as fragile as you think she is. Maybe she can handle it."

But could he handle the risk? "She's still flesh and blood. My job while I was married was far less dangerous, and you know how that ended."

It had turned his world so dark that he thought he'd never see again. Ripped the damn ground from beneath his feet and plunged him into the depths of hell.

"I know," Chandler said quietly. "But you need to live, or your life will just become one big cage."

His life was already a cage, with walls so high and strong they felt impenetrable. "Thanks for the information, Chandler."

He hung up and dropped his phone to the table, then he moved upstairs to the bathroom. He stripped off before turning the shower on so fucking hot that his skin burned. He welcomed the bite of pain.

He closed his eyes and lowered his chin to his chest, trying to drown out the voice in his head that told him he'd almost been too late tonight…just like he'd been too late to save his wife.

He pressed his hands to the wall.

Tonight had stirred up shit he'd tried to forget. He'd vowed to protect Vicky. He'd taken a fucking oath, but when she'd needed him most, he hadn't been there.

Then she'd died at the hands of his enemy.

He scrunched his eyes harder. Every time he tried to force himself to forget, to release the pain of the past, it felt like God laughed. Every bad memory had just gotten so much louder since returning to Redwood. Since meeting Hannah.

His breaths moved faster in his chest.

He'd killed the asshole who attacked Hannah tonight, just like he'd killed the man who murdered his wife. He'd thought ending his wife's killer would silence the voices in his head. It hadn't. The guy had torn his life to shreds, and his death hadn't sewn them back together.

What gave Erik purpose now was ridding the planet of animals. The ones walking around masquerading as people. He had tunnel vision when on a job. To hunt. Find. Kill. That purpose stripped him of any humanity that would have stopped a better man from playing God.

When he turned off the tap, he didn't feel any fucking better.

He'd barely managed to pull on briefs and shorts when a scream pierced the air.

THE GUN WAS *heavy in Hannah's hand, the tremble in her fingers so violent it was possible she'd pull the trigger without even meaning to.*

"Lower the gun to the floor, kick it over, then turn. If you make any sudden moves, I shoot."

God, why was there a tremor in her voice? Why couldn't she be strong and firm and brave?

The man lowered the gun, but he didn't turn. He just stood there, frozen. What was he doing? Waiting for her to shoot? Calling her bluff?

The quaver in her fingers grew stronger. She shifted her gaze around the small bathroom but stopped when she reached the mirror. Her lips parted, her heart thudding. That wasn't her staring back.

Well, it was…but not her today. She looked… God, she looked sixteen again.

Her gaze brushed over the pale green T-shirt, the ripped jeans. Why did she—

The man finally turned. She flicked her attention back to him. Her heart stopped and her lungs tightened to the point that no air got in. Because the person in front of her wasn't the man who'd broken into her home.

"Hello, Hannah. This is a nice surprise."

That voice…so familiar. And so utterly terrifying.

No. This wasn't real. He wasn't really here.

She blinked slowly, keeping her eyes closed for a beat, but when she opened them, the man was still there. And not only that, the room was different. The floor wasn't tiled. The red oak basin didn't sit to the left, and the shower wasn't at the back of the room.

It wasn't her bathroom at all…it was a bedroom. One she saw all too often when ghosts of her past tried to torment her. The small bed sat against the right wall. The closet, which was now empty, to the left.

"You've made my life quite difficult with your…accusations."

She stumbled back, foot catching on a piece of clothing. She righted herself. "You're supposed to be in jail." And the gun in her hand was supposed to be just a precaution. Something she had to feel safe but didn't need to use.

"Bail." He took another step forward. "Cost me a pretty penny too. Had to put my fucking house up as collateral. Something else you'll need to pay for."

She swallowed the nausea at his proximity. The terror that tried to freeze her mind and body.

"I don't want any trouble. I just came for my bracelet." The one that now sat on her wrist. The one she hadn't been able to leave behind. God, why hadn't she shoved it into her pocket and climbed back out the window faster?

He laughed. "You ain't taking that bracelet, girlie. Consider it compensation for my troubles."

"I am." Suddenly, the tremble in her voice was gone. Because no one was taking this bracelet from her. It was her one connection to her parents. A connection she couldn't give up. Wouldn't.

He stepped closer again.

"Stop moving or I shoot!"

He laughed. "You won't shoot me. You're too much of a good girl. It's why I liked you, you know. Usually, I get these no-good foster kids with a shitload of baggage and attitude. Not you. You were like a diamond in the rough. All pretty and clean and polite."

"They should've never let you be a foster parent." He'd probably done to countless other girls the same thing he'd done to her.

His stained teeth became visible as he grinned, evidence of years of drug and alcohol abuse. "They shouldn't have. But they did."

He undid his belt, and she felt the blood drain from her face.

"Now how about that payment, girlie…"

The second the belt was in his hands, he lunged forward. In that moment, it was as if the world slowed. As if every nightmare she'd ever lived and dreamed rolled into one terrifying reality.

The second he touched her arm, she reacted, screaming and shooting in a life-altering fraction of a second.

Hannah's eyes flew open, and she jackknifed into a sitting position. Sweat beaded her forehead, and her hands were clammy.

A dream. It was just a dream.

But it wasn't really. It was the merging of two memories, each one changing her, molding her into something different. Something a little more scarred.

Footsteps sounded from outside her door before Erik flew into the room. A gun was gripped firmly in his hand, aimed, and the expression on his face…it was so dark and dangerous, she almost shrank back. He scanned the room like he was looking for a threat. When his gaze eventually landed on her, he scanned her body, probably looking for injuries even though half of her was hidden beneath the blanket.

When his gaze settled on her face again, questions darkened his eyes. "Are you okay?"

She swallowed, the word *no* crawling up her throat, clawing to break free. "Just a bad dream."

If he was relieved, he didn't show it, just continued to look at her with his beautiful hazel eyes, so intense her breaths almost stopped in her chest. Then, slowly, he crossed the room. The pistol made a soft thud as he placed it on the bedside table then sat on the bed beside her. She wanted to lean closer. Burrow into him and take some of his warmth and strength. Because at some point during the month she'd known him, he'd become her safety net. Maybe even her sanctuary.

"Was the dream about today?"

She wanted to lie, but for some reason she felt like she couldn't. Not to him. "Yes, but it was also about a different day."

His brows slashed together. "The other day must have been pretty damn shitty if it rivaled this one."

"It was."

One of the defining moments of her life.

Erik seemed to wait for her to give him more, but she couldn't. She'd never told another soul about that day, about what she'd done…except one man. The only person in the world who'd known was the same man who'd saved her. But he wasn't around anymore.

She absently brushed her fingers over the cloud charm he'd given her.

Erik's gaze lowered to the bracelet. His frown deepened. "What does the cloud mean?"

For the first time in hours, she smiled. "Nico used to call me Cloud because I was always staring up at them. He gave me the charm on my eighteenth birthday."

The good memory of that day started to push away the nightmare. She lifted her gaze but stopped at Erik's bare chest, her belly doing a funny little flip. "Were you in bed?"

"No. I just got out of the shower."

Her gaze caught on a scar on the left side of his chest. Without thinking, she lifted a hand and traced it. Immediately, the muscles beneath her finger bunched.

"How'd you get this?" she asked.

"Knife wound on a mission gone wrong."

She swallowed. "Sounds dangerous."

"They were all dangerous."

Her finger trailed up his neck, finding another one. "And this one? Another mission?"

"No. That was during my cage fighting days."

A shudder rolled down her spine at the thought of this man in a cage fight. God, it's like he'd sought out as much danger as he could find.

She should pull her hand away, but she couldn't. Because touching him brought her that warmth and strength she so desperately needed. "You're fearless."

"I have fears."

She reached his cheek, finding another small, faint scar near his hairline. "Will you tell me one of them?"

Her gaze returned to his eyes, and the look in them made

her finger pause, because there was something different there now. The embers of a fire.

"I'm scared shitless of giving myself to another person."

The air stopped in her lungs. That was so much more truth and honesty than she'd been expecting. It was real and raw, and it punctured her chest.

She let her palm slide across his cheek so she was cupping him. "Then don't. Just give the pieces you can share."

The moment of silence that followed was so heavy it felt immovable. She looked up to see his eyes so dark, they were almost midnight.

"You make me want to do just that, Angel."

She swallowed, wetting her lips. And the second her tongue poked out, his gaze lowered. Burned her. Stripped her bare.

Like her hand had a mind of its own, it slid behind his head and tugged him toward her, so slowly it was as if there was no movement at all. Then, tentatively, she leaned forward and touched her lips to his.

This kiss was nothing like their last. It was a gentle graze of mouth against mouth. A cherish.

She swiped his lips again, getting a small nibble in return.

Then he growled, and, in one fluid motion, lifted her onto his lap to straddle him. She gasped and his tongue slipped into her mouth, melding with hers.

The kiss was life-giving air. It was refuge and protection. It was everything she'd been devoid of until now.

She slid her fingers through his hair, tugging him closer. Even the smallest space felt twisted and wrong.

When a hand at her waist slipped under her sleep top and trailed up, her belly clenched. Then he cupped her bare breast, and she whimpered. His thumb found her hard peak and swiped, and she gripped his hair, loving the extra sensation the rough pads of his fingers brought her.

She ground against him. He was thick and hard, and she

wanted more. She was just reaching down for him when she was suddenly deposited back onto the bed. Erik stood. His three steps back were accompanied by the pulling of his hair in both fists, like he was in pain.

"Fuck! I need to stop doing that."

She frowned, trying and failing to get her breathing under control. "Why do you need to stop?"

"Because I'm no fucking good for you, Hannah."

Hurt began to twist into frustration. "Who are *you* to tell me what's good for me? Shouldn't that be my choice?"

"No. Not when it comes to me."

Then he left. Stormed out of the room like he was being chased by demons, and she just sat there, wondering what the hell had happened to the man to make him run so fast from something that felt so right.

Chapter Fifteen

Hannah woke slowly, her eyes fluttering a few times before she took in the room around her. Not her room. Erik's spare room.

Her gaze shifted to the side of the bed where Erik had sat. Where he'd lifted her onto his lap and given her another of those soul-destroying kisses.

Oh God. She grabbed a pillow and shoved it over her face to muffle the groan.

It. Had. Been. Everything. Hot and passionate and safe… She'd never known a kiss to feel safe before, but his did.

With a long exhale, she tossed the pillow to the side and sat up. That's when she saw the note on the nightstand.

She lifted it to see messy, masculine handwriting.

I've gone to help Dad with something but didn't want to wake you. Eggs are on the stove, bread beside the toaster, and coffee maker ready to go. Take whatever you want, and when you leave, just pull the door closed and text me. I'll lock and alarm the house from my phone. Hunter.

Her stomach dropped. It probably shouldn't have, there was nothing blatantly unkind about what he'd written. It was just so…formal. No "Hope you slept well" or "Thanks for the earth-shattering kiss last night." Okay, maybe she hadn't expected the latter, but he hadn't even signed off with *Erik*. He'd used his damn last name.

With a sigh, she reached across the bed and grabbed her phone.

Holy shit! It was nine freaking thirty! She had an open house in an hour!

Shit, shit, shit.

The next forty-five minutes were a blur of showering, insulin, eating, and getting her ass out of the house. She had to take both long and short-acting insulin daily. The short-acting, NovoLog, was for eating and adjusting highs and lows. The long-acting insulin, Levemir, she took every twelve hours to help keep her leveled.

And as Erik had said, sometimes it all felt like a lot. Well, no, not sometimes—a lot of the time. Especially when she was in a rush.

At least *because* she was in such a rush, and had to focus on so much else, she didn't let herself freak out when she stepped into her own house to grab what she needed for the day.

Most people would just be able to call in sick after someone broke into their house and attacked them. Not her. Not if she wanted to make a sale and earn some commission. Taylor or James would no doubt help her if she asked, but she knew they both had their own open houses today.

She'd just jumped into her car when she sent a text to Erik.

Hannah: I'm out. You can lock up now.

Erik: Thanks. I hope your morning was okay. I forgot to write in the note that the guy who broke in was a confirmed small-time criminal. Now that he's dead, you're safe.

A tightness she hadn't realized she'd been holding released from her chest. She'd expected the attack to be random, because why would anyone target her? But still...having it confirmed was a comfort.

Hannah: Thank you, Erik. That's a relief.

She made a quick stop at the office, then got to the first house with minutes to spare. She had two open houses today, both lasting three hours each.

The first went fairly quickly, with a slow trickle of people coming through. There were a few promising buyers, which almost helped her forget the night before.

The second open was another at Angelo's home. And when two hours had passed and she'd had no one come through, nerves began to trickle down her spine. The place was expensive, so in a small town, she hadn't expected a huge number of people. But *no one*?

Give it time, Hannah. This is only the second open house, and there's still an hour left.

But thirty minutes later, there was still no one. She'd been nervously fiddling with her bracelet for fifteen minutes when a silver Ferrari pulled up outside.

No…it couldn't be—

Marco climbed out of the driver's seat.

Crap. What was he doing here? Was he here to see her? But how did he even know she'd be here?

She met him on the porch, where he leaned down and kissed her cheek, and she was so damn shocked she just stood there.

"*Cara*, it is nice to see you."

"Marco, what are you doing here?"

Humor danced in his eyes. "I'm here to view the house."

"You're looking to buy a house?"

"I have a wide portfolio and am always looking to expand."

She swallowed. She'd promised Erik she wouldn't go near the guy, but this was her job, and she couldn't very well send him away.

She forced a smile to her face. "Well, it's nice to see you again." She handed him a pamphlet. "Have a look at this, and if you have any questions—"

"Actually, if you have the time, I would love a tour."

It wasn't like she had anyone else here. "Sure."

She stepped into the expansive living area. "The home is less than five years old, and you'll find the owners spared no expense. To our left, we have a Swarovski crystal fireplace in the very well-sized living room. The flooring is all Macassar Ebony, which is quite rare."

Marco ran a finger over the fireplace mantel. "I do like expensive things."

Uh, yeah. She could see that. Even his watch screamed money.

She cleared her throat. "If you follow me into the kitchen, you'll find Carrara marble countertops and ILVE appliances."

When he remained silent, she looked up to see him watching her closely. So closely she wanted to squirm.

"You seem uncomfortable, *cara*."

Was she that obvious? "No, of course not." The words stuttered from her chest, awkward and heavy.

"You are worried about Erik, no?"

She swallowed, wanting to be professional but not exactly sure how to steer this conversation around. "Maybe a little."

"I am a bit hurt that he has spoken ill of me, as I consider him a friend, but I can assure you that I am not as bad as he must have described. And today, I am simply an interested buyer."

She opened and closed her mouth a few times. "He's just… overprotective. I'm sorry." She tried to smile with a bit more ease. "Follow me, I'll show you a laundry that'll make you *want* to wash your clothes."

ERIK LEANED back in his office chair as he read over the notes for tonight's job. He was returning to work earlier than planned because he was bored as shit.

Target was a senior member of a Middle Eastern terrorist organization who was currently in the country and close enough to Redwood to make Erik the obvious choice. He was here under a false name but had been positively identified by the FBI.

He flicked through images of the guy. They didn't have enough evidence of his participation in the organization to get him through legal means, but they still knew exactly who he was and what he was responsible for...so that was where Erik came in.

He read every page of the dossier, including what the asshole's organization had already done and suspected plans for the future. It fueled Erik's rage to get the job done quickly.

He spent the next hour planning his execution. It was only when his phone rang that he finally dragged his gaze from his computer screen.

"I've got it handled, Chandler," he said to his friend. "I might even be able to get this job done without you hacking into any systems."

"You expect me to believe you can complete a job without me?"

One side of Erik's mouth twitched. "Could do it without you *and* with my eyes closed."

"You're dreaming. My voice in your ear has been the only thing to save your ass on more occasions than I can count."

It was damn true. The guy had given him exit routes and penetrated alarm systems so many times, Erik would be a dead man a hundred times over without him. "Today, I've got it handled. Feel free to join me as backup, though."

Chandler scoffed. "Backup, my ass." There was a small

pause, and when Chandler spoke again, all traces of humor were gone. "But I didn't call about the job, Hunter."

Erik's brow quirked. "What is it?"

"You asked me to put a guy on Marco."

He had. Because he didn't like the guy being in Redwood and definitely didn't like seeing him with Hannah. Dancing with her. Touching her. "Yeah?"

Tapping of keys sounded. "Marco's still in town. And I just sent you some pictures my guy took today."

Erik's muscles were already tensing as he clicked into the email. Then his breath hissed from his chest. "What the *fuck*?"

The first photo was of Hannah standing by an open door of a huge house, and Marco's car out front. He clicked through the images, getting a play-by-play of the guy walking up to her. Kissing her fucking cheek. There were photos of Marco in a window, looking out. Then more of him leaving. But not before kissing her cheek again.

Erik's hands fisted tightly, and he wanted to lash out at something. A wall. The desk. The fucking face of Marco Salvatore.

He was up and moving before he could stop himself. Chandler's voice sounded behind him from the phone, but he ignored it.

He stormed out of his house and across their yards. When he reached Hannah's door, he told himself to knock, but he hit the wood so hard it was more of a pound. Her Honda was out front, so he knew she was home.

A beat passed, and he was about to pound on the wood again when the door opened and Hannah stood in front of him, looking so fucking radiant his chest constricted. And that just deepened his anger. Made it hotter. Fiercer. Because Marco had touched her...*again*.

"Erik—"

"Why didn't you tell me you saw Marco today?"

Her brows flickered, the surprise on her face shifting into confusion. "How did you—"

"It doesn't matter how I know. I told you to stay away from him, and you agreed to tell me if he showed up."

She cringed. "I know. I'm sorry I didn't tell you earlier. I just got home." She stepped forward. "I *planned* to tell you. I was actually going to text you in a few minutes."

He stepped back because he couldn't be so close to her right now, not when the rage was a living, breathing beast inside him.

Hurt registered briefly in her expression. "And I couldn't ask him to leave," she added, a bit more hesitantly this time. "Selling houses is my job, so I had to let him in."

Blood roared between his ears. He fucking knew that, but it didn't make this any easier.

"But, Erik," she started softly, "he doesn't seem like the bad guy you think he is."

He laughed, a twisted, ugly sound. "Hannah, you're twenty-three years old. You don't know evil."

Her spine straightened. "Excuse me?"

He turned. Coming here was a bad idea. He needed to get some damn space.

Soft footsteps padded after him. "Are you serious? You barely know me or what I've been through, yet you tell me I don't know evil?"

He spun around, and she just stopped herself from walking into him. When he spoke, he made sure she heard every word clearly. "If you knew evil, *real* evil, you'd know that it can masquerade as good. It can shift and change into whatever it wants you to see. And it will only strike when it has you exactly where it wants you."

Her frown was so deep it fully transformed her features. "Erik, that's—"

"A reality you never want to be exposed to. Promise me

you'll stay away from him. Promise me the next time he shows his face, you'll leave."

"I wish I could tell you I will, but if he's a client, I have to communicate with him."

The rage threatened to swallow him, so he turned around and walked away, not wanting her to see the fucking darkness threatening to overwhelm him.

Chapter Sixteen

"I feel naked, Brigid." Hannah tugged at the slit on her thigh as if she could stitch it together with her fingers. It ran from the floor nearly to her hip.

"Stop it." Brigid shoved her hands away. "You look hot."

It wasn't just the slit that had her feeling underdressed. It was the low cut of the front of the dress. It dropped nearly to the center of her chest. That, combined with the spaghetti straps on the shoulders…yeah, she definitely felt naked.

She stepped into the ballroom, closely following Henry and Brigid. Her gaze was still on her dress when Henry gasped.

"Holy shit, look at this place."

Hannah looked up—and gaped. Holy shit was right. The room was packed. Men in suits and women in long, elegant ball gowns. There were waitstaff in tuxedos carrying cocktail foods and a band playing at the far end of the room.

The cost of admission had been high, and if Henry hadn't bought them each a ticket, she wouldn't be here. But even if the proceeds weren't going toward a good cause, the ticket would be worth it just to see this elegant space.

Brigid's mouth dropped open. "This is—"

"Gorgeous," Hannah finished for her.

Everything looked spectacular, from the floating candle centerpieces on the tables to the huge heart foundation signage on the wall.

"It's a shame James is missing this," Henry said, side-eyeing Brigid.

Hannah tried not to cringe. The man had pulled out this afternoon, claiming he wasn't feeling well. It was bullshit, and Henry had made sure to let Brigid know. This wasn't the first time James had canceled a social commitment last minute.

Brigid rolled her eyes. "If you keep going on about him, I'm going to throw wine in your face."

"If you're going to throw alcohol at me, at least make it hard liquor, woman."

Henry and Brigid continued to squabble as they moved toward the bar. Hannah followed, unable to stop from searching the ballroom for Erik. They hadn't talked since he'd stormed over to her house and basically told her she was too young to recognize a threat. She'd barely seen the man, either.

And unless he approached her with a big-ass apology, they'd *keep* not talking.

She stopped at the bar and ordered her usual vodka soda before turning to glance around the room. That's when she spotted him. He was standing on the other side of the dance floor with the same man she'd seen leave his house a few weeks ago. The one who looked so similar to Erik. He had to be his brother.

Her brain short-circuited at the sight of the two men together. Both were incredibly tall, at least six foot five. And both filled out their suits in exactly the right way.

When Erik's gaze fell on her, his beer stopped halfway to his mouth. He didn't even try to hide the way his gaze slowly moved down her body. The hot look made her feel naked all over again. And what was more, she didn't want to cover up.

Brigid leaned over so her mouth was near her ear. "I told you that dress would be a hit."

Suddenly, Andi stood in front of Hannah, blocking her view.

"Hi, Hannah! I saw you from across the room and thought I'd pop over and check in. Also to tell you how freaking hot you look."

"Told you," Brigid repeated.

Hannah grinned. "Thank you, Andi. And I'm doing well."

"It's good to see the bruises have faded."

Mostly... "Makeup can work wonders. Andi, these are my friends Henry and Brigid. Guys, this is Erik's sister, Andi. The doctor who checked me over after the break-in."

"Oh, we've met," Henry said with a smile. "Dr. Hunter helped with that nail in my hand a few months ago."

Hannah's stomach turned. Henry had shown her a photo of that nail. She'd nearly puked.

"How's that hand doing?" Andi asked.

He held it up. "Good as new."

"Great." She smiled at them. "And thank you all for coming tonight. All ticket proceeds and money made from drink purchases go toward the American Heart Association, which is so close to my family's hearts."

"Is everyone in your family okay?" The words were out before Hannah could stop them. She wanted to cringe and tug them back.

Andi didn't blink. "My dad had a heart attack several months ago. He pulled through, but his heart still isn't great."

Immediately, Hannah wanted to seek out Erik. No wonder he'd moved back.

"God, I'm sorry," she said gently, touching the woman's elbow.

"Thank you." She tilted her head. "And thank you for

keeping an eye on Erik for us. Ignore him when he's an ass, though. It comes freakishly easy to him."

She laughed. God, she liked this woman.

Hannah spent the next hour moving around the room and talking to people she knew, which was basically everyone from their small town. Even Rita and Norman were attending. She found a few people she'd sold homes to, and a few more home-owners she'd sold houses for. Her small purse remained with her at all times, but then, her purse was always on her. It had everything she needed inside—her insulin, blood sugar meter, candy, and a Glucagon. Even setting it down to go to the bath-room felt wrong.

Eventually, she got so caught up in conversations with locals, she lost Brigid and Henry in the crowd. With a frown, she walked around slowly, looking for her friends. She'd just stopped at the bar to get a drink before doing another lap of the room, when she felt heat press against her back.

"You look beautiful."

A shudder ran down her spine at Erik's voice, and she had to stop her eyes from closing.

"Thank you." God, her voice was breathy. She didn't turn, instead remaining still, pretending the man didn't make every part of her want to fall into his arms.

There was a beat of silence. Then two words whispered close to her ear. "I'm sorry."

His voice was full of gravel, deep and rough. It brushed over her skin, causing the fine hairs on her arms to stand on end.

"For what?" she asked quietly. She knew what, but a little bit of groveling wouldn't go astray.

"I was an ass."

Well, it was a consensus, then. "You were."

"I was being reactive, but you're right. You did nothing

wrong. And you can't stay away from him if he comes to your work. I just hate Marco being anywhere near you."

Every word was spoken so quietly that it reached only her ears. Even though they stood in a room full of people, she could almost convince herself it was just the two of them.

Finally, she turned, and his proximity, in combination with his crisp pine scent and the heat in his eyes, was like an assault on her senses. "Has he done anything to make you think he would hurt me?"

"No. I just don't like dangerous men being around you."

She swallowed. "*You're* dangerous."

"I would never physically hurt you."

He'd told her that already. And just like the last time, his words seeped into her bones, creating new imprints.

When the burn in her lungs told her she wasn't breathing, she forced herself to suck in air.

He moved even closer. "Dance with me," he whispered.

Her mouth went dry. "You want to dance with me?"

"No. I *need* to. I've needed you in my arms since the second you stepped in here."

Her heart rattled against her ribs. Then she breathed out a single word. "Yes."

Relief slipped over his face. He slid a large, warm hand around her waist and led her to the dance floor. His touch seared her, made her skin blaze.

She finally caught sight of Henry and Brigid on one side of the room. They were standing in a small group with a few locals. Henry fist pumped the air while Brigid just stood there with a huge-ass grin on her face.

Erik stopped in the center of the dance floor, and the moment she was in his arms, her heart tripped and stumbled. There was barely any space between them. And, God, his arm was tight around her waist, his other hand firm around her own. She could almost convince herself he was holding her together.

"No matter how hard I try, I can't seem to get you out of my head, Angel."

Angel... Every time he called her that, she felt it everywhere. Across her skin. Deep in her chest. A spiraling low in her belly. "Is having me in your head such a bad thing?"

"Yes."

She looked up, not even surprised he was staring straight at her. "Why? And don't give me crap about you being a threat and me being twenty-three. You just said you would never hurt me."

His gaze skittered between hers. "I'm damaged. And that, in combination with everything else, is a cocktail that could ruin you."

Her brows tugged together. Damaged...that word didn't sit well inside her. "I don't believe people can become damaged. They just become different versions of themselves."

He took two heartbeats to answer, and in that time, she could almost see him turning her words over in his head. "Lesser versions?"

"Stronger." Hannah was absolutely firm on that. "Sometimes life makes us believe we're broken beyond repair. We're not. Everyone's fixable."

"And if the fragments don't slot together anymore?"

"They always slot together. The old cracks will be visible, but they're meant to be. To show everything a person has overcome." Unable to stop herself, she reached up and cupped his cheek. His eyes darkened, and God, she wanted to kiss him. "What happened to you to make you think you're damaged?"

Another heavy pause. "You don't want to know."

"Stop giving me guarded words and half-truths." This time, she touched a hand over his heart. "I want Erik. The real and the raw."

She craved him.

He gave a small shake of his head. "You don't want the real Erik."

"Why not?" When he didn't respond, she wanted to shout at him. Either that or dropkick him to the ground. She'd tried telling herself she didn't want him. That this was a simple crush, one she could wrap in a pretty box and put away. But every time he was close, every time he touched her, she realized how deep that lie ran. That whatever this was between them, it was real, and it was theirs to take.

"Let me in. Trust me. Allow yourself to have me."

His arm tightened around her. "I'm trying to protect you."

"From what?"

"Me." He almost sounded frustrated this time. "Angel, if we were a fairy tale, you'd be the girl in the red hood, and I'd be the wolf."

She slipped her hand into his hair, one side of her mouth lifting. "Then let's rewrite that fairy tale."

Chapter Seventeen

Rewrite the fairy tale? Like it was that goddamn easy. Like a million different things wouldn't have to happen to cement a happy ending.

He downed half his beer as he watched Hannah across the room. She danced with a small group of women that included Andi. She fit in with his sister. Hell, the woman would probably fit in with his entire family.

The thought made his fingers tighten around the neck of the beer bottle.

"You stare any harder, people are going to start thinking she's yours."

Erik stiffened at his father's words as the older man came to stand beside him. Not because he didn't want people to think she was his. He *did*. He wanted every man in the room to know exactly how much she belonged to him and that she wasn't free to touch.

In that silky green dress that showed off too much goddamn thigh, someone *would* eventually touch her. He'd seen men looking at her all night. Even without the dress, Hannah was the most beautiful woman he'd ever seen.

"She's too young for me," he said, clutching at goddamn straws.

"What is she, twenty-five?"

"Twenty-three. And I'm thirty-six."

His father laughed. "Thirteen years isn't that much of an age gap. Your mother's ten years younger than me."

Except his parents were perfect together, because they were each as whole as the other.

"Hey." His father touched his arm, and Erik finally dragged his gaze away from the woman. Michael Hunter had the same hazel eyes as Erik, and in them was a lifetime of wisdom so distinct it was almost visible. "I know you've been through a lot, son. And I haven't checked in on you nearly enough after what happened to Vicky."

Erik's chest tightened at her name. "It's been eight years. And I've been the one avoiding the family. You've had health issues."

"Doesn't matter how long it's been. Crippling pain will keep us down, no matter how much time has passed. And it doesn't matter what I'm going through. You're still my son, therefore mine to look after and love. I should have pushed harder to get you home."

He was right about one thing...time hadn't done a damn thing to diminish the roar of rage in his chest. The hollowness of sorrow in his limbs. "You had to look after yourself and Mom."

"I love you, Erik. And I need to know that you're okay."

He swallowed and dipped his head. The word okay felt foreign to him. "Vicky and I were young. We barely knew what love was."

"But she was still yours to protect."

His father said the words quietly, but they were like tiny little bombs detonating around him. How the man saw into his damn soul and pulled every crumb of guilt into the light, he had no idea.

"And it wasn't just her who died."

The familiar pain dug into his gut, almost making him keel over.

"Worse, it came straight off the back of losing half your team in the Middle East." His father clenched his shoulder, and he felt that touch right down to his bones. "I'm here. We're *all* here for you. And we'll be whatever you need us to be. Okay?"

He felt like a damn kid again. Fuck, he loved his dad. "I appreciate it, Dad."

His father nodded and dropped his hand.

Erik looked back to the dance floor. When he saw men encroaching on the circle of women, his fingers tightened on his beer bottle for a second time. His eyes narrowed on a particular guy who started dancing beside Hannah.

Too. Damn. Close.

Erik had no fucking right to be jealous, but he was. Every part of him wanted to tear the guy's arm off for a simple graze of her shoulder.

Stay still, Erik. Don't cross the fucking room.

The words were like shouts in his head…

Shouts that went silent when the asshole touched her hip.

Erik was moving before he could stop himself, weaving through the crowd, never taking his gaze off Hannah. When he reached her side, he wanted to tug her away. Pull her into the protection of his arms.

He only just stopped himself, instead touching her elbow and tugging her away from the guy before leaning down so he could whisper into her ear. "Can I see you home?"

He had no damn clue what time it was, but they'd been here long enough.

The other guy stepped forward. "Hey. What are you—"

One look from Erik and the guy stopped, swallowed, then turned and wove through the dancing crowd.

Good. He wasn't in the mood for a damn fight.

Hannah tilted her head, her bottom lip disappearing between her lips. Without even thinking, he reached up and pulled that lip out with his thumb before sliding the pad over it.

So fucking soft.

"Yes."

He was so transfixed by her mouth, he almost forgot what the question had been. He slipped an arm around her waist and tugged her toward the door. It was raining outside, and when she leaned into his body, he shielded her as they moved to his Corvette.

The ride home was quiet but charged. His hand twitched to touch her. Graze her thigh or slip his fingers through hers.

Silently, she checked her blood sugar as he drove. Had she eaten?

He leaned over and opened the glove box, then pulled out a granola bar.

Her brows shot up as she slipped it from his fingers. "Thank you."

When they finally reached their street, the rain was still heavy, so he drove down her long drive and parked close to her door. Even though they ran to the house, the rain still blasted them.

She unlocked and opened her door but didn't go in, instead turning to look up at him. Her chest rose and fell with sharp breaths, and her eyes...fuck, they seared him.

She took one small step into the bubble that was his space and pressed both her hands to his chest. That touch burned through the material of his shirt, penetrated his skin and slipped deep into his chest.

Then, slowly, she leaned her head forward and pressed a kiss right over his heart.

His pulse stopped, his hands going to her waist, gripping her so tightly he didn't know how he'd let go. "Hannah…I'm a man in pieces."

Jagged, ugly pieces.

"Beautiful pieces," she whispered, like she'd heard his unspoken words.

"I could be your ruin."

"Maybe." Her hands trailed up before curving around his neck. "Or maybe I could be your salvation."

Her words twisted his insides. Found the small crevices of wreckage and almost made them feel fixable.

One heavy heartbeat passed, and in that beat, an entire war raged inside him…a battle between doing what was right and doing what every part of him begged to do.

Her hands shifted up his neck, her breath brushing against his skin. Then she whispered, "Kiss me, Erik."

That was all it took. Three words from the beautiful woman in front of him, and the last thread of his restraint snapped as he crashed his mouth onto hers.

She moaned, and that sound tormented him. Choked him. Changed him.

When her lips separated, he slid his tongue inside, letting it tangle with hers. Every shift of her body against his had the heat inside him raging hotter, until it was like a wild inferno. And it burned for her.

He lifted her into his arms and moved down the hall after kicking the door closed with his foot. He didn't stop until he was inside the bedroom, and even then, he never broke away from her. Never moved his lips or hands from the beautiful woman against him. The woman who was becoming his calm. His flickers of light in a starless night.

He lowered her to the floor beside her bed. When she stepped away, he wanted to tug her back into his arms, keep her close and devour her. But then her fingers moved to the straps of her dress, and suddenly he was stuck, unable to move or breathe or feel the whispers of air on his skin.

Slowly, she slipped the silky material off her shoulders and let it fall to the floor.

Everything faded. Everything except her, the way she breathed new strength into his body. New life into his limbs. She became his world. A world he was irrevocably chained to.

He stepped forward. "You're so fucking beautiful."

―――

ERIK'S WORDS slid into her veins, making her blood pump so fast she almost wondered if her knees would buckle. He looked at her like she was perfect. Like every part of her was exactly as it was meant to be.

And that shredded her.

His eyes never left her as he threw off his jacket, unbuttoned and removed his shirt, and kicked off his shoes. Then he stepped closer. This time when he gripped her hips, he touched bare skin, and that touch singed her.

His mouth found hers again, but this kiss was softer than the first. He kissed her like he had all the time in the world. A million years for a million kisses.

His tongue explored her mouth while his body urged her back until her legs hit the bed. She lay back slowly, and he covered her. Surrounded her. He was everywhere, mind, body and soul.

When his lips left hers, she wanted to protest. To tug him back. But then they trailed down her neck and chest. As they neared her breast, her belly clenched. Then his lips closed around her tight nipple and she arched into him, a choked cry barely escaping.

His tongue swirled and swiped while he cupped her other breast in his palm. When the calloused pad of his thumb ran over one bud while his teeth scraped the other, she cried out his name. The sound rang so loud in the room that it cut through the air like a knife.

"I fucking love my name on your lips," he growled, breath whispering over her breast. One more suck, then he switched to the other.

It was the same explosion of heat and need. The same tornado of sensations. She tugged at the soft strands of his hair, needing an anchor. Something to hold onto, keep her here and grounded.

When his hand drifted down her body and slipped inside her panties, her breath caught in her throat. He moved his finger across her slit, and she whimpered, her body trembling so violently that she wondered if she'd ever be still again. Regardless, she'd never be the same. One touch from this man and she was different. And not just her—the entire world around her.

Erik pushed her panties down her thighs. She kicked them off with her feet before a finger slid to her entrance. Her breath stopped. Then he thrust inside.

She bowed, the only thing keeping her on the bed, his body. His thumb continued to move on her clit, and at every thrust, more heat pooled in her belly. More fire in her blood.

She lifted her hips to meet him, humming and purring as he strummed her body like it was an instrument only he knew how to play.

She reached between them to undo his pants and then slipped one desperate hand below his clothing. The second her fingers were around him, he stilled, the thick cords of his muscles tensing.

He was large in her grip, and as she moved her hand up and down his length in long strokes, he thickened further. With every little his of breath and tensing of muscle, she learned what he liked.

She felt like she'd barely touched him when he grabbed her wrist.

He leaned to the side and removed his pants and briefs. Before dropping his clothes to the floor, he reached into a pocket and pulled a foil from his wallet. Her breaths shortened as he tore it open with his teeth.

By the time he'd donned the condom and returned to her, her heart pounded so hard against her ribs she swore the beats could be heard thundering through the room.

As if sensing her nerves, he shifted some hair from her face, grazing her skin. "You sure you want to do this?"

She ran her fingers up his chest and over his shoulders, memorizing every hard ridge. If they did this, things would change. Shift into something else…something irreversible.

"There's no part of me that feels capable of walking away from you," she breathed. "I want this. I want you."

His eyes flared as he settled between her thighs. The tip of his cock pressed right there at her entrance.

"You make me want more than I've wanted for a long, long time, Angel."

"So take it," she whispered.

One sharp inhale from him, then his mouth crashed to hers and he slid inside her. Stretching her. Filling her.

She groaned and tightened her legs around him.

For a moment, he didn't move, just let her acclimatize to his size as their tongues fused together. It wasn't until she rocked her hips, pulling him deeper, that an almost strangled noise left his chest, and he slid out before thrusting back inside.

She groaned. He thrust again, and this time she ran her

nails across his shoulders, knowing she was almost breaking skin, incapable of stopping.

On every thrust, she lifted her hips, meeting him stroke for stroke. He growled and moved faster. Harder. It was ecstasy and torment rolled into one.

When he yanked her leg higher, hitting a new angle inside her, she threw her head back and whimpered. Erik took advantage, latching onto her exposed neck, sucking and nipping.

Her breaths shortened. "Erik…"

His name was both a gasp and a plea.

He reached for a nipple and thrummed it between his thumb and forefinger. That was all it took for her world to come apart. For her body to tense and spasm so violently that she screamed as her walls pulsed around him.

Erik kept pumping into her, kept grazing her nipple, and her cries continued to ring through the room, shattering every bit of silence, until suddenly, his growl rivaled her shouts. His mouth crashed back to hers and he broke. He kept thrusting until he must have had nothing left. Until they were both shadows of the people they'd been previously.

Then, finally, there was stillness. Stillness bar their heaving chests.

When he ran his fingers up the outside of her thigh, the touch was so gentle, so tender, her exhaled breath was a tremble.

How this man could think he was wrong or bad or dangerous for her, she had no idea. He felt the opposite of all those things.

When she met his gaze, she saw flickers of what almost looked like surprise. Because he felt what she felt? That what they'd done wasn't just physical? It went deeper. Rearranged and reshaped their lives, just like she'd known it would.

Their gazes held for three pounding heartbeats, then he

grazed his lips across hers one last time before lowering to the bed and tugging her against his side.

She sighed, finding refuge in his arms. And even though she tried to close her eyes, tried to rest, one thought rattled around her mind, refusing to let her sleep…

Maybe they were both right. Maybe she'd be his salvation, and he'd be her ruin.

Chapter Eighteen

Something kicked at Erik's gut. Something hard and intense…
something he had absolutely no control over. It was like a
sucker punch, so brutal his lungs refused to take in the next
breath.

Sun shone through the gap in the curtain, telling him it was
morning. Telling him he'd slept in Hannah's bed all night. Not
only that, but he hadn't woken once. That never happened.

Her soft cheek pressed against his heart, and her warmth…
it seized him, heating even the coldest part of his chest.

But the thing that really had his muscles tensing was the
fact he didn't want to move away. Because she felt right in his
arms. Like a piece of him that had been stolen was finally
being returned.

His hands twitched to stroke the hair that fanned over his
shoulder. Draw her closer even though she was already so
damn close there wasn't a breath of space between them.

He hadn't woken with another woman in his arms in…

His heart wrenched at the memory.

Then came the blaring fucking question in his head…why
didn't he want to run right now?

Because he'd already tried to stay away, and that just made him want her more? Because she made him feel like he could breathe, without the burn of pain inside his lungs?

A shrill beep trilled through the air. His brows slashed together, his gaze moving to her phone on the bedside table.

She groaned against his chest, then rolled over and grabbed her cell. His gaze flicked over the alarm—*Take your long-acting insulin now, Hannah, or I'll just wake you again in five minutes.*

His lips twitched as she ended the alarm. When she returned to his chest, he almost thought she was going to go back to sleep, but then he heard her breath stop, felt her body tense. Like she only just realized whose chest she lay on.

Slowly, she pushed up and looked at him. There was a moment of quiet where she studied his face like she was searching for... He had no idea what. Something.

"Hey." Her soft voice dug inside him, igniting a war. A battle over what he *should* do and what he *wanted* to do.

"Good morning, Angel." At least his voice didn't expose the turmoil inside him. "Do you need to take your insulin before your alarm goes off again?"

"I do. I usually set myself like five alarms because I get used to them and sleep through. When I was younger, Nico used to storm into my room and hit me with a pillow until I woke up."

Her eyes sparkled as she spoke, and it made too many damn emotions topple over each other in his chest.

Another second passed, and when the moment felt too heavy, he climbed out of bed and pulled on briefs and pants. The second he was separated from her, he felt the loss like he was leaving a part of himself behind.

"Coffee?" he asked in a voice that exposed too much emotion.

Her brows flickered and her bottom lip disappeared

between her teeth. "Sure. I just need to check my blood sugar and take my long-acting insulin and I'll be out."

Shit. The woman needed food too. His head was a damn mess.

When he only saw the pod machine in her kitchen, he groaned, tempted to go next door and use his café-quality machine. He didn't. Because then he'd be running, and he was trying like hell not to do that.

Erik heard the soft pad of her feet moving down the hall. He didn't turn right away, but when he did, he almost wished he hadn't. She was standing on the other side of the kitchen, hip against the counter, wearing panties and his shirt. The shirt was unbuttoned, so he had a perfect fucking view of the center of her chest.

His legs twitched to cross the room and pull it open.

But then she tilted her head and looked at him like she was dissecting some mysterious specimen.

His brows lowered. "What are you thinking about, Angel?"

She lifted a delicate shoulder. "Just trying to work out which Erik I have this morning. I'm not sure yet."

He opened a cabinet, finding a lot of pink animal mugs. "What are the options?"

"Grumpy, don't-care-if-my-grandfather's-flowers-die neighbor…or sweet, charming semi-friend."

A ghost of a smile played at his lips as he pulled out one pink and one pale blue mug. The blue mug had a sloth on it, but it was the least feminine of the lot. "I don't think I'm either of those today." And he was kind of glad psychopath wasn't on either list.

"Then what are you?"

He paused, not even sure himself. This all felt new to him. "I'm just Erik."

She laughed, and the sound hit him in the damn chest. "Okay, just Erik, I have a question for you."

Why did his muscles tense at those words? "Okay."

"When we had that fight the other day, you knew my exact age. How?"

He paused. Whatever he'd been expecting her to ask, it wasn't that. He could lie. He didn't. "In my line of work, I need to know who the people are around me."

It didn't really answer her question, but it also kind of did. Her brows shot up. "You did a background check on me?"

He opened the fridge door and searched for the milk. "*I* didn't. I got my guy to do it." When he couldn't find milk, she came up beside him. Her arm grazed his, and it felt like a shot of electricity. She leaned down and grabbed a carton.

He frowned. "That isn't milk."

"It's oat milk."

He took the carton as she moved to the cabinet and pulled out two bowls. It was only when she set the granola on the table a bit too firmly that he turned back to her. Was she angry about the background check?

He put some water into the nearly empty pod machine, but when he went to turn off the faucet, it kept dripping. He made a mental note to look at the pipe before he left.

As he finished the coffees, he saw her inject her insulin at the table. He also noticed some printed-out job advertisements on the counter. Was she changing workplaces?

He set the coffees onto the table and watched as she added a dash of lavender syrup. Of course the lavender oat milk latte had been hers.

Her brows were slightly pinched, and her knuckles almost white as she gripped her spoon. He waited for her to get a few mouthfuls into her granola before breaking the silence.

"It was only a surface-level background check," he said quietly. "Upbringing. Schools. Jobs. When nothing question-able popped up, we stopped digging."

"Only?" She swung angry eyes his way. "Erik, that's

personal. All of it. It's part of what makes me who I am. And it wasn't your place to learn any of it until I told you."

"I know. It's a safety thing." Then, because she was still looking at him like he'd run over her damn cat, he added, "I'm sorry."

"You owe me information about *you*. That's fair."

When he was silent a beat too long, she huffed and rose from the table. Before she could step away, he grabbed her arm and lifted her onto his lap so she straddled him.

She gasped and grabbed his shoulders. The shirt still covered her, but only barely.

"I grew up here in Redwood," he said softly. "I went to the local high school. Decided I wanted to join the military when I was thirteen, after soldiers visited us at school and talked about saving the world." He slid a hand inside the shirt and wrapped his fingers around her rib cage. "When I joined the Marines, I quickly worked my way into a special operations field. I got married to my high school girlfriend when I was twenty-one. I didn't realize I was too young to even know what love was."

Her breath seemed to stall for a moment. "You weren't too young. There's no such thing."

"You're probably right. We were just comfortable, since we'd dated all through high school, so we did what we thought came next." Her gaze flickered between his eyes as he continued. "I was twenty-eight when I did my last mission. It was the worst mission of my life."

"What happened?"

A familiar darkness tried to close in on him. "It was a mission in Syria to rescue some US citizens who'd been kidnapped from a university. We had a new guy on the team. He didn't like following orders. He was young and cocky. Thought he knew best. I was the team leader, and I should have pulled rank and refused to let him participate. I didn't.

When I told everyone to wait for a signal, he didn't listen. He fired, gave away our location, and a lot of blood was spilled."

He didn't tell her that he'd lost half his team on that mission, and that the weight of their losses almost destroyed him. He also didn't tell her about the call he'd made just before stepping onto the plane to return home. The words were there, bubbling in his chest, but every time he formed them with his lips, they cut new wounds into his flesh, making him bleed all over again.

"There's more to my story, but the basics are that my life changed that day, and I've been struggling ever since." He grazed his thumb across her ribs. "Eight years later, and I'm back here, trying to live again."

Questions flickered in her eyes. She wanted to ask about his wife. Maybe whether he'd lost team members on that mission. Instead, she went with two words.

"I'm sorry." She cupped his cheek.

He swiped her flesh again with the pad of his thumb. "What have you got going on today?"

"Two open houses. No rest for a real estate agent."

He wanted to protest at that because he couldn't think of her being at an open house without wondering if Marco would return.

As if she'd heard his thoughts, her tone softened. "I never heard from Marco after the one he showed up at."

It better fucking stay that way. He'd called the guy. Left messages. All warnings. He'd heard nothing back.

"Before I get up, I need to ask you something," she said.

"Okay."

"What's next…for us?"

The question he should have seen coming. "I don't know." His answer was honest, but if the sad tilt of her lips was anything to go by, it wasn't what she wanted to hear.

"But I know I can't stay away from you." Something inside

154

him needed to soothe this woman. He slipped his fingers through her hair. "If we try this, I can't give you all of myself. I have secrets, and I don't know when or if I'll feel capable of sharing them. Are you okay with that?"

She seemed to consider his words, her eyes flicking between his. "I have things I haven't shared too. But I *want* to share them. Because I want this to work." She paused, her blue eyes boring into him. "Baby steps."

He almost laughed. "And what would baby steps entail?"

"Well, I have a work function this Friday. You could come with me as my date. There'll be food. Some clients and Brigid and James. You can meet the other realtor, Taylor, and my boss, Reuben."

His gut tightened at the thought of dating her. He wasn't sure if the tightening was good or bad or a mixture of both.

"I could do that," he finally said, not willing to see her features fall again.

That beam of a smile made it worth it. "Good." She lowered her head so her lips hovered over his. "And don't you dare turn into grumpy neighbor Erik again. I will hunt you down and find the real you."

It sounded like both a promise and a threat. She moved that last inch and kissed him, and he finally gave in and tore the shirt open to drop his mouth to her breast.

———

"YOU'RE TAKING the property to another agent?"

No! This was a freaking nightmare…one she couldn't wake up from, occurring over and over again.

Hannah's fingers tightened around the phone, her foot starting a fast tap below the desk.

"I'm sorry, Miss Jacobs. There have been no offers and

only half a dozen people through, so once the thirty-day contract is up, I'll be taking back the keys."

She dug her fingers so deeply into her palm that she was sure she'd break skin. "High-end properties often take a bit longer to move. That's normal. And I have leads I'm still following up on."

"But no official offers yet?"

She cringed. "Not yet."

Angelo sighed. "I really wanted this to work, but it hasn't."

She didn't even know what to say to that. Empty words about it being okay that he was taking her listing when it didn't feel even close to okay?

By the time she hung up, she wanted to cry. She pinched her thigh to stop herself.

This was bad. Really bad. Not only had she made below-average sales for the last few months, but the homeowners she'd managed to list had been pulling their properties one by one.

She pressed her palms to her eyes, begging the tears to stay away. She *would not* cry. So her biggest client to date, the one whose sale could pay all her bills with a single commission, had pulled out. More would come.

"Hey." Taylor stood in the doorway, worry glazing her eyes. "Are you okay?"

Nope. She was drowning in a sea of bills with no way to pay them. "Angelo Bonetti is taking his property to another agent."

She cringed. "God, that's a big loss. I'm sorry."

"So am I." Fall-into-a-fetal-position-and-scream kind of sorry.

"I had a client pull a property a few months ago. It hurt. Especially because it was right as Elliot's father stopped paying child support, then up and disappeared."

Her heart went out to the other woman. Taylor was supporting her ten-year-old son on her own.

James appeared in the doorway beside Taylor. "You women talking about me and my good looks?"

Hannah rolled her eyes. "You wish."

He smirked, then his expression changed to one of concern. "Hey, Brigid said you left the fundraiser early with your neighbor last weekend. Everything okay?"

"Yeah. Things are really good, actually."

Taylor got an excited glimmer in her eyes, as one side of James's mouth tilted up. "That's good. I'm happy for you." He pushed off the doorframe. "Well, I'm going to Black Bean to grab a coffee and some lunch. You guys wanna come?"

Taylor shook her head. "Trying to save money by bringing lunch."

"Sure." Hannah checked the time. It was almost noon… why not? It wasn't as if she had anything else to do…like sell an expensive house.

Black Bean was close to the office, so the walk there and back didn't take long. But when she re-entered her office, she stopped at the sight of her boss standing in the room.

"Reuben."

He turned from where he was looking at a framed photo on her shelf. It was of her, Brigid, and Henry. Reuben wasn't smiling, and that made her belly fill with dread. "Hannah. I was wondering if we could have a talk."

The dread spiraled into something else. Something that felt a lot like panic.

She swallowed, trying to force it down. "Yes. Of course."

She moved behind her desk and pushed the coffee cup to the side, suddenly hating that she'd gone out to lunch at all. She shouldn't. She was entitled to a lunch break. But when work performance was low, she wanted her boss to think she was a workaholic who never took a break.

Reuben lowered into the chair opposite her desk, and when he sighed and looked at his hands, she knew it was bad. That's what people did when they prepared you for bad news, right? They sighed and looked anywhere but at you.

"Hannah, we need to talk about your sales these last few months."

She opened her mouth, but before she could get a word in, he continued.

"James's and Taylor's sales haven't been great either, but recently, they've improved. And I just got word that you lost the Bonetti property."

How the heck had he heard about that already? Had Angelo called him too?

She swallowed. "That's true. The combination of the competing company opening recently and hesitant buyers hasn't been working in my favor. But I've got some good leads on the houses I *am* selling."

He nodded and looked at her so closely she wanted to squirm. She felt like she was sixteen again and sitting in the principal's office, being lectured. But this was worse…this was her livelihood. Her health insurance.

"I'm going to be frank with you, Hannah."

Shit.

"You've been a fabulous employee for a few years…but sales have been really low, and the cost of employee benefits keeps going up."

Her breath caught in her throat. He didn't say the words directly, but she could read between the lines.

"I understand, Reuben. If I don't up my sales, you're going to have to let me go." He said nothing, and she leaned forward. "But I *am* going to sell the homes I have and get more properties. I've got a lot of leads on buyers, and I've already got fliers ready to pop in mailboxes."

She'd had them printed last week…thank God.

Reuben gave a slight nod. "Good." He rose, and she stood with him. "I trust I'll see you at our happy hour tomorrow night?"

"Of course. I wouldn't miss it." Even if she wanted to stay home and bury her head in the dirt.

Chapter Nineteen

Blood pumped hard and fast through Erik's veins as he moved quickly down the hotel hallway. On the outside, no one would know the storm that brewed in his gut. The utter fury that threatened to overflow and spill into the world around him. All because of one fucking man.

Marco.

He was still in Redwood. Not only still here, but he'd had coffee with Erik's goddamn sister!

Erik wanted to hit something. Tear something apart with his bare hands.

He couldn't have his two worlds colliding. His work and everything in it should be as far as fucking possible from his personal life.

He kept his face blank right up until he stepped in front of the asshole's door and pounded on the wood.

He didn't have to wait long. Two seconds. The door opened, and Erik grabbed Marco by the collar of his shirt and shoved him back into the wall, kicking the door closed with his foot. "What the fuck were you doing with my sister?"

Not one ounce of fear showed on the face of a man who, if

not a friend, was someone he at least trusted to have his back during a job. "I ran into her at the café. It was just a coffee."

Like hell it was. "You and I both know that isn't fucking true. Are you *trying* to make yourself my enemy?"

"I do not want to be your enemy. I simply want you to try out this new…business venture with me."

"I told you no," Erik growled.

"Choose differently."

Erik glared at him. "Let me make this crystal fucking clear, Marco. I will *not* be a private contractor. And if you don't leave town immediately—or if you go anywhere near my family again—I'll expose what you're doing."

"You would have to prove it first, and you and I both know that I don't leave any evidence behind."

"Neither do I, Marco. And I will do *anything* to protect my own."

Some might perceive that as an empty threat. Both he and Marco knew it wasn't. He could kill the man and get rid of the body and no one would know.

"I won't be leaving until you at least complete this one job with me."

Erik's fist connected with Marco's face in one violent punch. "Get out of my fucking town."

Blood dripped from the guy's mouth, but if it bothered him, he didn't show it. In fact, he almost looked pleased. "Wow. The great Erik Hunter has a weakness. More than one, actually…if your reaction to my being around that pretty neighbor is anything to go by."

The cords of muscle in Erik's arms pulled so tight they almost snapped. His hand twitched to punch the guy a second time.

Marco's eyes narrowed. "Careful, Hunter. I let you get in one hit to appease you. But try another, and I won't be so understanding."

Erik lowered his voice. "If I hear you've gone anywhere near either of them again, I'll tear your tongue out and shove it so far down your throat you won't take another fucking breath."

That smirk on Marco's face...it made every part of Erik want to do what he'd promised right there and then. He barely stopped himself.

He shoved Marco against the wall, hard, then left the room. He had to fight his internal animal the entire drive home, convincing himself to not turn around and finish what he'd started.

He'd only known about Andi's little coffee date because of Chandler's guy. It hadn't been hard for Chandler to get Marco's room number at the hotel, but he'd only given it up after Erik had promised not to kill the guy.

A promise he'd almost broken.

Andi had received a fucking earful from him on the way to the hotel. He hadn't answered her questions about how he'd known where she was, who she was with, or why she should do as he said, but he knew she'd heard the danger in his voice. How serious he was.

He was almost home when a text came through on his phone.

Hannah: Hey! You almost ready to go?

It took three seconds for realization to hit him. Shit. The drinks at her office—that was tonight. With everything that had happened with Marco, he'd almost forgotten.

Erik: Sorry. Running late. Will be home in a couple minutes, then we can go.

He wasn't going to admit that he'd forgotten. It was bad enough he'd spent the week trying to digest what was going on between them while barely seeing her.

He was just pulling up in front of her house when Hannah stepped outside the door. She wore tight jeans that hugged every damn inch of her, from ass to ankles. And the red heels she'd paired them with…

His dick twitched as he climbed out of the car. She held a large bowl in her arms and had just turned when he stopped in front of her.

Her lips curved up into a smile. "Hey."

He slid a hand around her waist. "Hey, Angel."

Unable to stop himself, he leaned down and kissed her. It was everything he hadn't realized he needed. The peace that had eluded him for hours. The quiet to the loud fucking shouts in his head.

When he came up for air, her eyes were half-hooded, and it took every ounce of self-restraint to not pull her back into the house and take her.

He forced his voice to work. "You ready to go?"

"I am. You?"

No. He needed more of those damn kisses. "Yes."

"Great. Your car or mine?"

He didn't even look at her beat-up Honda. "Mine." He slipped his hand into hers and led her toward his Corvette.

She laughed. "Hey, your mechanic fixed Hondi up well. She's good to go. Something I still haven't paid for, by the way."

And she wouldn't. Just like he didn't expect anything in return for fixing her pipes. He wanted to take care of this woman.

He opened the passenger-side door. "Hondi?"

"Has a good ring to it, doesn't it?"

He shook his head as he moved around the car and slid behind the wheel. As he pulled out of her drive, he eyed the salad. "Did you make that?"

"Well, I certainly didn't let Brigid anywhere near it. That woman can massacre a fried egg."

His brows flickered. "So you knew the muffins tasted like shit?"

"Oh my gosh, they were terrible. I can't believe you swallowed that mouthful."

He laughed. A full laugh right from his gut. It felt good. Foreign, but good.

Hannah kept him entertained the entire drive to the office, including telling him a story about Henry forcing her and Brigid to sit in a bar out of town for three hours just so he could get a glimpse of a guy he liked. Her stories almost made him forget about Marco…almost.

When they stepped into the office, the place was already full of people, all drinking and eating. Immediately, his chest felt tight. He hated crowded places like this.

As if she could feel his unease, Hannah slipped her hand into his and whispered, "Thank you for coming."

And that touch, combined with the softness of her voice, was all he needed for the tightness to loosen.

They spent an hour and a half moving around the room so Hannah could greet clients and network. Erik was introduced to a lot of people, none of whom he remembered by name.

When they eventually approached Brigid and James, Erik was glad to stop moving for a while.

"My God, it's busy tonight," Brigid gushed, her gaze zipping around the large room. "Good job, guys. Lots of people means lots of sold houses, and hopefully, lots of returning clients."

Hannah's brows flickered, and he was almost certain he saw a small cringe. The expression was so subtle that no one noticed. No one but him.

Why? Because she hadn't sold many houses? Because she didn't have a lot of return clients? Was that why she was short on cash…and why she had those job printouts on her kitchen counter?

"We're doing well over here, Brig."

When James side-eyed Hannah, Erik's muscles tightened. The look was almost smug. Because he was selling more than her?

Asshole.

Hannah didn't seem to notice, instead getting pulled into a conversation with Brigid. When James excused himself to get some fresh air, Erik watched him the entire way down the hall.

Fresh fucking air? What was he, a house plant?

For some reason, he didn't like the guy. Call it gut instinct.

"You look good with Hannah on your arm, Erik."

Brigid's words tugged his attention back to the women. "Hannah can make anyone look good."

"And a charmer too." Her eyes twinkled. "God, you're gonna make this woman want a ring and babies soon."

Every fucking bone in his body froze at those words. He knew she was joking, but it didn't quell the panic that crawled up his throat. The sweat that beaded his forehead.

"Kids aren't in my future." The words came out clipped and short and so much harsher than he'd meant them to.

The smiles dropped from both Brigid's and Hannah's faces.

When his phone rang, air he hadn't realized he'd been holding whipped out of his lungs. He bent down and pressed a kiss to Hannah's cheek. "I'm just going to step out and take this."

She nodded, and he hated the uncertainty on her face. The questions in her eyes.

He waited until he was in the hall to look at his phone. A smile tugged at his mouth when he saw the name of an old friend. Actually, the person who'd gotten Erik his current job.

"Rachel. You've been MIA for a while."

Wind whistled in the background of the call. "I could say the same about you, buddy. A text on my birthday, then nothing?"

He laughed. He'd done more than send a damn text and she knew it. A very nice, very expensive bottle of tequila had found its way to her place. "You know that's not true."

"Yeah, you're right. I'm the one who didn't send anything on *your* birthday. But, hey, at least I remember to call and check in once in a while."

It was true. She was a good friend. Eight years ago, when his entire damn world had imploded, this woman had been by his side. He probably wouldn't have survived that time without her.

"How's Rex?" Erik asked, pushing outside.

"Ha. I dumped that idiot months ago. He couldn't handle me."

He laughed. "Can anyone?"

"Just you."

Even *he* could only handle Rachel for short periods of time. She may be the closest thing to a best friend he had, but she was also spontaneous and liked to do dumb, dangerous shit way too often.

"Honestly though"—her tone softened—"I'm sorry I haven't checked in on you more since you've been back home. You doing okay?"

He blew out a breath and looked up at the sky. A small collection of stars scattered across the black canvas. "Most days. Every so often, I'll be walking down the street and I'll remember walking down the same street with Vicky. I'll remember how easily I smiled back then. My hope for a future that was so different to what I got."

Rachel sighed. "Shit. I'm sorry."

"But I'm here."

"You are. And your family must be loving that. How are they?"

"Mom calls every day, and I've started going to their place

for dinner on Sunday nights. It's not as painful as I thought it would be."

She laughed, and he remembered the sound so well. It was a throw-the-head-back, put-the-entire-body-into-it kind of laugh. "You want painful? You should sit down with my train wreck of a family. You'll get a lifetime of trauma in the span of one meatloaf."

This time *he* laughed. Her parents weren't that bad. Sure, they talked a lot and asked invasive questions. They also gave shit advice, but always with the best intentions.

He moved toward the side of the building—and frowned when he heard a distant voice.

James. And he sounded angry.

Rachel said something, but his focus remained on James's voice.

"I'll get you the fucking money. Back off!"

Erik muted the call for a moment and peered around the side of the building. James stood in profile, phone to his ear, and he looked jittery as hell. His movements were jerky as his head swiveled to look around, his foot tapping so damn fast that it looked unnatural.

Then Erik saw what dangled from his hand. A small transparent bag of white pills.

———

HANNAH TWISTED her hand in Erik's. Words bubbled just under the surface as he drove them home. Questions. But she didn't know how to ask them. How did you ask someone why they didn't want kids, especially someone you were barely dating, without making it sound like you were desperate?

It had been on her mind since Brigid's poor choice of joke. It wasn't so much what he'd said, but the way he'd said it, like the very idea of having children of his own both scared him and made him angry as hell.

Just do it, Hannah. Ask the hard questions. You won't die.

She cleared her throat. "Was it an important call?"

Okay, not the question she wanted to ask. She'd ease into it.

"It was an old friend of mine. Her name's Rachel."

Her name? Suddenly, a million more questions rushed to the surface. How had they met? How close were they? And most importantly, had they dated?

Jealousy skittered in her chest that he might be friends with an ex.

"I met her my first year in the Marines," he said quietly, as if reading her thoughts. "We've been friends ever since. She lives in Arkansas."

Friends…just friends. Still, the stab of jealousy was there, and she hated it. Not just jealousy over their history, but the way Erik's voice softened with affection when he spoke about her.

"She was just calling to check in," he added.

She nodded. "I look forward to meeting her one day."

There was the slightest tensing of his jaw. It was so small, she almost missed it.

She cleared her throat. "Erik—"

"Hannah—"

She laughed at the way they both said each other's name at the same time. "You go first."

The corner of his mouth lifted. "You sure?"

"Yes."

"Okay. I saw something while I was outside tonight."

"Hope it wasn't Bigfoot." His lips didn't even twitch at her joke. She frowned, nerves tickling her belly. "What?"

"Does James do drugs?"

"Drugs?" Her voice came out as a squeak. "No. Absolutely not. He's been with Brigid for as long as I've known them, and she would have told me. Plus, I've known him for four years myself and have never seen him take anything. Why?"

"I overheard him talking to someone about owing money. Then when I looked around the corner and saw him, he was holding a small bag of white pills."

Her breath cut off. "No. That…no. It had to be something else."

She'd definitely know if he did drugs…right? At the very least, Brigid would know, and she told Hannah everything.

He squeezed her hand. "Okay."

For the rest of the drive, every other thought left her head, and James was all she could think about. Because what if Erik was right? What if he was doing drugs and Brigid didn't know?

Then she needed to tell her friend…didn't she?

Chapter Twenty

Hannah fiddled with the cloud on her bracelet. It was a nervous fiddle.

Her gaze shifted out the window of her car to Brigid's lingerie shop. The store didn't look busy.

Good. Not busy was good. No listening ears for this hard conversation.

Now, she just needed to get out of the car and do it. Tell her best friend that her boyfriend might be doing drugs.

Oh God, she hated this.

There was the chance it was all a big misunderstanding. That James wasn't a drug addict who owed his dealer money and was keeping it a secret from his girlfriend. But if there was even the tiniest possibility of Erik's suspicions being true, and Brigid didn't know, Hannah needed to tell her.

All right. Time to rip off the Band-Aid.

She grabbed the tray of coffee and climbed out of the car. If there was anything that could put her friend in a good mood before a bombshell, it was caffeine.

She'd only taken one step onto the sidewalk when she almost ran into a crisp white shirt. She looked up and nearly groaned at the sight of Ezra Hall, the top-selling realtor at the new competing agency.

A smug smile spread across his face. "Hannah, hi."

"Hi, Ezra." She'd met him once before when he'd come over and introduced himself at a café. Everything about the man had screamed arrogance.

"I just finished with an open." His gaze shifted to the coffees in her hand. "I heard business has been tough over at Reuben's."

Heard from whom? "Not true at all. We're thriving." The lie just slid off her tongue, because no way was she letting this guy know about her low sales. "I've been showing homes all day." *That* part wasn't a lie.

"Really?" His eyes glittered. "I got a call from Angelo Bonetti the other day."

A shot of air sucked into her lungs. "He's giving his property to you?"

God, she wanted to strangle this guy. It wasn't his doing, of course, but she had to put the anger somewhere.

"If you can't sell it within the month, then yes. And that month is just about up, isn't it?"

She ground her teeth together. "Fortunately, it only takes one offer to sell a house. Excuse me, I have somewhere to be." She had to grit her teeth as the man watched her walk into her friend's lingerie shop.

She blew out a long exhale, immediately spotting Brigid at the back desk behind the computer. The second her friend's gaze lifted, all thoughts of Ezra left her head.

"Coffee," Brigid gushed. "Thank God. I need caffeine or I may kill someone. And when I say *may*, I mean *will*. You'd have to help me bury the body."

Hannah's lips tilted up as she set the drinks on the desk. "I've brought you a Black Bean macchiato and an iced latte."

Double the caffeine, so double the softening of the blow, right?

Brigid reached for Hannah's hand and closed her eyes. It almost looked like the woman was praying. "Thank you. You have just saved a life, my friend."

Brigid grabbed her macchiato and took a big gulp before groaning. Christ, didn't the woman burn her tongue? The beverage was steaming hot when she'd grabbed it.

The cup hit the counter as Brigid asked, "Okay, now that I have some caffeine in my system, tell me, how were your open houses today? You had two, right?"

"They went well. I had some very interested buyers." She hadn't shown Angelo's home today, but she'd given a few people tours yesterday before happy hour at the office. She just had to pray one of them made an offer before she had to return the keys to Angelo. "I also had a couple of callbacks already from those mailbox drops this morning."

Brigid's features softened. "Oh, Han, that's great."

"It's a huge relief. I might even go back to the office today and follow up on some leads." It wasn't like she had any huge plans. And she had time to kill before dinner with Erik, or she'd show up at his house three hours early. "How's the shop?"

Brigid lifted a shoulder. "It's fine. Business has been a bit slow, but nothing I can't handle. It just sucks that both my and James's incomes are short at the same time. I wish you guys had more houses to sell."

Her heart thudded. Were they also having money issues?

Brigid leaned forward, eyes widening in excitement. "Have you heard about Henry's new guy?"

She frowned. "When did he meet a new guy?"

"Last night, while we were at your office, he met a Tinder date. His name is Rob, and Henry says he's cute."

"Henry thinks a lot of guys are cute. But I'm glad and I

hope it works out. That man needs a partner. He's been on the lookout for too long."

"I know. I hope he finds his James."

Hannah cleared her throat, the familiar tingle of nerves running over her skin. "I actually have a question about James, and I hope it's okay to ask."

"Girlfriend, if it's a sex question, you know I'm an open book."

Usually, she'd laugh at that kind of comment. Right now, she couldn't even muster a smile. "Last night, when Erik took that call, he went outside. James was on the phone, and Erik heard him say something about owing someone money." She swallowed, rushing the last words out. "And when he glanced around the corner, he saw James holding a bag of white pills."

Some of the color left Brigid's face. "What?"

"He also said James looked…jittery."

Brigid's mouth opened and closed. It was the first time Hannah had ever seen her friend speechless. "Are you saying… you think James is doing *drugs*?"

"No. I…" She shook her head. "I'm just telling you what Erik saw, in case you don't—"

"In case I don't realize my boyfriend's hiding a drug problem." There was a bite to her words now. "That's he's such an addict he owes money he can't pay back?"

"Brigid—"

"How long have you known Erik?" Her eyes were narrowed now, her words flat. "A month? Maybe two? And how long have you known James?"

She swallowed. "Four years."

"Four years. Yet you believe this new guy when he says your best friend's *partner* is a drug addict?"

"He never said he was a drug addict, just that he—"

"Had a bag of drugs, probably took said drugs, and owes people money for them."

Oh God, this was not going the way she'd hoped. "I'm not saying I believe it or that I don't. But I *had* to mention it, Brigid. Imagine if I didn't and something happened. You're my best friend. I want you to be safe."

If anything, those words seemed to enrage Brigid further. "I *am* safe with James. He's my world, Hannah. Something you should know." Her chest expanded and she straightened. "As a friend, I would encourage *you* to think really carefully about where you put *your* trust. Erik's barely told you anything about himself. Hell, you don't even know what he does for work."

"Brigid—"

"I actually have a lot of ordering to do, so if you don't mind…"

Hannah's mouth dropped open. She searched her friend's face, but there was no leeway there. God, she'd never seen her so angry, and she had no idea how to navigate it.

With numb fingers, she lifted her own untouched latte and left. It wasn't until she was sitting in her car again that she sucked in her first long breath.

What did she do now? She and Brigid had been friends— no, *best* friends—for four years, and they'd never fought before. Sure, small squabbles here and there, but never like that.

The entire drive back to the office, she ran over the exchange in her head. Could she have done it differently? Used different words so her friend didn't get so offended? Or maybe she shouldn't have said anything at all. Maybe she should have just stayed out of it.

Christ, she had no idea.

When she reached the office, she didn't get out right away, instead lifting her phone and typing out a text to her friend. But every time she wrote something, she immediately deleted it. What could she say to make things better?

She went with something simple.

Hannah: Brigid, I'm sorry. I love you. X

Sent. There. Done. Now it was in Brigid's court.

Why did that thought make her chest feel unbelievably tight?

She blew out a breath and sped up the steps to the front door. The office was dark and empty, but then, it was Saturday afternoon, so she'd expected to be alone.

She was moving down the hall when something sounded... footsteps, maybe? Was she *not* alone?

She stopped. "Hello?"

When she didn't hear anything else, she took slow steps forward. That's when she heard the soft creak of the back door.

She walked faster down the hall to find the back door closed, but not locked. She tugged it open but saw nothing.

Still, a chill swept over her skin that had nothing to do with the cool breeze. This entire scenario was too much like the break-in at her house.

When her phone dinged with a message, she closed the back door and clicked the lock before tugging out her cell.

Erik: How does vindaloo sound?

She forced herself to forget the back door. Maybe she'd been hearing things. Or maybe she hadn't, and it was Taylor grabbing something? She'd left the office door unlocked once before, when she'd been in a rush to get her son from school.

She focused on the text in front of her, but even though she smiled at his question, she couldn't get Brigid's words from earlier out of her head. She was right. She *hadn't* known him for long, and she didn't know what he did for work. She'd told him she was okay with not knowing for now, but what if that time stretched into months, or even years?

Yes, his job may be classified. But surely he could tell her *something*? The very foundation of a relationship was built on honesty.

She lowered to her seat and tried to push everything to the

back of her mind as she started making calls to prospective sellers and buyers who'd emailed her thanks to the mailbox drops. It took a while, but she didn't mind. She loved her job, and after such a long slow period, it felt good to be busy.

When she was done, she grabbed the keys from her open houses earlier that afternoon and headed to her small office safe. After keying in the code, she opened the door and placed the keys inside. She was about to close it—but stopped.

The keys for Angelo's property were supposed to be in the safe…but they weren't.

Shit! Had she put them somewhere else? Had she taken them home after showing those prospective buyers yesterday? She'd done it before, so it wasn't outside the realm of possibility.

She tried to think back to the tours. The last had been at the end of the day, and she *had* gone straight home after…but she could've sworn she'd replaced his keys this morning, when grabbing the sets for the open houses.

Panic bubbled in her chest, but she forced it down. It was fine. She'd go home and search there. She'd also search her car and work bag. She'd find those keys.

Still, her heart rattled in her chest. Because what if she didn't?

Chapter Twenty-One

Erik's watch lit up when Hannah stepped onto his property. Good, he'd been getting damn worried.

Since last night, the idea of her working with James made him uncomfortable. If people were after the man for money, they might target anyone close to him, and that could include coworkers.

He tugged the front door open. Hannah stood on the other side, smile a mile wide on her lips and bottle of wine in hand. "A red to go with the vindaloo."

He tugged her straight into him and crashed his lips to hers. He couldn't be in the woman's company without needing to touch her. Kiss her. Feel her soft against his hard.

She sighed, and when her lips parted, he slipped his tongue inside, tasting the fucking sweetness that was Hannah.

When they finally separated, her eyes were soft, lips red. "Hm. That was a nice greeting."

"What I really want to do is take you against the damn wall."

Heat blasted through her eyes. "And the problem with that is…?"

He lowered his head again, his lips hovering over hers. "The problem, Miss Jacobs, is that I'd need hours to get my fill of you. And then you'd never be fed."

"Who needs food? I already ate lunch, I'm good."

If it wasn't for her diabetes, he might believe her. Instead, he gritted his teeth and pushed the door closed after her. "Come on, before you completely corrupt me."

In the kitchen, Hannah lifted the knife he'd just been using and started slicing the mushrooms while he opened the wine.

"Did you see James today?" Erik asked, knowing his voice came out harder than he'd intended.

"No. But I often don't see him, Taylor, *or* Reuben on a Saturday."

Good. "How'd it go with Brigid?"

Her chopping paused, and the sad tilt of her lips gave her away. "Worse than I could have imagined. She wasn't happy. In fact, she was offended that I believed it might be true."

His brows flickered as he slid a glass of wine toward her. "James said what he said, though. And those were definitely pills in the bag."

She swallowed. "I know. I think she was more questioning how well I knew *you* and trusted what you saw."

That was fair.

"She's not texting me back," Hannah said quietly. "I asked Henry to check on her, so I'm just waiting to hear from him."

Unable to stop himself, he moved behind her and gripped her hips, setting his mouth close to her ear. "She'll come around."

A small shudder made her tremble in his arms. "I hope so. I've never had many important people in my life, but when I do, I always seem to lose them. I don't want to lose her too."

Something shifted in his chest. He applied some pressure to her hips and waited until she was facing him to cup her cheek.

"Give her time. Once the shock is over, she'll come back to you."

"And if she doesn't?"

"You still have me."

She smiled, but the smile didn't quite reach her eyes. "Thank you."

He kissed her, hating that he knew exactly what she was thinking. That they were new and hadn't even labeled what they were. That secrets still lay between them.

He shifted over to the pantry and took out the spices, but he could feel her eyes on him.

"So," she said softly. "When's your next…job?"

He stilled, the muscles in his forearms flexing. "I leave Monday and will be gone for three days."

She gave him a slow nod. "Will it be dangerous?"

His jaw clenched. "I can't talk about that, Angel."

Disappointment flashed in her eyes. "Do your parents know what you do?"

"No." And he planned to keep it that way.

"Your brother or sister?"

He shook his head, although he was pretty sure they all suspected.

She seemed to think about that for a moment, and he wasn't sure exactly what she'd settled on. A part of him knew he wasn't just keeping the information from her because it was classified…he was keeping it from her because he wasn't sure she'd accept what he did. That she'd accept *him*.

She looked like she was about to go back to the chopping, then stopped. "Can I ask you another question?"

Dread snapped through his limbs like a whip. "Sure."

"Why don't you want kids?"

He set the spices onto the counter with a bit too much force.

"I'm not asking because I'm saying we're going to get

married and I'll want kids," she rushed to add. "God, we've only just started exploring this thing between us. But if there's never even a possibility, I'd like to know why. Because I've always seen kids as part of my future."

He swallowed, trying to make himself link a few fucking words together. "There's never a possibility with me." He didn't look at her as he said it.

"Why?"

He grabbed the edge of the counter, his fingers so tight that he felt like he was going to crack the damn thing. "Hannah. I told you there are things I'm not ready to talk about."

The hurt on her face deepened before shifting into anger. "You won't tell me why you don't want children. You won't tell me what your job entails. How am I supposed to know who you are?"

"You're not."

Her lips parted. "Really? You seriously don't want me to know you?"

When he remained silent, she shuffled away from the counter. "I know I said I was okay with slow, but I need to know who I'm dating. I need to know if I'm just keeping your bed warm until something better comes along." Hurt tangled with her words.

His gaze cut to her. "I haven't dated another woman since Vicky. You mean something to me."

"Vicky. Your ex-wife. Is she around?"

When he didn't respond because of the vise gripping his chest, he thought he saw tears in her eyes. Then she blinked.

He forced softness into his voice. "I can't change who I am."

"Can't or won't?"

"Both."

She cocked her head, the sad tilt of her lips becoming more

emphasized. "See, that's the thing. I think you *can* change, and deep down you know it. You just don't want to."

"You think I can change? I have *blood* on my hands." His voice rose so much louder than he meant it to. "So much I can actually feel it most days."

"Tell me about it then. Let me in. Let me help you."

"I'm not doing this, Hannah."

He turned because he couldn't look at the hurt on her face. The hurt *he'd* caused, like the damn asshole he was.

She sighed, and said quietly, "You weren't doing it anyway."

They were the last words he heard before her footsteps moved toward the door and she left.

━━

HANNAH SCRUBBED AWAY a tear before it could slide down her cheek. She was so mad, and she wanted to hold on to that anger. Keep it from changing into something deeper. Something she didn't want to name.

God, they'd barely started dating, yet tonight *hurt*. So much more than it should have. And she knew why. The man had snaked his way to her heart and already started cracking through the protective outer shell.

Pressing her hands to her kitchen counter, she tried to breathe. Brigid's words had affected her today, and too quickly, she'd let them slip into the relationship she was trying to build with Erik.

She swallowed the avalanche of emotions. Falling apart wasn't an option. She was stronger than that. Pain and loss had assaulted her before, and she'd come out the other end just fine.

She tugged out her phone and called the only person she wanted to speak to. The second the call to Brigid went to voice mail, she wanted to throw the cell to the floor. Stomp on it and watch it shatter.

A text came through, and she couldn't stop the flash of hope when Brigid's name popped up. Then she read the message.

Brigid: I'm sorry. I know I was awful today. I just need some time.

She closed her eyes and let the hurt in her heart settle. She'd call Henry, but there was a chance he was with Brigid.

All right. She needed to pull herself together, get some insulin, and eat something. The last thing she felt like doing was eating, but she didn't really have a choice.

God, she even wanted to cry about her damn diabetes. She hadn't done that in a long time. Not that diabetes ever got easier, but she'd been dealing with it most of her life.

She gave herself a shot of insulin, then grabbed a bowl, the Frosted Flakes, and some milk. She was only halfway through her hasty dinner when her phone rang.

She frowned when she saw it was one of the homeowners she'd spoken to today.

She cleared her throat before straightening. "Hi, Allen. How are you?"

"Hi, Hannah."

Her heart jolted at his tone. "Is everything okay?"

"Actually, we've had a change of heart. We're going to go with another agent."

No…this couldn't be happening. Just a couple hours ago, he'd been so happy with her. Excited even. "Why? We had a great talk today and were all set to work together."

There was an awkward, heavy silence.

"Please," she begged. "I just need to know why you've decided to go elsewhere."

Why *so many* people were deciding to go elsewhere.

He cleared his throat. "Honestly, another agent spoke to us about some issues others have had with you."

Another agent? "Who?"

"I don't want to say. But they told us there have been some issues with your property sales and work ethic."

Her jaw dropped. "*What*? That's not true."

Particularly not about her work ethic. Heck, she lived and breathed her job.

"I'm sorry, we're just not comfortable maintaining the relationship at this point."

The line went dead, and she just sat there, looking at her phone like it had sprouted heads.

Another agent was bad-mouthing her? Was it Ezra? Another agent in his office? Hell, it could even have been Taylor, or…

No. James wouldn't do that.

But then, did she really know *what* he would do? The man was possibly taking drugs and owed money to his dealers, something she never suspected would be possible a few days ago.

God, she was ready for this day to be over. Or better yet, she wanted a complete redo so she could make sure this day never actually happened.

Chapter Twenty-Two

Hannah rose from her desk and stretched, the crumbs from a cherry strudel scattered across the desk. Stress eating. She'd done a lot of that over the last week.

But it was Friday...finally. And as far as she was concerned, this week could go die in a hole. Brigid was still barely talking to her. James hadn't shown his face in days, claiming he was sick. And Erik had gone away for the job she wasn't allowed to know the details of, and even though he'd said it was a three-day thing, he hadn't yet returned home.

Yeah, it had been a week to forget.

She blew out a breath and moved over to her key safe. There were three open houses this weekend. She entered the code, opened the door...and paused. Was that...

It was the key to Angelo's home.

What the hell? That had not been there last Saturday. And she'd never found it in her home or car. Had someone taken it and put it back?

"Hannah."

She jumped and turned to see Reuben standing in the doorway. "Hi. Yes?"

"I'm just leaving for that client meeting. Do you want to drive together or meet us there?"

"I'll meet you there." That would make a quick getaway easier. "Just about to leave now."

"Great."

"Reuben…"

He stopped.

"You haven't opened this safe over the last week, have you?" Reuben had the code to all the safes here. Taylor also had the code, because Hannah had asked her to grab a key for an open once when she'd been running late. But surely Taylor wouldn't take any of her keys…

"No." He straightened "Why? Is one gone?"

"No." The word came out too quickly, like word vomit. She didn't want to give her boss any reason to question her competence.

He frowned. "Okay. Good. I'll see you at the restaurant. He should be there in a few minutes."

Crap. Quickly, she grabbed the keys she needed—including the one for Angelo's home—and closed the safe, then rushed to her desk to shut down her laptop. She'd almost forgotten about the dinner, but there was no way she would have told Reuben that. It was with some client with big money who wanted to meet with Reuben and an agent to see what properties they could offer.

She dropped the keys into her bag, popped the last bit of strudel into her mouth, and rushed out. She'd parked on the street today, so she ran out the front. She locked the door and turned—then gasped at the sight of two large men in front of her.

Her heart thumped in her chest. Where the hell had they come from? She tried to force calm into her voice, but God, they screamed danger. "Can I help you?"

"We're looking for Paley."

Every hair on her arms stood on end. "James hasn't been in this week."

The guy stepped toward her, and her heart took off at a gallop. She wanted to step back, but there was nowhere to go. "Then we need you to do something for us."

Did she have a choice? "Okay."

"Tell him Vincent is looking for him, and the longer he hides, the worse it'll be for him."

The ice that slid over her skin was so sudden that she almost shuddered. Her nod was more of a jerk, and it was only when they turned and walked away that she finally breathed again.

It took her a few long seconds to finally force her legs to move. To unlock her car and slide behind the wheel. Immediately, she hit the lock button. Her fingers clenched the wheel tightly during the short drive to the restaurant, and her gaze kept darting to the rearview mirror.

Before getting out, she pulled out her phone to text Brigid.

Hannah: Hey. I just need to let you know that two not-so-friendly-looking men were waiting outside the office just now, looking for James. Stay safe, Brig. X

If they'd gone to the office to look for him, they'd definitely already gone to his home—where Brigid also lived. God, she hoped her friend was okay. She sent a text to Henry too, letting him know what had happened and that Brigid might need a place to stay.

Once that was done, she felt better...kind of. After this meeting with the client, she'd also tell Reuben. She hadn't told him about the phone call or the drugs because she'd had no way of confirming if the suspicions were true. But he needed to know about this visit. It wasn't nothing. Having big, intimidating men block her path to her car was most definitely not *nothing*.

Quickly, she layered on some lipstick and a touch of foundation. Argh. Was it the lighting, or were the bags under her eyes as dark as they looked? Who the heck cared? How she looked was at the bottom of her problems list. Like absolutely last on the list.

Grabbing her bag, she climbed out of the car and walked into the Italian restaurant. It was busy, with almost every table taken, and most definitely fine dining—not anything she would choose herself.

She was approaching the hostess stand when someone lightly touched her arm. She bit back a groan at the sight of Ezra. "Hi."

The guy lifted a brow. "Hannah. What are you doing here?"

"Meeting a client. You?"

"A client?"

"Yes. So excuse me." She felt the guy's gaze on her the entire way to the stand. Creep.

A hostess appeared in front of her. "Good evening, ma'am. Do you have a reservation?"

"Reuben Caster made our reservation. He should already be here."

"Right this way."

Hannah followed the woman to a small table. She could only see the back of the man who sat opposite Reuben, but even sitting, there was no missing how tall and broad he was.

"Hi, I hope I haven't missed anything," she said as she reached the table. She smiled at Reuben, then turned to the man opposite—and the air in her lungs ground to a halt.

Marco Salvatore. He was the client?

Marco stood.

"Hannah, this is Marco Salvatore," Reuben said, oblivious to her shock. "Mr. Salvatore, this is Hannah Jacobs, one of my agents."

His eyes sparking with amusement, Marco leaned in and

kissed the back of her hand. She couldn't step away. She may not be in a good place with Erik right now, but she knew he'd hate this.

"It's nice to meet you, Miss Jacobs," he said in his smooth Italian accent.

She swallowed. "You too, Mr. Salvatore."

"Marco, please."

She dipped her head and lowered into her seat. Her limbs were numb, and she was moving on autopilot. Questions spun in her head. Was he here because he wanted something from her? Or to anger Erik?

"Marco was just telling me what he's looking for in a property."

"Oh?" Interesting, seeing as she'd shown him a property, then never heard back. Clearly, Marco hadn't shared that little detail with Reuben.

The next half hour was a blur of property talk, all of which she knew was bullshit. It had to be. She tapped her foot nervously under the table. When a text came through on her phone, she glanced down at the table. Her heart twisted when she saw Erik's name. It was the first text he'd sent her all week.

Erik: I just got back and noticed you're not home.

She tapped her foot faster and locked her phone to make the message disappear.

"Hannah, why don't you tell Marco about the current market."

She didn't know what came out of her mouth next. Words about interest rates and the speed with which properties were selling. When Reuben took over, she looked down to see another message.

Erik: I'm sorry. I miss you. Can we talk?

Her chest tightened. While Marco and Reuben were deep in conversation, she moved the phone to her lap and quickly typed out a response.

Hannah: I'm at a work dinner with Reuben and a high-end client. Marco's the client.

Immediately, three dots came up, then his reply.

Erik: Where are you?

"Hannah."

Her head shot up at Reuben's voice.

His lips were pulled into a thin line. "Could you tell Marco about the properties you currently have listed?"

"Sure." She forced her gaze to Marco, again talking on autopilot.

It wasn't until their food came that she was finally able to push her chair back and excuse herself. "I just need to pop into the restroom."

As she walked away, she heard Reuben telling Marco about her diabetes. She cringed. God, that was a *huge* invasion of her privacy. The world, including Marco Salvatore, did not need to know about her medical history, something Reuben should understand.

When she reached the bathroom, she quickly used the facilities, then tested her blood sugar levels and sighed. She was high. Damn stress eating. She'd already known she was though, not just because of what she'd eaten, but because she was thirsty and could feel the beginnings of a headache.

Quickly, she gave herself a shot of insulin, then checked her phone, cringing again when she saw the three missed calls from Erik. She didn't have time to deal with him right now.

Dropping her phone into her bag, she stepped out of the bathroom—only to run smack into a black buttoned-down shirt. Marco's shirt.

"Hello, *cara*."

She opened and closed her mouth two times before getting words out. "Marco...what are you doing back here?" The men's bathroom was the other way.

"I came to talk to you."

"Well, I think we should talk at the table." She attempted to sidestep him, but her arm was tugged in the opposite direction, and he pushed her against a wall. "What are you—"

"I need a favor."

She tried to pull her arm away, but he tightened his fingers.

Trickles of unease ran down her spine. Because *this* was the Marco Erik had always warned her about. She was finally seeing the threat. Feeling it in the strength of his hold. Hearing it in the deep, dangerous tone of his voice.

Her spine straightened and she lowered her voice, anger competing with the fear inside her. "Marco. Let go."

With his spare hand, he ran a finger down her cheek. She tried to shift away, but it was futile. There was no getting out of his hold.

"I need you to convince Erik to take a job."

She swallowed. "What job?"

His finger kept trailing down, and she gasped when he ran it along the outside of her breast. She tried to shove him away, but he didn't budge.

"He knows which one."

Her jaw clenched. She was a fraction of a second away from nailing this asshole in the balls. "And if he doesn't?"

His smile was slow—and it made the hairs on the back of her neck stand up. "You really want to know?"

She opened her mouth to say yes, absolutely yes, but before she could utter a sound, the man was torn off her and thrown against the opposite wall.

***

THE SECOND ERIK SAW MARCO, blood roared between his ears.

He crossed the distance in seconds and grabbed the guy off Hannah before shoving him into the wall.

"What the fuck are you doing here?" Erik growled, making sure to position himself between him and Hannah.

Marco tilted his head, almost looking pleased with himself. "I am here to talk to your beautiful woman, of course."

Erik's fist twitched to hit the guy. "I told you I'd tear you apart if you touched her again."

"A threat you knew was empty, because you know what I can do."

He dipped his head and lowered his voice. "And you know what *I* can do."

"Careful. People are watching. If you end up in jail, how will you protect the women in your life?"

The fucking scumbag.

He shot his gaze to the side. The few people with a view of the hallway were all watching. Even a waiter had stopped and was staring at them. Probably a second away from calling the police.

"Take the job and I disappear, Hunter."

Erik's hands fisted so tight—all he wanted to do was throw a punch and make sure the asshole never got back up. "I do the job and you leave?"

"Yes."

He hated it. But the fucker had made it clear he was going nowhere until he got what he wanted.

"Fine," Erik bit out through gritted teeth. "I'll do it. But you don't show your goddamn face in Redwood again. Got it?"

Marco's smug smile made Erik's blood boil. "Deal."

Erik turned and grabbed Hannah's arm. They didn't say anything as he tugged her through the restaurant.

"You're not gonna fight me on leaving?" he asked through gritted teeth.

"No. I'll text Reuben that I wasn't feeling well."

Thank fuck.

Carefully, he helped her into his car. "We'll come back and get yours tomorrow."

Again, she didn't argue, just nodded.

The second he was behind the wheel, he nodded toward the glove box. "There are some M&M's in there if you need them."

Her brows tugged together. "Why do you have M&M's in your glove box?"

"For you." He'd made sure he had some form of sugar in every room of his house too.

Her eyes softened. "I don't need them, but thank you."

When she massaged her temple, his gaze whipped to her again. "What's wrong?"

"Nothing. Just a headache from high blood sugar."

If she'd told him that Marco had hurt her, he'd turn the car around right now and murder the fucker.

"How did you find me?"

Erik's jaw clicked. "You said high-end, so I got Chandler to hack into the reservation systems of the most expensive restaurants in Redwood."

She frowned but said nothing. The rest of the drive home was silent. When he reached her place, he climbed from his Corvette. She didn't say anything as he followed her to the door.

She turned once it was unlocked and opened. "You don't need to come in, Erik. I'm fine."

He stepped closer and ran his fingers over her arm, right where the fucker had grabbed her. She wore long sleeves, so he couldn't see her skin, but he was sure she'd have marks. "I'm sorry."

She swallowed, her gaze shifting between his. "About Marco, or…"

"Both." He touched his other hand to her hip, relieved as hell when she didn't step away. "I *do* want to share everything with you. Every little detail of my life. I just need some more time. I don't know how much. But soon, I promise."

She seemed to roll that over in her mind. "But you want a relationship with me?"

"Yes." Hell yes. "I wasn't lying. I did miss you. When we're apart, I *crave* to be around you. To touch you. To have you as mine."

She swallowed. "I feel all those things."

Her words shot into his chest like a bullet, hard and fast. He took a small step forward, testing whether she'd back away. When she didn't, he lowered his head, closing the distance so slowly she had all the time in the world to turn. Instead, she allowed his lips to touch hers.

It was a long, slow kiss, like he was re-familiarizing himself with her. Relearning what this woman did to him.

She moaned and pulled him inside. He closed the door with his foot and pushed her against the wall.

Quickly, the kiss changed. Deepened. Shifted into something more desperate.

Her hands went to the buckle of his jeans.

"Hannah." Her name tore from his lips. He wasn't sure if he was trying to stop her or encourage her.

"I need you," she breathed.

When she slid her hand into his briefs and her fingers wrapped around his cock, his muscles pulled so tight he thought they'd snap. He palmed her breast as her hand slid over his length, but it wasn't enough.

With a deep growl, he shoved his hand beneath her skirt and yanked her panties down, then lifted her into his arms. His tip was at her entrance, and he fucking burned to push inside her. Take what was his.

He reached between them and swiped her clit with the pad of his thumb. The cry from her lips sank its teeth inside him, tormenting him.

He touched a finger to her entrance to see if she was ready for him. Fucking soaked. She trembled in his arms, so damn sensitive. He swiped her again, and his cock slipped an inch inside her.

"Erik…" she breathed. "You're not wearing anything."

Fuck. He'd forgotten. How the hell had he forgotten?

He started to set her down, but she tightened her legs around him. "I'm on the pill. And I'm clear."

The world darkened, everything disappearing until it was just her. His fucking light. His angel.

He thrust inside.

She cried out, her walls so wet they fucking coated him. He eased out, then thrust again, this time crashing his lips to hers and catching her next scream.

God…this woman. She'd dug herself so deep inside him that he was empty without her. She didn't seem to care how imperfect he was. She made him feel like he was enough.

He thrust harder. Faster. Needing more of her. Needing everything she had.

He wrenched open her shirt, then yanked down her bra to palm her bare breast. Her nails bit into his shoulders and he welcomed the pain. He rolled her nipple between his thumb and finger. Suddenly, her back bowed and she tore her mouth from his to scream. The sound cut through the room, echoing off the walls.

He tried to hold off, needing to stretch this moment out, make it last as long as he fucking could. But at the feel of her walls pulsing around his cock, he shattered. Broke so violently and fiercely, he didn't know what kept his feet on the ground.

When he had nothing left, nothing but her, she touched his cheek. And suddenly he knew how his feet remained planted. How he could breathe even when his lungs felt constricted.

Her. Always her.

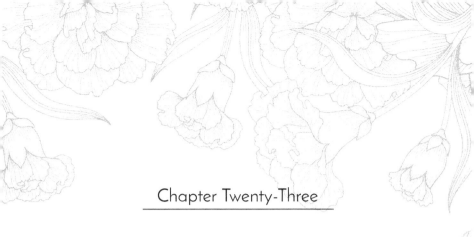

Chapter Twenty-Three

Erik: I'm coming to get you in ten.

She frowned at the message, then shifted her gaze to the time on her phone. Shit. It was almost six. Where had that time gone?

She'd only managed to fix her hair so far, because she'd gotten home late from her open houses.

Erik: Tick tock.

She flew into her closet, shoving dress after dress aside, looking for something that screamed "meet the parents" while giving off I'm-a-great-fit-for-your-son vibes. Was there such a thing?

An organized person would have made this decision days ago when she'd been invited, but with all the time she was dedicating to work, she'd put no thought into it.

There was nothing. Absolutely—

She stopped at a beige dress with white flowers. That could work. Pair it with some leggings and a black cardigan.

Quickly, she yanked the outfit from the closet and threw off her clothes. Thank God she'd already showered.

She changed quickly and had just applied some foundation and blush when the doorbell rang.

Her heart sped up, but that had nothing to do with meeting the family and everything to do with Erik and his effect on her. They'd woken up together this morning, so she shouldn't be so nervous. But it didn't seem to matter how much or little time passed—he took hold of every one of her senses.

With a long inhale, she walked out of the bedroom and down the hall. The second the door was open, her chest constricted.

God, how could one man be so beautiful? He only wore jeans and a dark T-shirt, but it was like every inch of him was sculpted to perfection.

"Hi, Angel."

"Hey." She swallowed, trying to get her bearings. "You look…"

He stepped forward and curved an arm around her waist. "Handsome? Strong? Like a warrior?"

"All three."

"Hm." He leaned down and kissed her, and God, those lips catapulted her somewhere else. She had no idea where. She didn't care. As long as he was there with her, that was the only place she wanted to be.

He slid his tongue between her lips, and she hummed. His kisses, his taste, his earthy pine scent…it had all become so achingly familiar to her now.

When his head rose, she groaned. She wanted more. She wanted every part of this man to be hers.

He chuckled. "We're going to be late, Angel."

Argh. Anything else, and she'd miss it. Throw her bag down and drag him to the bedroom. But she wanted to have dinner with his parents and siblings. She wanted to spend time with this man's family, weave herself into his life so they could intertwine and build one together.

"You're right," she grumbled.

He laughed again. And God, she loved that. He didn't laugh often, but it was a beautiful sound. One she wanted to play over and over again in her head.

Once they were driving, he reached over and wrapped his fingers around her thigh. Touching each other seemed to be something neither of them could resist. "How was your day?"

"Really good, actually. I went into the office and did some paperwork for a house that's about to sell."

"On a Saturday afternoon?"

She lifted a shoulder. "I love my job, and sales haven't been great, so I'm happy to work whenever I have to."

His brows flickered. "A few weeks ago, I saw some job advertisements on your counter…"

She cringed. She hadn't realized he'd seen them. And his statement just now wasn't really a question, but it kind of was. "I've been applying for second jobs. When I renovated my house, sales were great, so I put all my savings into it. Since then, things have been a bit tougher."

A bit? Ha, that was an understatement.

At his silence, she lifted a shoulder, feeling awkward about the topic. "I'm managing."

If the narrowing of his eyes was anything to go by, he didn't like that answer. But it was the best she could do without lying.

"If you need money, Angel—"

"*Don't* finish that sentence. I'll be okay. Really." Taking money from the man she'd only just started dating? Nope. Absolutely not. She'd stood on her own two feet her entire life, and that was not changing now.

His fingers tightened on the wheel. "Fine. But you'll let me know if you need help, won't you?"

Sure. Once she was homeless and insulin-less…then her ego might be so fractured she could reach out. "Yes."

His jaw clenched as if he'd heard her thoughts. "How's your blood sugar today?"

Thank God, a change of topic. "Always hanging on by a thread," she joked. "I'm fine. And I brought my diabetes bag, so I won't be passing out on your family."

He tightened his fingers around her thigh. "I still think Reuben should be upping your health insurance to cover a monitor and pump."

"Unfortunately, that's only one part of the equation. Some people actually have two insurance companies, and they still have to pay thousands of dollars for pumps." To say she thought little of companies that didn't cover the cost of vital equipment would be a big fat understatement.

She set her hand on top of his. "I've managed to keep myself alive this long without those things." Another narrowing of his eyes. All right, time for a second change in topic. "Have you seen your family much since moving back to town?"

"Weekly dinners. We usually do Sunday, but my brother Nate, who's a SEAL, is leaving tomorrow. He's been here on leave since the fundraising ball."

"Oh, I'm sorry. Everyone must be sad to see him go."

Erik nodded. "Yeah. Mom in particular. But everyone understands it's his job. I think Mom's just been happy to have all three of her kids in the same town at one time. That hasn't happened in years."

She wet her lips and began to trace a vein on the back of his hand. The closer they drew to his family's house, the higher her nerves peaked.

When he finally pulled into a long drive, her eyes widened. "Holy shit, your parents live *here*?"

Her gaze brushed over the multistory brick facade. The high, perfectly cut hedges and massive doorway. The place was a mansion.

So, it wasn't just Erik who had money.

"Yeah. They're comfortable."

She laughed. "Comfortable is code for rich. Did you grow up here?"

"I did. Both my dad and his dad, Stanley, were great businessmen and investors."

Uh, yeah, she could see that. She tilted her head, trying to get a better view from the passenger seat. Erik just shook his head and climbed out of the car.

They were halfway to the entrance when she touched his arm. "Hey. Before we go in, I just want to check in on you after what happened with Marco yesterday. You have to do a job with him now?"

A job she had no idea about, other than he didn't want to do it. She felt him tense.

"Yeah. I'll be okay."

Okay? That's what *she* said when things *weren't* okay, but she didn't want to go into detail. "I'm just…I'm sorry. That you have to do something you don't want to do because he targeted me."

He stopped at the door and turned to cup her cheek. "Hey. You do not need to apologize for that scumbag."

"I know. But I'm worried."

"Don't be. I can take care of myself." One side of his mouth kicked up. "Haven't you heard? I'm badass."

She smiled. How the man could put her at ease so quickly, she had no idea. "Really?"

"Mm-hmm." He lowered his head. The rhythm of her heart sped up. His lips were almost touching hers when the door opened. She gasped, and Erik's jaw ticked as they both turned to see his sister, Andi, standing in the doorway.

"Sorry, am I interrupting a moment?" Mischief gleamed in her eyes.

Hannah laughed.

Erik straightened before leaning forward and kissing his sister's cheek. "Timing is impeccable as always, A."

She lifted a shoulder, a ghost of a smile still on her face. Hannah stepped forward and Andi tugged her into a hug. The embrace felt oddly familiar, like she'd known this woman a lot longer than she actually had.

Before separating, Andie whispered in her ear, "I'm so glad he has you." She pulled back but kept hold of Hannah's shoulders. "I was wondering when the big grump would bring you to a dinner."

Erik shook his head, his hand returning to Hannah's waist as he tugged her inside. Her mouth dropped open at the sight of the grand staircase. At the crystal chandelier that centered the entrance.

The place was just as grand on the inside as it was on the outside.

Erik led her to the right, into a beautiful formal sitting room, which opened into a huge dining room and kitchen.

An older man stood from the couch and moved forward. She recognized him as someone who'd visited Stanley regularly, although she'd never met him. "Hi, son."

"Dad, this is Hannah. Hannah, this is my father, Michael Hunter."

He beamed at her. "It's nice to meet you, Hannah," he said, before kissing her cheek.

A younger guy, the same man she'd seen leaving Erik's house not that long ago, stepped forward. "And I'm the better-looking brother, Nate." He leaned forward and kissed her cheek too.

Erik slid an arm around her waist and tugged her closer. "Also the delusional brother."

She grinned. "It's nice to meet you, Nate."

Finally, an older woman moved around the kitchen island toward them. She was shorter than her kids, with a few grays and kind, dark brown eyes. She recognized the woman as another regular visitor of Stanley's.

"My boy." She tugged Erik into a big hug. Her eyes closed as she leaned into him. The love was so vivid, Hannah almost wanted to step back and give them space.

When she turned to Hannah, her smile was wide.

"Mom, Hannah. Hannah, my mom, Jennifer Hunter."

Jennifer wrapped her into a tight, warm hug, and Hannah could only sink into it. The embrace felt so maternal that she didn't want to let go.

"It's nice to meet you, Hannah." She eased away but kept hold of Hannah's shoulders. "Thank you for joining us. And thank you for keeping a watch over my son."

Hannah swallowed. It sounded like there was another meaning behind her words. What, exactly, she wasn't sure. But deep emotion shone in the woman's eyes, almost making Hannah feel equally emotional.

"Thank you for *raising* such a wonderful son," she said quietly.

For a second, there was a thin sheen of tears in the woman's eyes. But then she blinked them away.

Michael headed to the corner bar. "What can I get you to drink, Hannah?"

"Just water would be great."

Andi clapped her hands. "And I'll give you the house tour. If you want one, of course."

Did she want a tour of this mansion of a house? "Yes, please." The place was like a museum.

"Great." Andi linked their arms and patted a stony-faced Erik on the shoulder. "You'll get her back...after I've told her all my stories."

Hannah only had time to send a quick smile Erik's way before she was tugged down the expansive hall.

CONVERSATION TOOK place around Erik at the table. His dad and Hannah were laughing at a story Nate was telling. Andi was telling his mother something about her best friend, Finley. While Erik couldn't stop watching Hannah.

She fit so fucking well. But then, he'd known she would. Somehow, a part of him had just expected her to fall into his family unit, like she was an unknown missing piece.

It should make him scared. Hell, the Erik of a few months ago would be running hard and fast by now.

He wasn't running.

His fingers tightened around her thigh under the table. Because as well as watching her, he couldn't stop touching her, either.

When his phone rang, he tensed before tugging it out. Chandler. Hannah looked up at him with questioning eyes.

"I'll be right back." He kissed her temple before leaving.

He didn't answer until he was in the office. "Chandler."

"Hey, brother. Sorry to call on a Saturday night."

He ran his gaze over his father's myriad of books, not really seeing a single one of them. "You know you can call anytime."

"I just wanted to let you know that I'm with you on this job."

He'd told Chandler about the situation he was in with Marco, but Erik was shaking his head before his friend had finished speaking. "No. It's off the books. *I* shouldn't even be doing it. No way am I dragging you into it."

"You're not. I'm with you by choice."

Erik dropped his chin to his chest, so many fucking emotions coming to the surface. "Thank you, friend."

"Of course. Still in two days' time?"

Erik's jaw clenched. "That's what Marco told me."

"Send over all the information. I'm going to make sure your ass is covered."

Fuck, he was lucky to have Chandler. He ran a hand through his hair. "Have I told you how much I appreciate you?"

"Nope. But feel free to send me a bottle of Dalmore 64 Trinitas for Christmas."

Erik laughed. That was a serious top-shelf whiskey. "Done."

He hung up, hearing the steps from the hallway before he turned. His mother stood in the doorway, the smile from earlier not currently present. "Everything okay, honey?"

He shoved his phone into his pocket. "Yeah, everything's fine, Mom."

She walked further into the room. "I'm not just talking about right now. I've asked you a couple of times since you've been back, and I always get the same answer. I'm going to push you for some honesty now. *Are* you okay?"

He ran a hand through his hair. She was right, she *had* asked him before, and he'd always brushed it off with pretty little lies.

"Better than I thought I'd be." It was more honesty than he'd normally give. "How are *you* doing?" he asked, ready to deflect the attention. "Since Dad's heart attack?"

"It was a scare. For a moment there, I thought I was going to lose him." There was a slight sheen to his mother's eyes. "And after losing *you*, I don't think I would have coped very well."

A rock formed in his throat. "You never lost me, Mom."

The sheen became thicker. "Oh, but I did, honey. Eight years ago, I lost my oldest son. My first baby. But I understand that the pain of the past kept you away, and you did what you needed to do to survive. There were too many memories in this town from the person you used to be."

It was so fucking true. He'd never voiced any of that out loud, but of course, his mother knew.

"When you first got back, I was worried you'd come in body, but that was it," she said softly. "Tonight's the first night I've seen beyond the man you put on for show."

His heart pounded in his ears, drowning out nearly everything else. "She almost makes me feel like I can *be* that man again."

"I can see that." His mother stepped forward and grabbed his hand. "I love you. So much. And I can see that this thing between you and Hannah is real. Cherish that. Nurture it. Sometimes love can pull us away from the brink and bring us the salvation we need."

Every word fell into his chest like a perfectly placed explosive, detonating the shadow of a man he'd become. "I'm starting to learn that."

His mother cast her gaze down, and when she looked up, there was something new in her expression. Something harder. "This job of yours…are you staying safe?"

She said it like she somehow knew what he did. Suddenly he felt like a kid again, trying to keep secrets from his all-knowing mother. "Yes."

"I'm not just talking about physically, Erik." She held his gaze so long that his breaths started to shorten. "I know you don't shy away from danger, but if you sit on the edge of life and death too long, you eventually lose more than you're willing to pay."

"It won't be forever."

How long then? The words were a whispered question he'd never asked himself before. How long did he want to play God? How long did he need to spend clearing the world of assholes just to allow himself to breathe?

She squeezed his arm. "I hope not, honey. I want you to have the peace you deserve."

Peace. Something he never thought he'd find again. But since Hannah…there was hope.

"Whoops. Sorry."

His mother stepped away, and he looked up to see Hannah in the doorway. "I was, um, looking for the bathroom, but I obviously went the wrong way."

"I'll show you, Angel." But before he left the room, he leaned down and kissed his mother's cheek. "Thank you, Mom. I love you."

Chapter Twenty-Four

Hannah pulled out a bowl and a box of Corn Pops. Yep, cereal for dinner...again. But the word "corn" in the title made her feel like she was being semi-healthy.

She wasn't being lazy, *per se*. Erik was away for the evening for work, and cooking for one no longer felt as practical as it once had.

She poured half a bowl of cereal and topped it with some milk before her gaze shifted to the window. All day, she'd been trying to convince herself that Erik would be okay tonight. But a pesky voice in her head questioned if that was true. What did this job entail? And why had it been so important to Marco that Erik, specifically, do the job with him?

She sighed and lifted the spoon to her mouth, but before it reached her lips, a text came through on her phone.

Henry: Put the cereal down and come to the door.

She stopped. What the hell? Was the man watching her or was she just too predictable?

The latter. Of course, it was the latter.

She lowered the cereal to the counter and moved to the door. When she opened it, it wasn't just Henry standing there.

"Brigid…" Her friend's name fell from her lips in a surprised whisper.

Brigid held up a box of Honey Nut Cheerios. "Forgive me for being an awful friend?"

Hannah released the door and tugged the woman into her arms. "I missed you, Brig."

"I missed you more."

She stepped back and let her friends inside. She noticed Henry had a to-go bag. The smell alone made her salivate.

It wasn't until they were in her living room, Chinese food on the table and plates in hand, that she was able to ask Brigid what she needed to ask. "How are you?"

Tears immediately gathered in her friend's eyes. "James left. I asked him about what Erik saw the night of the office party, and he got *so* angry. He ended up packing a bag and storming out. I haven't seen him since. I don't even know where he's staying. I've texted him a couple of times, and he just tells me lies about being with family, but I know he's not there. I texted his sister."

"I'm sorry, Brigid."

She blew out a breath. "Some men came to the house, looking for him."

Hannah gasped and clenched Brigid's knee. It had to be the same men who'd come to the office. "Are you okay?"

"I told them he wasn't there. I even let them check the place, but that was mostly because I was scared of what they'd do if I didn't. Once they were satisfied, they left. But I immediately packed some stuff, and I'm staying with Henry now."

"Oh God. I'm so sorry!" Her friend didn't deserve that.

She lifted a shoulder. "Our relationship hasn't been great for a while. I felt him pulling away from me, and I never understood why. Now I do. I just never suspected it would be this bad."

"Of course you didn't."

Brigid swallowed. "I called him after the men showed up, and he didn't answer. I sent him a text…still nothing. It's like he doesn't even care that he put me in danger."

Anger boiled Hannah's blood. The scumbag.

She lowered to where Brigid sat on the floor and wrapped an arm around her shoulders. "You've got me and Henry for whatever you need."

She sniffed. "Thank you. And I really am sorry for saying what I did about Erik and icing you out for so long. Being angry with you felt safer than the pain of believing the truth."

"It's okay. You weren't wrong. I *haven't* known Erik for long."

The first small smile stretched her friend's lips. "Henry said you guys are doing well though."

"I'm kind of obsessed with him."

Okay, there was no "kind of" about it. She was one hundred percent, forget-everything-else, fixated on the guy. Maybe even falling in love. But that was a secret she wasn't ready to say aloud yet.

Brigid's eyes softened. "I'm really happy for you."

"My Tinder date didn't work out, if anyone cares."

Hannah and Brigid looked up at Henry.

"I thought it was going great?" Hannah said.

"Me too, until he hinted at wanting a key to my town house on the third date. Then the hourly texts started coming in, asking where I was and what I was doing."

Hannah cringed. "That's a bit much."

"Uh, yeah. So I'm ready to eat my feelings and finish it with ice cream and *Fifty Shades of Grey*."

Hannah perked up. "Ice cream?"

"Chocolate chip. I put it in the freezer."

Well, her night just got a whole lot better.

ERIK KEPT his steps silent as he moved down the dark street. It was late. Too late for anyone else to be around.

Three guns were strapped into holsters, and two knives— one around his thigh, the other his ankle—were in sheaths. If everything went to plan, this job would be an easy in and out… but nothing was ever guaranteed. Things had gone to shit before, so he needed to be ready.

He stopped at the entrance of the apartment building.

"I've seized control of the cameras," Chandler said through the earpiece. "Code is four-eight-two-zero."

Erik typed in the numbers with a gloved finger. There was a clicking sound, then he pulled the door open and slipped inside. Instead of taking the elevator, he used the stairs. The apartment building was large, and there was another set of stairs at the back. Those were the stairs Marco would be using.

Erik ground his teeth at the mere fucking thought of the guy. At the reminder that he was completing this job under duress.

His steps were quick but quiet as he moved up. Even though he was in the middle of a dangerous op that required all his attention, he couldn't get his mother's words out of his head. They'd been on replay since Saturday night.

Sit on the edge of life and death too long, you eventually lose more than you're willing to pay.

The thing was, he fucking knew that. He felt it. When you spent too much time in the darker corners of the world, that darkness started to become a part of you.

He wouldn't do this forever, and now that he'd met Hannah, he was starting to realize how much he didn't need to. He could heal. He could live without needing the rush of danger. The satisfaction of knowing he was eliminating assholes.

The thought of telling her what he did, though…fuck, it made a sharp blade of fear slice across his flesh.

Would she understand?

When he'd almost reached the top floor, Chandler's voice sounded in the earpiece again. "One armed man guarding the top of the stairs."

Erik forced his mind to still as he stopped and pulled out a gun and silencer. He let the deadly calm settle inside him, one that only grew from years of training and missions. Only when he knew his entire focus was on the job did he move, weapon raised.

The second the guy came into view, Erik fired, not giving the man time to react. One kill shot between the eyes. He raced up the final flight of stairs and caught the guy before he hit the floor. He laid him down quietly, not feeling a flicker of remorse for the kill. He'd done extensive research over the last two days and knew the guy was part of a group responsible for drug money laundering. It was also whispered they had a hand in trafficking women. They all deserved to die. Every single one of them. In fact, a bullet to the head was too kind.

"When you step out onto the roof, you'll be hidden by an alcove around the entrance to the stairs," Chandler said. "The men won't be able to see you, and if you go quietly, they won't be able to hear you. Marco's already up there, hiding behind the alcove to the set of stairs across the roof. You'll be able to see him."

"Got it."

He waited two beats, then opened the door slowly, pistol at the ready. Just as Chandler had said, there was no one in front of him. But he heard voices, all coming from behind the stair-well, near the edge of the roof.

He stepped into the cool night air, spotting Marco on the other side of the roof, hiding behind a similar stairwell exit. Marco held a hand up, fingers splayed, indicating they were going in five.

Erik closed the door silently, then shifted to the edge of the staircase enclosure, focusing on the voices. On differentiating them.

Chandler had already reported eight men on the roof. Four on each end, all supposedly watching the streets to the front and back of the building. When he was down to his final minute, he dragged in a long breath, blanked his mind, and raised his weapon. He looked back at Marco...

When he got the signal, he stepped around the alcove and fired, getting the three closest assholes in the span of a second. All shots to the head.

The men dropped.

Marco got three as well before return fire came.

Erik swung back behind the structure as bullets peppered the bricks. He turned his head to see Marco also crouching.

Two men remaining. They were covered by the backside of each alcove, firing in the opposite direction, Marco's man pinning down Erik and vice versa.

The bullets continued to spray the area—until they didn't.

During the tense silence, Erik quickly shifted to the other side of the alcove. He was about to move when a large figure appeared in front of him, gun aimed.

Before he could get a shot off, a bullet exited the asshole's forehead.

Erik eased his head around the structure carefully and flicked his gaze toward Marco, seeing his fourth guy was also dead.

Marco's smile shone from his position across the roof. "You're welcome," he shouted.

Erik rose and crossed the roof. "We're done, Marco." He removed the silencer from his weapon. "I did you a favor tonight, helped you kill your enemies. You do *me* a favor and stay away from Redwood. You and I don't have anything more to do with each other."

Marco lifted a shoulder. "Until the next job pops up."

Erik stilled, every muscle in his body going tight. "This was it. This *was* the last job. We're *done*."

Marco smiled slowly as he crossed the remaining distance between them. "Come on. Separately, we are good. Together, we are the best. We could make great money."

"No." When the asshole just smiled again, Erik took two steps closer. "The agreement was one fucking job, then you leave."

"Maybe I changed my mind. Maybe there are very lucrative jobs out there for you and me. Jobs I've already accepted on our behalf."

Erik lunged, grabbing him by the shirt and shoving the muzzle of his gun against Marco's head. "I'm not doing more fucking contract jobs with you."

"You said that about *this* one. Didn't take much to get you to change your mind. Tell you a sob story about my brother. Threaten your loved ones. And here you are."

Erik growled. "I'm gonna kill you."

"No, you won't."

The door to Marco's stairwell opened—and two men stepped out, both aiming pistols at Erik.

"These two men are already part of my new business."

"Why the fuck have you pulled me into this?"

"Because we're both the best," he said simply. "Imagine if we team up. We can charge whatever the fuck we want."

Every part of Erik was begging to pull the trigger.

"I suggest you walk away and think about my offer."

He didn't move, not a single fucking muscle.

"Don't do anything stupid, Hunter."

Three heartbeats passed before he lowered his weapon and hissed, "I *will* kill you. Not today, but soon. Watch your fucking back." He shoved Marco away and moved back into the stairwell.

His words were a vow. The guy would pay. Erik would make sure of it.

Chapter Twenty-Five

Hannah was pulled from sleep by the sudden warmth behind her. It curled around her body, surrounding her.

A hum slipped from her throat as a hand cupped her bare breast. When it started to massage, the hum turned into a moan, and she writhed, rubbing her backside against Erik.

He found her nipple and rolled it between his thumb and forefinger. It caused every inch of her body to tremble.

"Erik," she breathed, reaching a hand behind her head and running her fingers through his hair.

She had no idea what time it was. Her friends had left at two a.m. and she'd slipped straight into bed. It was clearly still the middle of the night, but time didn't exist. One touch from Erik and he was all she knew.

Another roll of her nipple, and her groans grew louder.

"I need you so much right now, Angel," he rumbled, his chest moving with his words. "I need your goodness, your softness, and your fucking light."

She turned her head and tugged forward so his mouth was a mere inch from hers. "You have me."

The distance closed, and they kissed. It was hard and passionate, and it twined them together like they were one.

His other hand slipped between her side and the bed, easing inside her panties. Her breath stopped. When his finger parted her slit, a full-body shudder ran down the length of her spine.

He swiped her again, this time accompanying it with a palm of her breast and a kiss to her lips. She was on fire, every little touch making her burn for him.

His lips trailed down her cheek before latching onto her neck. His teeth grazed her flesh, then he sucked.

She cried out as the need in her lower abdomen grew, taking on a life of its own. Every part of her needed this man, to a point it almost scared her. She needed his touch and his strength and the way he made her feel like she was *it*. She was all that existed for him.

When he slid a finger to her entrance, she bit down on her bottom lip so hard she almost drew blood. Then he slipped it inside her. Her cry echoed through the room.

He began thrusting his finger, his mouth never leaving her neck, his hand on her breast. It was an overload of sensations. An annihilation of peace and calm.

With desperate fingers, she reached behind her to find his cock. Her heart doubled its beats. She wrapped her fingers around him, loving the way he hardened further in her palm. The way his body tensed and trembled.

When she started to move, exploring his length, he groaned. She slid her hand from his base to his tip, loving the effect she had on him. That she could bring such a powerful man to the edge.

"Erik," she whispered. "Now."

The word had barely left her lips when he tore her panties off. Then he was at her entrance, replacing his finger.

He slid into her folds, and it was a riot of sensations. He

began to move, long, deep thrusts that cut off her breath and ignited her heart. He quickly took her to the brink, threatening to push her over the edge.

He reached for her chin and tilted her face to take her lips again. His tongue tangled with hers, like they were tasting each other for the first time. But he never stopped thrusting his hips.

She pushed back against him, wanting more. Wanting him deeper. Harder.

His finger returned to her clit, his hand to her breast, and he began to stroke and play, his even thrusts unrelenting. She moaned. It was too much. She felt like a string that was about to snap.

When he pinched her nipple, she threw her head back and screamed as she broke. Fell so hard she wondered if she'd ever be strong enough to rise again.

———

AT THE FEEL of Hannah's walls pulsing around him, Erik groaned and drove harder inside her, her shuddering and trembling spurring on his own need.

He needed her like he needed air. Like he needed food and shelter and *life*. She gave him everything. She gave him calm when every other part of his world was in complete fucking chaos.

This woman had stolen her way into his life, giving it new meaning.

She moaned, and that sound goaded him to move faster, until he couldn't fucking stop. White-hot fire ripped through him. He got three more thrusts in before his entire body convulsed, and he broke.

When he was finally still, he didn't try to move away. His hand remained on her breast and his other between her legs, while her walls hugged his cock. So damn connected.

Their quick breaths cut through the otherwise quiet room. He kissed her neck. Her hum was soft this time, barely discernable. The next kiss was to her jawline, then her shoulder.

When he finally pulled out, he groaned.

Immediately, she turned and nuzzled into his chest. "That was…"

"Perfect," he finished for her.

"Yes. Perfect." She pushed up on his chest and looked at him. Those blue eyes…they pierced him. Looked like they could see into his damn soul. "Are you okay?"

His chest tightened. He didn't want to talk about the blood on his hands when he was in bed with her. The scum of the earth he interacted with. "It's done now."

A sadness washed over her eyes…because he hadn't answered her question. Because he couldn't. He couldn't tell her a pretty little lie, and he couldn't tell her the dirty truth.

She swallowed. "Okay." Then a small smile spread across her lips, and fuck, it was glorious. "Giving you a key was a good idea."

He tightened his arm around her. "If you hadn't, I would have found a way in."

Nothing would keep him from this woman. Not when she'd become so fucking vital to him.

The smile slipped and an emotion he couldn't name took its place. "Good."

His gaze caught on a small scar between her breasts. It was dark so he could barely see it, but he remembered it from the first time they'd been together. He hadn't asked about it…but now something cold and hard slid through his blood.

"What's that from?" He didn't really have to ask. He knew a knife scar when he saw one. Gently, he grazed his finger over the old wound.

She swallowed. "When I was sixteen, I was placed in a… not-so-safe home."

His hand fisted involuntarily. "What happened?"

"It was the middle of the night. My foster father came into my room and attacked me. He cut my bra down the middle with a knife. That's what the scar is from."

The anger inside him turned into a rage so dark, he almost couldn't control it. "Did he—"

"No. He was drunk, and I fought him off. The attack was classified as a sexual assault but not rape."

Still too fucking much. "Tell me he's dead, Angel." If not—

"He's dead."

Something flickered in her eyes. Some emotion he couldn't name. But she sighed and leaned her head against his chest. Whatever it was, she didn't want to share.

He stroked her soft, silky hair. "Sleep, Angel. You're safe with me."

"I know."

His arm tightened around her. Her feeling safe with him... fuck, it was everything.

He needed to get up and shower, but not right now. Now, all he wanted was to hold her. To listen as her soft breaths lengthened in her sleep. She was so damn peaceful. And he fucking needed that. He'd never wanted to need another person again, because then you had someone who could be taken away. Someone who could be used to destroy you.

But the choice wasn't his anymore. She was here, and she was his. And there was nothing that was going to fucking change that.

He wouldn't fail her like he had Vicky. He'd protect what was his, no matter the cost.

Chapter Twenty-Six

Two contracts signed in a single day, both properties selling for above asking, and three new inquiries from prospective clients to sell their homes. Hannah was happy, but there was also something else there...guilt. Because some of her good fortune was due to James up and disappearing, which meant more clients for her and Taylor.

Reuben hadn't been happy about the men approaching her outside the office, or about James's disappearance. He'd tried to make contact with James several times since then, with no luck.

Her phone vibrated from the desk, and her smile grew when she saw Erik's name.

Erik: Dinner at my place. Don't be late, or I'll come find you.

Hannah: Is that a promise?

Erik: Always.

Her heart rattled.

She and Erik had been in a great place since dinner at his parents' house a week ago. Dinners every night, usually at his place. He'd even invited her to go to his parents' home for Christmas dinner.

Christmas with a real family. She'd sometimes gone to Brigid's or Henry's Christmas celebrations, but this felt different. This felt…important.

She was just responding to an email when Taylor popped her head into her office. "I'm leaving now, and Reuben's already gone. Are you okay to lock up?"

"Yes, I'm about to go too."

"Great." She turned to leave.

"Taylor," she called, and the other woman stopped and faced her again. "You didn't happen to take some keys from my safe the other week, did you?"

She still hadn't gotten to the bottom of Angelo's missing keys.

A frown creased Taylor's brow. "No. Why? Is one missing?"

She studied the other woman's eyes, seeing only honesty. With a shake of her head, she smiled. "No. Everything's fine."

"Okay. Well…have a good night."

Once the other woman had left, she quickly typed out a response to a client's email, then did a finger prick to test her blood sugar. It was good. Still, she pulled out a granola bar and had a couple mouthfuls before shoving the rest into her purse.

She was halfway to the door of her office when Marco suddenly appeared in her doorway.

She stopped, her breath cutting off in her chest. "Where did you…I didn't hear you come in."

He lifted a shoulder. "I can be quiet when I want to be."

She took a small step back, her hand itching to reach into her purse for her phone. "You need to go. Erik will be here any minute to pick me up."

It was a lie, and by the gleam in Marco's eye, he knew it. "Your Honda is in the lot, *cara*. No one is picking you up."

Shit.

He ran a finger along one of her shelves as he moved further into the room.

"What do you want?" she asked in a voice that wasn't nearly as steady as she would have liked.

His smile was slick, and it made her skin pebble. "What do I want? I want what everyone wants. Money. Freedom. Prestige."

"I can't give you any of those things, so why are you here?"

He was now so close that if he reached out, he could touch her. And every step she took away from him brought her closer to the back of her office. She could always try to dodge around him, but the man was big. There was no way she could outrun him.

"*You* may not be able to give me those things, but Erik can help. You see, both of us have made names for ourselves in our…industry."

"Names for yourselves?"

"Yes. I am stepping into a career change, and I would like Erik to come with me."

She shook her head. "He won't do that." No way would he do anything with this guy, let alone go into business with him. Not after how he'd been acting for weeks.

Marco ran a hand down her arm.

She pulled away as if he'd burned her. "Don't touch me!"

"You fear me, *cara*."

She ground her teeth, not wanting to answer.

"You should," he said quietly. "I am good at hurting people…just like that boyfriend of yours."

She forced the air to move in and out of her chest. The urge to shove him away was overwhelming. Or to kick him between the legs, but that would be a bad idea. This man was a predator. Threaten him, and she'd pay. "Erik was a special forces soldier. Of course he knows how to hurt people." He probably knew a thousand and one different ways.

Marco shook his head. "No, *stella*. He has far more recent

blood on his hands. Do you know where he was Monday night?"

"Doing a job with you."

He raised a brow, like he was waiting for her to explain what that job was. At her silence, he lowered his head. "He was on the roof of an apartment building, murdering a group of men. Family men. Some had wives. Children."

Erik had never told her details about his job, but he'd told her enough for her to suspect. "He works for the government. If he's killing people, they need to die."

"Has he *told* you the people he kills are bad? Or just that he has blood on his hands?"

Her heart started to beat faster. He'd only told her the latter.

At her silence, the corners of his lips tilted up. "And I wouldn't be so quick to believe that all his kills have been government sanctioned." He leaned down and whispered in her ear, "They haven't."

A cold numbness slipped over her skin. "You're lying." The words were so quiet, they barely touched the air.

He straightened, hands going to the wall on either side of her head, caging her. "No. Your boyfriend is an assassin who doesn't always do what's right, Hannah. The best in the business, in fact."

Nausea crawled up her throat, threatening to break free.

"You are associated with a dangerous man. A man with many enemies." His breath brushed over her face. "You know what happened to his wife, don't you?"

She swallowed, unable to form words.

"No?" His hand returned to her arm, but now she was too shocked to do anything about it. She could barely feel the touch, she was so numb. "She was murdered, *cara*. His enemy entered their home and killed her. Stabbed her so many times, she was almost unrecognizable."

222

It took every ounce of strength she possessed to stay upright. To not keel over and be sick at the picture he presented.

His mouth barely touched her cheek as he whispered, "Tell him to take the next job he's offered and not to make an enemy of me. You don't want to end up like her."

———

ERIK RAN a towel over his hair, his gaze shifting to his phone again. It was getting late. Hannah should've been here by now. But not only had she not arrived, and her car wasn't next door, she also hadn't answered his last text.

He threw his towel into the laundry basket. He'd finished his workout, expecting her to arrive during his shower. She hadn't.

He lifted his phone as he left his bedroom and called her on his way down the stairs.

It went to voice mail. *Dammit.* Where the hell was she?

The sound of pounding rain filtered in from outside. He didn't like that he didn't know where she was, not when Marco was still in town.

Fuck it. He was going to look for her. He didn't give a shit if he was overreacting. He needed to know where she was, and he needed to know *now.*

He moved to the entrance and grabbed his keys. Every step had the dread in his gut intensifying. He'd just opened the door when he saw her car pull up in front of her house.

Thank fuck.

Hannah climbed out into the rain. Her head was down as she moved toward her door and inside the small house.

He stepped outside and pulled his own door closed, then jogged across the yard and through the gate. He tried the handle. Locked. That should make him happy. It was safe. But

Hannah rarely locked her doors. Had something happened today?

His gut twisted and he pulled his keys from his pocket to unlock it.

He was just heading down the hall when she walked out of her bedroom, overnight bag on her shoulder. She stopped, and his chest tightened at her tear-stained face.

His limbs went cold.

"What happened?" he growled, storming forward.

When she stepped back, he abruptly stopped, brows slashing together. It wasn't just the way she'd stepped back...it was the look on her face.

Fear. Fear of *him*? No. That wasn't possible.

"Is everything okay?"

Her throat bobbed. "I'm staying at Henry's tonight."

The cold turned to ice, and he had to forcibly restrain himself from moving toward her. "Why?"

Her chest moved up and down a bit faster, and tears glistened in her eyes, but she stayed silent.

Screw the distance.

He took two steps forward, but she matched them, moving back. "Don't."

The word was a whisper that felt like a blow to Erik's abdomen.

His body locked as it came to a standstill. Everything about this moment killed him. The distance. The pain on her face. The inability to comfort her. It tore him into so many fucking shreds, he wanted to tear down the world to find out what was wrong.

"I need you to tell me what's happening right now, Hannah."

Her bottom lip trembled like she was about to break. Like the weight of whatever she was carrying was too big of a burden to bear.

"Hannah…"

She straightened, resolve hardening her eyes. "I got a visit from Marco today."

Anger exploded inside him, and his next words were dangerously low. "Marco was at your office?"

"He told me to tell you to take the next job…" She swallowed. "Or I'll end up like your wife."

The anger morphed into something so dangerous, for a moment, his vision went dark. A need so tangible he could feel it slip into his blood, pumping it harder. A need to find and kill the man who'd threatened his woman. "What else did he say? Did he touch you?"

"He told me what you do for work. That you kill people."

He shouldn't be surprised. The asshole had nothing to lose, so why make sure his job remained classified?

"I would never hurt you, Hannah. You *know* that." He stepped forward, hating every time she stepped away from him.

"Tell me it's not true," she said quietly, a tear sliding down her cheek.

Words clawed at his throat. Lies that would keep this woman here. But he couldn't release them. He couldn't lie. Not to her.

Her face paled further. "I need…time."

Fear catapulted into his chest. He couldn't lose her. Not after she'd so easily crumbled the walls he'd built. Slipped into his life and fit like she was always meant to be there.

His fingers itched to touch her. Draw her into his arms and be whatever she needed him to be. He had so many fucking words to say. About why he did what he did. Why his missions were so important. Who the targets were.

But the door opened behind him, and he turned to see Henry and Brigid. Hannah moved past him and he had to physically stop himself from grabbing her. From wrapping his fingers around her arm and tugging her into him. It was the closest to torture he'd ever been.

Henry ushered Hannah outside, but before Brigid turned, she stopped and looked at Erik. "She just needs some time. A day or two. Then try again."

Then he watched as both Brigid's car and Henry's drove away, meeting Hannah's gaze in the passenger seat of the latter.

Devastation. It cut into every corner of her face and darkened every scrap of light inside his woman.

The second they were out of sight, he turned and slammed his fist into the wall. The pain was nothing compared to what was inside him. The utter agony.

He stormed out and ripped his phone from his pocket.

Chandler answered on the second ring. "Hunter, are you—"

"I want a fucking location for Marco."

There was a heavy pause. "I don't think that's—"

"He's fucking *mine*, Chandler. Make it happen, or I'll do it on my own."

Chapter Twenty-Seven

"It's a beautiful home. We'll definitely be in touch."

Hannah smiled, and that tiny lift of her lips took so much more energy than it should have. "Great. I look forward to hearing from you."

The second the couple slid into their car and disappeared, she heaved a deep sigh, letting her lips fall and the ache in her chest return. Her cheeks hurt from all the smiling. Thank God this was her last open house of the day.

It wasn't just the open houses that had dragged on—the last twenty-four hours had been brutal.

Henry and Brigid were amazing, reassuring her everything would work out. Constantly trying to bring a smile to her face, even though Brigid was grieving the loss of her own relationship.

She moved around the house, turning off the lights one by one. She had to call Erik. He'd been texting and calling since last night, but she'd just been so shocked, hurt, and alarmed by Marco's words that she'd barely been able to think, let alone talk to Erik.

It was unfair of her not to listen to his side though. She

needed to hear him say the words out loud. Tell her about his job and explain why he did what he did.

Tonight. She'd call him tonight.

There was still fear inside her…but she knew that fear was because she loved him. At some point in the last couple months, her heart had begun to beat for Erik. The air she breathed, every emotion inside her, it was all for him. How he'd cocooned himself inside her so quickly, she had no idea. But she couldn't deny it.

And now, it might turn out he was a ruthless killer.

Her heart squeezed as she locked the house and got into her car.

On the way to Henry's, she called Coalfire Pizza to order dinner. There was no part of her that felt like cooking, and for once, cereal didn't sound appetizing. Plus, Henry and Brigid never said no to takeout.

When she stepped inside the pizza place, her eyes widened at the sight of Andi by the counter. A woman who looked to be the same age stood beside her. She had straight brown hair just past her shoulders and big brown eyes to match.

When their gazes collided, Andi beamed and pushed off the counter.

"Hey!" She stepped forward and wrapped Hannah in a hug.

God, these Hunter hugs…they really wrapped her up in warmth and love, two things she could really use right now. "Hi, Andi."

Andi pulled back and turned to the other woman. "This is my childhood best friend, Finley. She's basically part of the family. She would have been with us at dinner last week if she'd been in town. Finley, this is Erik's partner, Hannah."

Her insides knotted at the label, but she used all her strength to keep it off her face. "It's nice to meet you, Finley."

"You too, Hannah."

She cleared her throat. "Pizza for dinner?"

Andi laughed. "Yeah. Finley's out of town a lot, so when she's here, we make the most of it. She's leaving again soon for some big Christmas fair in Canada. She's a bigwig social media marketer slash influencer."

Finley rolled her eyes, but there was a hint of a smile on her face. "I am not a bigwig. I just have a big following."

"She's lying," Andi whispered. "Every event organizer wants her."

Almost on cue, Finley's phone rang.

"See," Andi said. "People call her left, right, and center to market their events."

Finley shook her head. "Not true, but I *am* going to take this call. It was a pleasure to meet you, Hannah."

When the other woman stepped away, Andi turned back to her. "You here to pick up dinner for you and Erik?"

Hannah tried not to cringe. "Actually, I'm staying at Henry's place tonight."

"Oh." It took less than two seconds for suspicion to widen Andi's eyes. "Is everything okay?"

"Um…" She considered lying, but she was a terrible liar. Plus, she didn't want to lie to Andi. "Not really. But I'm hoping it will be."

Andi nibbled her bottom lip. "I'm sorry. I really hope you work things out. Since Erik's met you, I almost feel like I have my brother back."

"Back?"

There was a sad tilt to her eyes. "After Vicky and their baby were killed, Erik became less than a shadow of the man he used to be."

Her heart jolted painfully. "Baby?"

A frown transformed Andi's face. "God. He didn't tell you? She was six months pregnant when she was killed."

A chill swept over Hannah's skin and nausea bubbled in her stomach. "That's…"

There weren't any words.

"It was a devastation I thought he'd never come back from, honestly," Andi said softly. "Since then, he's barely been surviving. Never returned home. But *you*…you've healed some of that hurt. Slotted him back together. I really hope you two can work things out, Hannah."

Andi's pizzas were set on the counter just as Finley returned. Andi squeezed her arm gently before both women said goodbye.

Every word Andi had said flickered through her head on repeat on the way to Henry's house. No wonder the man didn't want children. He'd lost a child before he'd had a chance to hold them. That would ruin the strongest person.

She scrubbed a tear from her cheek as she pulled onto Henry's street and parked outside his town house. It was a balancing act to get out of the car without dropping her bag or the pizzas. When she reached his door, she set the bag on the ground to unlock it.

"Henry? Brigid? I've got pizza," she called as she walked inside.

She frowned at the quiet house and lack of response. They should both be here tonight. She set the pizzas on the counter and looked down at her phone, only to see that she'd missed a text.

Henry: Forgive us, but we couldn't sit around and watch you be so sad for another day.

Her frown deepened. What was he—

"Hi, Angel."

Her breath caught in her throat at that voice…a voice she'd heard whispering in her head in the dark last night while she'd tried to sleep.

Slowly, she turned, and her stomach clenched at the sight

of Erik walking through the door she'd not yet locked. He wore a gray shirt and jeans. His hands were in his pockets and his gaze firmly aimed at her.

"What are you doing here?"

"I need to talk to you." He stopped in the living room, like he was afraid that if he crossed the remaining distance, she'd run.

She was too scared to move. Hell, she didn't even want to blink, but not because she was afraid of him. In case he disappeared and that hole in her chest, the one that filled when he was close, hollowed again.

"Marco told me you're an assassin." The words that had been repeating in her head for the last day spilled out. "That not everyone you…kill is government sanctioned."

Erik's jaw clenched. "Only one job has ever been a private contract—the one he forced me to do. But even then, I made sure those assholes deserved to die." He stepped forward. A little more of that hole inside her filled. "I'm contracted by a covert government agency. I'm one of many people who are called in when they need to eliminate the scum of the earth but can't get a target through legal means."

"He hinted that they weren't all bad people."

"They're *worse* than bad," he argued, voice hard. Another step forward. "They're terrorists. Murderers. Drug and arms dealers. Sex traffickers."

That was so different to what she'd been told. "So you save people? Because by killing evil men or women, you're helping others?"

"I like to think so."

Another inch of the hole closed. She swallowed. "Do you do this job because you need it to ease the pain of losing—"

"Everyone." One word, said so forcefully and with so much pain she almost crossed the room and went to him. "Something I didn't tell you about that final mission as a Marine—I

231

lost half my team that day. In a matter of minutes, they were gone. Men I considered brothers. I thought that was as broken as I could get. Then, just before my military flight back to the US, I returned a call to my mother. She told me about Vicky and our baby."

Tears gathered in her eyes. Tears of sorrow for this man. For the suffering he went through. Was *still* going through.

"That kind of pain carves itself into your bones," he said quietly. "It forces you to choose between giving in and giving up…or learning how to live a different way."

She forced air to move in and out of her lungs. "I'm glad you chose to live."

"But the only way I could do that was by living close to the edge of death myself. Doing a job that brought me purpose. I know not many understand it. Not everyone likes that my targets don't get the benefit of the justice system."

She understood. Not just what he did, but why. His job had become his reason. With every kill, there were fewer victims. Fewer Vicky's.

He stopped in front of her, his hands still deep in his pockets, clearly trying not to touch her.

"I'm sorry…" she whispered. "About everything. I'm sorry you lost your team. And I'm so damn sorry about your wife and baby." Her voice broke, and he finally tugged his hands from his pockets and gripped her hips. The touch was healing. It was peace and salvation.

"Hannah—"

"And I'm sorry I didn't give you a chance to explain. I was in shock, and I was afraid that if you confirmed it was true, it would destroy me. But I should have given you a chance."

"It's okay."

A tear slid down her cheek, and he wiped it away with the pad of his thumb.

"The last twenty-four hours have been so hard without you," she whispered.

"For me too, Angel." He lifted her up onto the counter and stepped between her thighs, then touched his forehead to hers. "Being apart from you…it made everything so fucking clear."

Her heart thudded. "What's clear?"

"I was a shattered mess when you met me. I've been trying to dull the pain with my job and boxing…but the truth is, it hasn't helped. I've been a mess for eight long years. And somehow, in the span of only a few months, you unbroke me."

She pressed her hand to his chest, feeling the thuds of his heart against her palm. "Erik…"

"I love you, Hannah Jacobs. And I need you in my life. Not for a moment. Not for now. Forever."

His words both broke her and pulled her back together. Freed her and caged her…to him. Always to him.

"Love is when a person feels like home," she whispered. "And you, Erik Hunter, feel like home to me. I love you."

⊂===⊃

ERIK CLOSED his eyes and let Hannah's words fill him. Drown out every other fucking voice but hers. Kill every emotion that wasn't love.

Home. He was her home, as she was his. And it was the first fucking home he'd had in so long.

Somewhere along the way, this woman had changed him. Twisted him into something new. Something whole. And he needed that…he needed *her*.

He lowered his head and touched his lips to hers, letting her softness and goodness fill him. Calm him. Annihilate him. Her lips parted and he tasted her sweetness. It was something he needed with every fiber of his being.

In the kiss, he took and gave everything. Then he lifted her into his arms, wanting her as close as possible. Wanting to feel all of her against him.

She hummed, and when he lifted his mouth and touched his forehead to hers for a second time, they both just breathed and let this moment weave its way inside them.

The single night without her had been the worst kind of hell. Something he never wanted to experience again. And he wouldn't. He would love this woman and protect her. That was both a promise and a vow.

Chapter Twenty-Eight

"Why are you staring at me, Angel?"

Crap. She tugged her gaze away. He'd caught her staring *again*. To be fair though, he was a lot prettier than the sidewalk in front of her. "Because you're nice to stare at and I love you."

His fingers tightened around hers. "I love you too."

Oh, those words... Over the last week, she'd probably told the man she loved him a dozen times, and he'd said it just as much. And every time, they made her feel the same thing...peace.

They'd barely been apart since that night at Henry's. In fact, he'd declared himself her unofficial bodyguard, which meant he was with her all the time. Even while she was in her office, he was usually close. He was paranoid about Marco returning. And if she was honest, she was a bit nervous about that too.

For that reason, she'd barely been at the office. And fortunately, Reuben didn't mind.

"I feel guilty that you're spending all your time with me."

He kissed the top of her head. "Don't. There's nowhere I'd rather be."

She nodded, not entirely sure she believed him.

When they reached Reuben's Real Estate, she unlocked the door, and he followed her inside.

"Reuben's been okay with the locked doors and buzzer system?" Erik asked, following her to her office.

"He's been great with everything. So much better than I thought. I guess Marco coming in here and threatening me, after those guys had already come looking for James, made him realize we needed some serious security."

Erik stopped abruptly. "*What* guys came here searching for James?"

Shit. She hadn't told Erik about them. With everything that happened with Marco that evening, she hadn't wanted to give him anything else to worry about. She'd told him about James's disappearance, just not the other part.

She cleared her throat. "The night Marco met me and Reuben at the restaurant, some guys showed up outside as I was leaving the office. They were looking for James."

A vein in his neck popped out. "How many guys?"

"Two. They told me to tell James that Vincent was looking for them. Then they left."

The look that crossed Erik's face was scary.

She touched his arm. "I'm okay. James isn't here anymore, and they clearly know that, because they haven't come back."

That hard look remained as they continued toward her office.

She took one step inside, then it was *her* turn to stop abruptly, startled by the sight of the man waiting inside, sitting across from her desk.

"Angelo! Do we have an appointment?"

Reuben had been in the office when she went to lunch, so he must've let Angelo inside. The man had never managed to come by for his keys, so she'd run them by his place the previous week. His assistant had assured her he'd get them.

The older man rose to his feet. "No, we don't. Forgive me, but I have something to discuss with you. It's about the property you were contracted to sell."

"Oh, okay. Sure. Of course." She turned to Erik. "I'll see you in an hour?"

Erik's gaze ran over Angelo, a new hardness swirling in their depths, before he looked down at her. "Okay." He lowered his head and kissed her cheek, but before moving away, he whispered, "Are you okay with him?"

She smiled, understanding Erik's hesitation in leaving her. Angelo had "rich Italian Mafia" written all over him. "Yes. Thank you for lunch."

He squeezed her arms, and his gaze moved to Angelo one last time before he stepped out of the office.

She crossed the room and lowered her bag into a desk drawer before indicating to the chair opposite. "Please, resume your seat."

He nodded and lowered. "Thank you."

"What can I do for you today?"

Angelo cleared his throat. "I went to my property this morning for the first time since receiving the key."

Her brows flickered at his tone. "Was everything okay?" God, there hadn't been a break-in, had there?

He took a moment to answer, and that short pause made her heart clench. Something was wrong.

"As you well know, I have some very expensive artwork in that house."

Instantly, sweat beaded her forehead. Someone *had* broken into his home...and stolen the art? Is that where he was going with this? "You do," she agreed quietly.

"One in particular, a Charles Cham worth over fifty thousand dollars, was a favorite of mine. It was a gift from a good friend."

Her heart beat so loudly she could almost hear it in her ears.

He leaned forward. "I like you, Hannah. Which is why I'm going to give you twenty-four hours to return it before I take this matter further."

Her eyes widened as a shock so cold and unfamiliar trickled through her limbs. "You think I broke into your home and stole it?"

"No, Miss Jacobs. The home was not broken into. You took the painting while you had the key, after tampering with my surveillance. Fifty thousand dollars is child's play to me. This isn't about the money. It's about the principle. Doing the right thing."

Oh God. "Angelo, I didn't—"

"Please do not tell me lies. You had a key. And you are one of very few people who had the code to my alarm system."

He stood, and she all but jumped to her feet. "Please believe me, Angelo, I didn't take anything!"

"What else am I to think, Hannah?" At her silence, he almost looked disappointed. "Twenty-four hours. I really hope we don't have to do this the hard way."

He turned and walked out, and it was while he was walking away that her gaze flicked to her safe. Suddenly, she remembered Angelo's key had gone missing for a time. And the alarm code had been written on the key ring.

Had someone taken the key and used it to steal the painting before returning it?

Only Reuben and Taylor had the code to her safe. But it *couldn't* be one of them...could it?

⊂⊃

"YES, there's a Vincent who runs a drug operation out of Tacoma. Vincent White. Authorities have been trying to shut him down for years."

Erik cursed under his breath as he watched Hannah's office building.

"This guy's dangerous, Hunter. You don't want him anywhere near Hannah."

No shit, he didn't. He didn't even want to leave her damn office. There were too many threats. "I want you to find everything you can on him."

"You got it."

"Also, before you go, I need another favor."

"If it's about Marco, I'm still working on his location. The guy's good at staying hidden. And considering he's starting his own business, he's probably been planning his disappearance for months."

"No. It's something else. I need you to run a name for me."

He knew he was pushing their friendship here. Chandler was only supposed to use his resources for Erik, but fuck, Hannah was like an extension of him.

Chandler huffed out a breath. "Okay. Give it to me."

"Angelo Bonetti. Owns a property here in Redwood. Approximately mid-fifties. And he may drive a Jag." Erik's gaze skimmed over the expensive car outside the agency as he read the plate numbers to his friend.

"Give me a second." The tapping of keys sounded. The couple minutes that passed felt like a fucking lifetime. "Got him."

Erik straightened. "Is he clean?"

Chandler's whistle had Erik's chest tightening. "He owns and runs a casino, and the government has him flagged as possibly being involved in money laundering. They don't have the evidence to do anything about it yet. There are photos in the system of him meeting with various criminals."

"Fuck."

Erik ended the call as he climbed out of his Corvette and strode back to the office. He reached the door just as it opened. When Angelo met his gaze, the guy's eyes hardened, then he dipped his chin and walked around him, heading to his car.

Erik caught the door before it closed and went straight to Hannah's office. She was sitting at her desk, her gaze flickering across the wood as if her mind was racing. And her face…fuck, it was so pale.

He was across the room in a second, spinning her chair to face him. He lowered to his haunches in front of her and cupped her cheeks. "Angel. Talk to me. Are you okay?"

Did he need to go and kill that fucker?

A beat passed while she just looked at him with worried eyes. She shook her head.

He cursed and ran his gaze down her body. When he found no injury, he looked at her again. "Tell me what he did."

She swallowed. "Someone took the key to his house from my safe. A few days later, it was back, so I forgot all about it."

"What did they do with the key?"

"They stole a painting from him. It's worth over fifty thousand dollars, but he said it's not about the money." She sucked in a sharp breath. "He's given me twenty-four hours to return it."

The muscles in Erik's forearm tightened as he tried to contain his anger. When footsteps sounded in the hall, they both looked up to see Taylor and Reuben walking in the direction of the office kitchen. Taylor noticed them first, then Reuben did. They both stopped.

"Hey," Taylor said with a frown. "Are you okay?"

She shook her head. "Taylor, I need you to be honest with me. Did you take Angelo Bonetti's keys from my safe?"

A gasp sounded from the woman. "What? No! Why would you think that?"

She swallowed. "Someone took the key and used it to access Angelo's home, where they stole a fifty-thousand-dollar painting. Other than me, the only people with the code are you and Reuben."

"Oh, shit."

Everyone's gaze shifted to Reuben.

Erik's voice lowered. "What?"

"I gave James the code." His cheeks reddened. "About two months ago, one of his clients wanted to see one of your listings, Hannah. You weren't here, and I gave him the code so he could grab the key. I meant to tell you so you could change it, but it just slipped my mind."

Hannah's face paled and Erik pulled out his phone, once again calling Chandler, this time putting his friend on speaker.

"You need me to look into someone else?" he asked without greeting.

"Hannah's in trouble, and we need your help."

"What do you need?" Chandler's tone was hard.

"You're on speaker. Hannah's gonna tell you."

"Hey, darlin'," Chandler said, his voice softening. "How can I help?"

Hannah took a moment before answering. No one rushed her. They just waited for her to gather her thoughts. "I think a man named James Paley stole a painting from a client's home —Angelo Bonetti."

"Shit," Chandler cursed.

"Angelo thinks I took it," she added.

"Double shit!" Tapping sounded. "Do you know what type of painting it was?"

Her nose wrinkled. "He said it was a…Charles Cham. And that it was worth fifty thousand dollars."

Chandler whistled. "That's a nice chunk of change. Okay, give me some time. I'll see if it's been put up for sale anywhere. I'll also run a search for James."

She blew out a long breath. "Thank you."

"You got it, darlin'."

The second Chandler hung up, Erik pulled her into his arms.

"I'm going to try to contact Angelo," Reuben said from the door, his face now pale.

"And I'll try James," Taylor said quietly. "I know it's a long shot, but I need to do something."

None of that would help, but Erik appreciated they were willing to try. James wouldn't answer, and if Angelo hadn't believed Hannah when she'd said she hadn't stolen the painting, he wouldn't believe Reuben either.

He had a feeling this Angelo guy was a man of his word. He wouldn't stop harassing Hannah until he had either the painting or solid evidence that she was telling the truth about not stealing it.

Reuben let her leave work early, probably because the fucking color never returned to her face. As they stepped into Erik's house, his phone rang. Again, he put it on speaker so Hannah could hear.

"Chandler, what do you have?"

"Good and bad news. The bad news—I couldn't find the painting, which means he may have had a buyer lined up before he took it. *But* I found the next best thing."

Hannah sucked in an audible gasp. "You found James?"

"Bingo. He's staying at the Thompson in Seattle. There are records of his booking and footage of him drinking at their rooftop bar every night for the last four evenings. He goes up there at about six-thirty. So, if he continues to follow that pattern, and you leave now, you might just be able to catch him."

"But we have no evidence of what he's done," Hannah said quietly.

"I'll make him talk," Erik growled.

She shook her head. "No. He knows who's after him, so he's probably carrying. I don't want you or any innocent people in that bar put in danger."

Fuck that. *She* was in danger, so he'd do whatever the hell he had to do. "I can take care of myself and make sure no one else gets hurt, Hannah."

"You can't guarantee that." She nibbled her bottom lip. "I have an idea."

Erik's eyes narrowed, a bad feeling churning in his gut. "What?"

"I could ask Brigid to talk to him. Get him to admit what he's done while wearing a wire or something. Then we can give the recording to both Angelo and the police, and no one gets hurt."

"Why would James tell her anything?" Erik asked.

"They dated for over four years. She knows him, and she's smart. If anyone can get him to admit to what he did without any blood getting spilled, it's her."

There was a beat of silence.

She grazed his chest. "Please, Erik."

"Could be worth a try," Chandler said quietly. "We don't have a lot of time."

Erik ground his jaw. He didn't want to agree to any plan that didn't involve him pounding into the guy for putting Hannah in this position. And he also didn't want to leave her unprotected, which meant she would have to go to Seattle with him if he…*coerced* a confession from James.

If Brigid could do it, it would be cleaner and easier.

"Fine," he said between gritted teeth. "But if she can't get what we need, I go in and force the fucking confession."

Chapter Twenty-Nine

Hannah hated how nervous Brigid looked. Her friend never looked nervous. She'd once walked into a bar wearing only a bikini on a dare and hadn't batted an eye.

She glanced at her in the rearview mirror, where Brigid sat beside Henry. "Are you sure you're okay to do this?"

"Yes." She nodded and straightened. "I *want* to do this. If he did take that painting to frame you, then he's an even bigger scumbag than we thought, and he should pay."

That was a bit of the friend Hannah knew.

Henry squeezed her arm. "Damn straight."

God, she was grateful to have the friends she did.

Erik pulled the rented SUV into a parking structure close to the hotel. They'd made a reservation for Brigid and Henry on the balcony area, while she and Erik had booked a table inside, in a private corner.

The story for James would be that Brigid and Henry were having a weekend getaway. Brigid would act surprised when she saw James, go over and talk to him, and she'd mention Hannah being accused of stealing the painting. She'd slip in comments about missing him. About James having her loyalty.

Basically, she'd attempt to make him trust her. Hannah truly did believe that if anyone could get James to admit what he'd done, it was Brigid.

Her friend wore a small wireless listening device on her chest and a tiny earpiece that was covered by her hair. She'd argued she didn't need the earpiece, but Erik had wanted two-way communication.

Before her friends could open the back door, Hannah turned. "Brigid…be careful."

The corners of her friend's lips lifted, but the smile didn't quite reach her eyes. "Always."

She climbed out, and before Henry followed, he whispered, "I'll look after her."

Hannah fiddled with her bracelet as she watched them leave the car and walk down the street toward the hotel. It was only Erik's hand on her arm that had her tearing her attention away.

"She'll be okay," he said quietly.

She was less worried about her physically and more worried about emotionally. Brigid was strong, and she liked to put on a brave face. But she'd loved James for a long time. That kind of love didn't just go away.

When it was time for them to go, Erik slid an arm around her waist and led her to the hotel. As soon as they were inside, they headed for the elevator. The rooftop bar was called The Nest, and from what they'd researched, the place got busy. They were lucky they'd been able to reserve the tables they had.

When the elevator doors opened, they stepped into a dimly lit bar. Music boomed and loud voices competed with one another. Erik tugged her toward a small stand.

"Hi. Do you have a reservation?" a waitress asked.

"Yes, for two, under Silver."

Hannah barely paid attention to the exchange, instead

shifting her gaze to the open doors that led to the balcony. Was James out there? Could Brigid and Henry already see him?

Her belly did a little dip.

"This way."

Erik pulled her forward as they followed the waitress to a shadowy corner.

"Here you are," she said as she stopped. She handed them each a menu. "I'll be back in a few minutes to take your order." They had a great view of the entire bar, including everyone who came and left through the elevator, yet people didn't even glance their way as they passed.

"It's okay, I know what I want," Hannah said before the woman could leave. "A vodka tonic, please."

The fewer visits they had, the better.

"Pacifico, please," Erik added.

The second the waitress left their table, Erik pulled out a laptop. He was tense. Probably because she was with him. The only reason she was here at all was because Erik wanted her in his sights at all times. Worked for her. There was nowhere else she wanted to be.

He pulled out two earpieces and handed one to her. Then he spoke into the laptop microphone.

"We're here, Brigid."

Voices and music sounded through the earpiece. Some wind. Then Brigid's voice.

"We can see James," she said quietly. "He's standing by the railing but hasn't seen us yet."

Hannah leaned in. "Remember, it's not too late to pull out."

"Hannah. Relax. I'll be fine." Brigid sounded confident. "I want to do this for you. And also, for me. If it was a lie for all those damn years, that asshole can tell me to my face."

"Okay. Just…be careful." She'd said it before, but she had to say it again.

"I'm going over now."

"Good luck," Henry said, his voice sounding distant.

Hannah dug her nails into her palm until Erik unfurled her fist, slipping his fingers through hers.

"Hi, James."

Hannah straightened at the sound of Brigid's voice.

"Brigid! What are you… How did you find me?"

The wind was loud when she continued. "Henry and I are having a weekend away, and I saw you over here. Henry's over at our table."

There was a brief pause. "Is Hannah with you?"

Hannah's finger tightened on Erik's, anger coursing through her. The asshole sounded nervous because he knew what he'd done to her.

"No. It's been a really hard week for her, so she stayed home." Brigid cleared her throat. "One of her clients accused her of stealing a painting."

Another pause before he spoke. "Really?"

"Yeah. She didn't do it, but the guy didn't believe her. He actually threatened her. Luckily, Erik paid him off, and she's safe now."

"Seriously?" Relief spidered through that single word from James.

"Yeah. I'm glad she's okay." Another pause, this time from Brigid. "I've missed you."

James cleared his throat. "I thought you'd be angry at me."

"Oh, I'm definitely angry. But I'm also struggling to live without you."

Hannah exhaled softly, because she knew there had to be some truth behind her friend's words.

"Brigid…I've missed you too. And I only left because—"

"Bad people were after you. I know. They came searching for you. You left to keep me safe, didn't you?"

No! The word was a shout in Hannah's head.

"I did."

Lying scumbag.

"The thing I don't understand," Brigid said quietly, "is why you didn't ask me to go. I would have disappeared with you."

"I thought you'd say no."

"No, James. I wouldn't have said no. I would have come with you and done anything I could to protect you." There was another pause. "Just like I protected you when I heard about the painting. I know you took it."

Three heartbeats of nothing passed. Then...

"I didn't—"

"You did. I know Hannah, and I know *she* wouldn't have taken it. You had the means and the motivation. You needed the money. But I didn't say anything because I *love* you. And I know you did it so you could get yourself out of trouble. Now that all that's finished...we can be together again."

At the next small break in conversation, Hannah thought her heart was going to beat from her chest.

"It's not sold yet," James said. "I have a buyer lined up."

Hannah's skin turned cold. It was true. He *had* taken it. He'd set her up. She'd known...but hearing it? It hurt far worse.

"I'm meeting them tomorrow night," he added in a lower tone.

Hannah closed her eyes and let the confirmation of James's betrayal slice through her like a dagger, sharp and unforgiving.

A kiss pressed to the back of her hand, then Erik whispered, "I'm sorry, Angel."

—

ERIK WANTED to go out there and lay into the asshole. The guy stole something that wasn't his, ran out on his girlfriend, not caring that his enemies would pay her a visit, and framed Hannah for his crime.

As far as Erik was concerned, he didn't deserve the air he breathed.

He was still clenching his jaw when the elevator doors opened and two large men entered the bar. They weren't dressed like the other patrons. They were too casual in T-shirts and jeans. They both had shaved heads and tattoos.

But it wasn't just those things that had the pit forming in Erik's gut…it was the fact that he recognized them from a collection of photos Chandler had sent him this afternoon, before they got on the road to Seattle.

Mug shots of Vincent's men.

He lowered his head. "Brigid. Get out of there. The dealers are here."

There was a gasp over the line before Brigid spoke. "What? They're here?"

"Who's here?" James asked in a rush.

Erik cursed as he rose and closed the laptop. "If they see you together, they'll assume you're with him." He pulled out one of his Glocks and handed it to Hannah. "Keep this on you. If someone comes toward you, shoot."

Hannah's eyes were wide, but she nodded.

He ran out onto the balcony to see it was too late—both James and Brigid were being chased and running toward the staff stairs. But Brigid was slower. One of the men grabbed her before she could make it.

She screamed while the other man disappeared down the stairs behind James.

Erik pulled out his second Glock and aimed it at the asshole. "Let her go or I shoot."

The guy spun, gun to Brigid's head. "We're gonna go down these stairs, and you're not gonna stop us."

Gasps and screams sounded around them. The footsteps of

people running away from the violence. Erik ignored them all. "Not happening. She's not part of this."

"She was with him, so she *is* part of this. My boss'll want to have a little chat with her."

Brigid's face lost its color, and Erik fucking hated that. "I'm not letting her go with you. So your options are, join your friend and chase the asshole who owes your boss money—or die."

The guy's chest rose with a deep breath, his mouth tight. Then, suddenly, he shoved Brigid toward Erik and took off down the stairs.

Erik didn't bother going after him. If the guy wanted James, he could have him. Instead, he holstered his weapon and steadied Brigid. "Are you okay?"

She nodded vigorously. Henry appeared beside him and tugged Brigid into his arms. Erik spotted Hannah behind Henry, gun in one hand, laptop bag in the other. She was just as white as her friend, but one look at Brigid had relief spiraling over her features.

Police sirens rang in the background, and everyone on the balcony had run out of the bar.

Erik tugged Hannah to his side and breathed in the scent of her. They didn't have James…but they had a confession.

Chapter Thirty

Hannah leaned her head back, the dull thrum of the engine background noise for her racing mind. Tonight had not gone the way she'd envisioned. Yes, they'd gotten James's admission of guilt, but Brigid had been held at gunpoint. Then the police…it had all been one giant nightmare.

Erik reached over and covered her hand with his own. "You okay, Angel?"

"Yeah, just tired."

It was only nine-thirty, but it felt later. They'd gotten food and ate it while driving home before dropping Brigid and Henry at his place.

"We'll be home in a couple minutes."

She found a vein on his hand and traced it. "I hope Brigid's okay."

Her friend had been quiet the entire drive home, which was nothing like her. Not that Hannah blamed her. Tonight had been a lot. Brigid hadn't meant to give away that those thugs were at the venue, but in doing so, she'd also given herself away.

"She's tough," Erik said quietly.

She was. But she had been with James for a long time, and that hurt would cut deep.

"James is just such a…" God, she didn't even have words. "Brigid deserves better."

Apparently, he'd made it out of the building, and when the police checked his room, there was an overnight bag but that was it. The painting wasn't there. She almost hoped the thugs *did* catch him after everything he'd done.

"Your place or mine?" she asked quietly.

"Mine. More security."

He was right. And after tonight, she needed all the security she could get. "Will you call Angelo?"

"Yes." His answer was immediate.

Good. And this would finally be over.

He pulled into his garage, and they moved into the house, but when he went for the stairs, she went toward the front door. "I'm just going to run home and grab some more insulin and an overnight bag."

He snagged her wrist and tugged her back. "I'll come."

She was about to argue that she'd be quick, but one look into his steely gaze and she knew she wouldn't win that one. So she slipped her hand into his and headed out the front door. They'd just reached her house when Erik's phone rang.

He tugged it out and checked the screen. "I'll wait here for you, but leave the door open. Don't take long." He pressed a quick kiss to her cheek before answering the call.

Quickly, she raced through her house to the bedroom.

She'd just turned on the light when a hand slipped over her mouth, followed by a voice in her ear.

"I have a man out front. Make a noise, and they shoot Erik."

Marco.

Fear and panic swirled together in her chest, creating a

deadly concoction. She worked hard to control her breathing, but it was almost impossible.

"Unfortunately, *cara*, you've pissed off the wrong person."

She frowned. Was he saying…she was a *job*? God, had someone hired him to kill her?

"My job tonight is to retrieve either a stolen piece of art, or you," he said, as if reading her thoughts.

The painting? Oh God, this was Angelo's doing? But he'd said she had twenty-four hours!

"Do you have the painting, *cara*?"

At the small shake of her head, he began to drag her from the room. She made a noise from the back of her throat, and he stopped, fingers tightening. "Remember what I said about the shooter?"

She pulled at his hands, begging the man without words to let her speak.

"Make enough sound for him to hear you," he whispered. "And you both die."

When the hand finally left her mouth, she sucked in a deep breath, then whispered, "I was set up! I don't have the painting. But I have a recording of another person admitting to taking it."

"Something you can share with Bonetti when we get to him. Now, let's move quietly to the car. It's on the other side of the woods."

He tugged her toward the bedroom door, and her throat closed. He was going to take her, and if she alerted Erik, he'd die.

Her mind moved a million miles a minute. She couldn't let him get her into a car. He said he was taking her to Angelo, but what if Angelo ignored her pleas of innocence again? She didn't have the recording with her!

"Wait!" she whispered. "I need my insulin."

He stopped and his brows flickered. "What?"

"I'll need to take it in an hour. If I don't, I pass out, and then I won't be any help to Angelo." She breathed through her lie. "Angelo wants me awake to answer questions, doesn't he?" She'd taken her dose in the car when they'd gotten drive-thru burgers, but he didn't know that. "It's right here in my bedside table."

"Fine," he growled. "You have ten seconds."

She hurried to the bedside table, intentionally opening the wrong drawer and pretending to look through it. When she found the small stone, she absently placed it on the bed, pretending to continue her search. She opened the next drawer and grabbed an insulin pen, which she pushed into her pocket.

"That's all you need?" he asked.

She nodded.

He wrapped his fingers around her upper arm so tightly, she winced, then he tugged her through to the back door. When he dragged her toward the opposite side of the property from Erik's home, all she wanted to do was fight and scream and battle for her freedom. But that would just get her knocked out and Erik shot. She needed the protection of the woods. Somewhere to run and hide.

Her hands trembled as they walked, the insulin heavy in her pocket. Tonight, it was the closest to a weapon she was going to get. It was a needle, and if she used it correctly, it could help her get away.

She worked hard to control her breathing as he moved through the trees. Once they were in the densest section, she slowed, lagging just slightly behind him.

"Hurry up," he growled, tugging her forward.

In one fluid move, she pulled the syringe from her pocket, uncapped it, and plunged it into Marco's right eye before tugging it out.

He cursed, his hand dropping from her arm to grab at his face.

Hannah ran.

⸺

"HE'S STILL NOT ANSWERING," Chandler said quietly.

Erik's muscles tensed. Chandler had been trying to contact Angelo on any line he could find for the guy, but the asshole wasn't picking up.

After speaking to the police at the hotel, he was sure they'd also make contact with Angelo, particularly if they found James with his painting, but that wasn't enough, dammit. They needed to make contact *now*.

"So we just wait?" Erik growled, the words tasting like acid in his mouth.

"Hang on. I'm hacking into his phone records to see who he's been in contact with."

Erik ran a hand through his hair, his pulse drumming at the base of his neck. He fucking hated this. He wanted any and all threats to Hannah eliminated.

After too many goddamn minutes, Chandler cursed.

A vein throbbed in Erik's temple. "What is it?"

"Angelo's been in contact with Marco several times in the last twenty-four hours."

Blood roared between Erik's ears, and he scanned around the area.

That's when he saw it...a gun, glinting in the moonlight from behind a tree.

He turned away quickly, rage moving through his veins like acid.

Half a second later, he spun, whipping out his pistol and firing three times at his target. Then he crashed into the house.

"Hannah?"

Silence. And that silence was so fucking loud, it deafened him.

He took off down the hall, scanning the living room and kitchen as he went before finally running into her bedroom. The light was on, but the room was empty. A quick check of the walk-in closet and bathroom told him he was alone.

His heart pounded against his ribs as he returned to the bedroom where his gaze stopped on something he'd missed at first glance. The drawer in her bedside table where she kept everything for her diabetes was open…

But it was the small stone on the bed that caught his attention. The one he'd given to Hannah by the river.

That was intentional.

The woods… Marco had taken her through the fucking woods.

Erik was moving before the thought had fully formed in his head. Outside, the soft ground sank beneath his feet, and wind slapped his face as he ran. He ignored it all, focusing on one thing. *Her*. If Marco had harmed a fucking hair on Hannah's head, he was going to tear the asshole apart piece by piece.

Erik knew these woods. He'd grown up in these woods. If they were here, he'd find them.

Chapter Thirty-One

Hannah's fingers tightened around the insulin pen. It was covered in blood, and that blood ran down her arm, making her want to be sick. A choked sob tried to break free from her chest. A sob at the bullets she'd heard in the distance. Three. Had they been for Erik?

Her foot caught on a rock and she almost stumbled, barely righting herself.

She pushed down the emotions. The dread and anxiety that tried to drown her. She couldn't think about that right now. She had to believe that Erik was okay. That he'd spotted the shooter and got him first.

The water grew louder. Usually, the sound would make her break out in a cold sweat, but right now she welcomed it. Beelined toward it. Because the sound of running water was loud in the quiet night. And she needed loud so that any noise she made would be drowned out.

But that wasn't the only reason she was heading for the water. This is where Erik had given her that stone. She just had to pray he'd find it and make the connection.

Her foot caught on another rock, and again, she barely caught herself.

Everything in her had screamed to run back home to Erik, but that would have left her open, an easy target for a bullet. This was the safest plan. The trees were the best cover.

She worked hard to control her breathing. How much time had passed? Five minutes? Ten?

Suddenly, she heard the faint sound of footsteps. Then his voice.

"Get the hell out here, you fucking bitch, or I start shooting!"

Another stumble. This time she caught herself on a tree, skirting behind it so she stood almost on the water's bank. There was anger in Marco's voice, but also pain. And he sounded close. So much closer than she'd been hoping.

"I can't believe you stabbed me in the fucking eye!" he shouted.

Yesterday, she wouldn't have believed it either, but drive a person to desperation and there was a lot they could do.

"You know I'm going to find you, right?" His breaths were short and loud. "And I'm going to make sure you suffer for this."

She closed her eyes, begging her shaking limbs to still.

More rustling of wet leaves sounded, then a thud, almost as if he'd tripped. "When you die at Angelo's hand," Marco continued, "if Erik lives through the night, he'll be a wreck. He'll have no idea I was part of this, and he'll come running back to his old friend Marco with a fuck-the-government attitude."

Her hands fisted. The asshole was underestimating Erik. If she died, he'd find every person responsible and make sure they paid.

Her heart nearly seized when he passed her tree. For a

handful of seconds, she held her breath, afraid even the subtle sound of air moving through her lungs was too loud.

But it didn't matter, because Marco whipped around and pointed a gun at her head.

Out of reflex, she threw her hand forward to stab him with the pen a second time, but he grabbed her wrist, his fingers tightening to the point she cried out and the syringe dropped.

He spun her around so her back was against his chest, the muzzle of the pistol pressed to her skull. "I should just fucking kill you now for being a bitch."

His chest was moving fast against her back, and when he stepped forward, he stumbled. Her heart skipped a beat. What if he accidentally pulled the trigger?

He took two more steps, then stopped—but this time, it was for a different reason. A noise in the distance. A quiet scuffling of footsteps.

Her heart skipped a beat.

Erik.

Suddenly, Marco moved toward the river, obviously coming to the same conclusion. A new panic welled inside Hannah. One that had her vision tunneling.

She kicked and screamed, trying to throw a foot into his leg, an elbow into his gut. Nothing worked.

Her belly dipped when he stopped right on the edge. "No, stop! I can't swim! Throw me in there and I'll drown!"

The water ran quickly and made every part of her come alive in fear.

"You'll figure it out."

She didn't have time to process his words before she was lifted from her feet and thrown into the icy water.

ERIK'S FEET pounded the soft, uneven ground. Every second that passed was a second too long.

Even though it was nighttime, the moon cast a dull glow over the woods. It was still dark, but he didn't mind. In fact, he welcomed the darkness. He knew these woods and Marco didn't—that could only benefit him.

Suddenly, a distant voice sounded.

Marco.

Erik took off toward the sound, pushing his body to run faster than he'd ever run before. His arms pumped, branches lashing his body, scraping against his skin.

The scream that pierced the air next had the fear in his chest expanding, choking him, blackening out everything but Hannah.

He'd almost reached the river when the splash of water made a fresh wave of terror fill his lungs. The second he reached the bank, he saw her. She'd grabbed onto a boulder in the center of the river, but the current was strong, and she barely seemed to have a grasp on it.

"Hannah?" He kicked off his shoes, preparing to jump in.

Her head bobbed above the water. "Marco…!" Her attention flew to his left.

Erik turned his head just as a gun fired. The bullet hit the tree beside his head, and Erik dropped and rolled behind it, knowing a second shot would come.

His gaze flicked to the water. Hannah's head was still bobbing up and down.

Fuck, he had to end this quickly.

Marco'd had a clear shot—and he'd missed. That *never* happened. Was he injured? If he was, Erik needed to use that to his advantage.

"Show your fucking face or I start shooting the water, Hunter."

His stomach clenched. He looked at Hannah again. This

time her head went down…and it didn't come back up for too damn long.

"I'm shooting!" Marco yelled, his words slurring slightly.

Erik gritted his teeth and dropped to the prone position. He eased his head out from behind the tree.

The second he saw Marco's arm extend, weapon in hand, Erik fired, getting the asshole in the forearm.

Marco released a loud curse, the gun dropping from his hand as his arm disappeared. Erik rose and raced forward. Before he could get another shot off, Marco lunged from the other side of the tree and wrapped his arms around Erik's middle, sending them both crashing to the ground.

Marco grabbed Erik's wrist, slamming it into the dirt above his head. Erik spared one glance at the guy's bloodied right eye before headbutting the asshole and following it up with an elbow to the face. They rolled. He easily overpowered Marco, aiming his gun.

"Don't you fucking—"

He pulled the trigger, cutting off Marco's words with a bullet to the head.

He didn't stick around to watch the life leave his eyes, instead turning back to Hannah.

Only, she wasn't on the rock anymore.

A depth of fear he'd never felt in his life seized his limbs. Then he was running. Racing down the bank, leaping over rocks and tree roots. When he finally spotted her, she was being swept away by the current.

He ran faster, pushing himself to beat the current and only slowing when he was in line with her.

He dove into the river. Cold blasted his body but he barely felt it, instead putting all his focus on swimming toward her.

The second he was within reaching distance, he wrapped an arm around her waist. She coughed uncontrollably, her lungs crackling with water.

"Breathe, Hannah!" he shouted, rolling her to her back so her head was on his shoulder. "I'm getting us out of here."

The current was strong. He swam as hard as he could toward the bank, and the moment he could stand, he did so with Hannah in his arms.

As soon as they were on land, he lay her down and rolled her to her side, hating how damn cold she was and the coughs that still racked her body. "Breathe, Angel."

She choked and spluttered. It took a few minutes, but her chest finally stilled. "Erik." She reached for him, and he tugged her tightly against his chest.

"I'm here, Angel. You're safe."

Chapter Thirty-Two

Erik watched the slight tightening of Hannah's eyelids. He'd been up for hours, unable to sleep even though the night had been a late one. For the second time in as many months, police had come to her house, and so had paramedics. Hannah hadn't wanted to go to the hospital, but because of her diabetes and what stress could do to blood sugar, they'd pushed her to go anyway.

Fortunately, she hadn't had to stay the entire night and was resting in his bed now. Where she belonged.

His muscles tightened at the fact Marco had gotten his hands on her yet again. If it hadn't been for her quick thinking with the insulin pen, the way she'd attacked and run...

Fuck, he couldn't think about that.

A part of him wished she'd yelled for him when Marco had first grabbed her. But at the same time, he knew why she hadn't. That could have cost Erik his life.

Just like Marco, that shooter on her land was found dead.

A small hum sounded from her throat, then she rolled to her side. There was a quick batting of eyelids before she opened them fully.

She frowned at him. "How long have you been sitting there?"

"Not long enough." Wasn't a lie. He could watch this woman all day. Hell, after last night, it would take a damn army to get his eyes off her.

She slid a hand beneath her cheek.

He ran a finger down her shoulder and arm, loving the tremble through her limb at his touch. "How are you feeling?"

"Like yesterday wasn't real. Like it was a nightmare I've just woken up from."

"It *was* a nightmare. But it's over now."

"But Angelo's still—"

"Chandler made sure he got the recording, and the police know what he did. We still need to keep an eye out for Angelo though. Men like him don't leave proof when they hire people like Marco to do their dirty work, so I doubt he'll do time. But he may be pissed we told the police about him."

If Erik ever saw the asshole around Hannah again, the guy was as good as dead.

She swallowed, gaze shifting between his eyes. "I'm sorry about Marco."

"I'm not."

Her brows flickered. "He was your friend."

"No. He was a work colleague. A man I knew was dangerous. A man I knew could easily tip to the other side." He should have known better than to ever be even remotely friendly with the guy.

"Still, I'm sorry. And I'm sorry that it's happened so close to Christmas."

"The only thing I need to do for Christmas is be with you."

Her smile softened. She took his hand and pressed a kiss to his palm. He felt those lips everywhere, even deep inside the little crevasses of his heart he didn't know were waiting to be filled.

He grazed the pad of his thumb over her bottom lip. "Thank you for fighting last night. If he'd gotten you in his car…"

He could have lost her. And then he would have had to tear down the world to find her.

"It was just lucky I was able to convince him to let me grab my pen."

"Not lucky. Smart."

A small smile stretched her lips. "So, my diabetes kind of saved the day."

"*You* saved the day, Angel." Because she was all strength.

Her eyes softened, and she opened her mouth to say something, but his watch beeped and when he looked down, he frowned.

"What is it?" she asked, pushing up onto her elbow.

"Someone just pulled into my driveway."

"Who?"

He lifted his phone from the bedside table and clicked into his cameras. The muscles in his forearms knotted when he saw a Bugatti stop by his front door.

Angelo climbed out, two other suited men coming around to his side.

Erik stood, air hissing from his teeth.

"Erik—"

"Stay here, Hannah. I'll be back in a second."

He moved out of the room, closing the bedroom door before heading down the stairs. The fury in his chest threatened to overflow into violence. Fury that the asshole would dare show his face here after what he'd done.

He moved into his office and opened his safe, then pulled out a pistol.

When he opened his front door, he aimed his gun at Angelo's chest. "What do you want?"

The men behind him reached for the guns in their holsters.

Erik wasn't scared—he could shoot all three men in under a second.

But Angelo held a hand up and they stopped. "I am just here to talk."

"Yeah? And did you just send Marco Salvatore to Hannah's home last night to fucking talk?"

"That is what I would like to explain. Is Hannah here?"

"You think I'm gonna let you anywhere near her?"

"How else will I apologize?"

Erik could have laughed. "You want to apologize for sending a fucking hit man after her?"

"May we come in?"

"No." And he wasn't lowering his fucking weapon either.

"Mr. Hunter. Please."

The fuck was wrong with this guy? "Go. Before I give in to the voice in my head that's telling me you need to die."

Angelo sighed. "If you do not let me in, I will find her another time. I am a man of honor, and when I wrong someone, I make it a point to right that wrong."

"Anyone touches her, and I cut off their fucking hand."

Movement sounded upstairs, and Erik wanted to growl.

"Mr. Hunter—" Angelo tried again.

"Get off my land!" Erik shouted.

Fast footsteps were loud on the stairs…then her voice. "What are you doing here?"

His muscles tightened, his gut twisting at the sound of Hannah's voice behind him.

HANNAH ROSE and pulled on some track pants and a T-shirt. Thank God Erik had grabbed some comfy clothes from her house last night. She needed comfort right now.

A shudder raced down her spine at the thought of everything that had happened. The stolen painting. The bar fight. The attack from Marco.

Dead. Marco was dead because Erik had killed him to protect her. It didn't feel real.

She lifted her phone and sent a text to Brigid. She hadn't yet told her friends what had happened when she'd gotten home last night. Not only because it had been late, but Brigid was already dealing with everything that had taken place in Seattle.

Hannah: Hey, Brig, just wanted to check that you're doing okay. X

Three dots popped up, then disappeared. Her heart gave a little sad thump, then the response came.

Brigid: Yeah, I'm doing okay. Henry's cheering me up with chocolate chip pancakes and mimosas.

She laughed. That sounded like Henry. She was about to respond when a raised voice sounded downstairs.

Her brows flickered. Erik.

Quietly, she opened the bedroom door and crept to the top of the stairs.

"Mr. Hunter—"

"Get off my land!"

She jolted. Oh God, it was Angelo.

Without thinking, she rushed down the stairs, needing to know Erik was okay.

She stopped at the base as Angelo's gaze hit her from beyond the front door.

"What are you doing here?" she whispered, not even sure her words crossed the space.

"Get back upstairs, Hannah," Erik said, not taking his gaze from Angelo.

"I am here to apologize," Angelo said, seemingly unfazed by the gun in his face. "I explained to Mr. Hunter that if I do not apologize now, I will simply do so later. I always repay my debts."

"The fuck you will," Erik hissed.

She swallowed, then slowly crossed to Erik.

"Hannah—"

"Are you here to hurt either of us?" she asked, cutting off whatever Erik had been about to say.

"No. I give you my word. I will even come in alone if you wish."

She touched Erik's back. "We need to let him in. I don't want to be looking over my shoulder every time I go out, searching for him."

For a moment, Erik was silent, then he growled. "Fine. But your men stay outside, and so do any weapons."

"I am unarmed."

Erik didn't look like he believed him, but he lowered his gun and wrapped an arm around Hannah, pulling her back to give Angelo space. "You have two minutes to say whatever you want to say."

Angelo dipped his chin, then turned to his men. "Wait at the car for me."

In the living room, Angelo took a seat on the recliner, looking so at home, anyone would think this place was his. Hannah perched on the edge of the couch while Erik remained standing beside her, gun still in hand at his side.

"I have come here to apologize, Miss Jacobs. I am sorry for not believing you when you told me you didn't take my painting."

Hannah swallowed. There was a ring of sincerity in his voice. But even if he was sorry, that didn't take away from what he'd done. "You sent Marco to hurt me."

"No." His response was immediate. "I sent Marco to acquire the painting."

"But if she didn't have the painting?" Erik bit out.

"Then he was to bring her to me, but not hurt her."

Erik's fingers visibly tightened on the weapon. "And what would you have done to her?"

Hannah swallowed, almost dreading the answer.

"I would have learned the truth the hard way."

The hard way for Hannah…

A shudder rolled down her spine.

Angelo's gaze shifted back to Hannah. "I cannot simply do nothing when something is stolen from me. But I *am* sorry. It was a mistake on my part. I should have listened to you. To show my remorse, I have spread word to everyone I know that you are the best agent to sell their properties. I know some very successful businessmen. You should receive a great amount of work from this."

Her brow furrowed. "I really don't want to sell properties for people who are—"

"They are clean." Angelo rose, and she did too. "I believe that my time is up. I hope you both have a lovely afternoon."

He was halfway to the door when she spoke. "Angelo, what are you going to do about James?"

He stopped and turned, and for a moment, he almost looked like a different man. The anger…the hard edge…it was meant to incite fear, and it did. "He is not your concern. He is *mine*."

The fine hairs on her arms stood on end. Even though James deserved whatever happened to him, she couldn't help but feel just a bit of sympathy for the guy.

The door closed and Erik waited until the car left his driveway before moving to his office with his gun. When he returned, his hands were empty, and he slid his arms around her waist. "If I ever see that asshole again, I'm shooting."

She dipped her head, James still firmly on her mind. "I know James made his bed, but I'm scared for him. And also for Brigid."

Erik's jaw visibly clenched. "The asshole framed you. He

didn't care about what happened to you or Brigid. He doesn't deserve your sympathy."

"I know." She skimmed her hands down his chest, forcing the other man out of her head. "So, what are we doing today?"

Without warning, she was lifted from her feet. She yelped.

"You're staying in bed."

She laughed as she skimmed her hands over his shoulders, feeling every ridge and muscle beneath the shirt. "Really? And will you be staying with me?"

"After last night, I'm not leaving your side for a fucking month."

In his bedroom, he lowered her to the mattress. He was about to rise, but she pulled him back down. "Hey. You said you weren't leaving."

"I need to get food into you, Angel," he said softly. It was the only soft thing about him.

He was right. She needed to eat something. She also had some calls to make. Firstly, to Reuben. But right now, she needed something else. "Kiss me first."

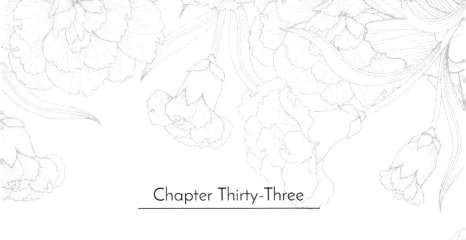

Chapter Thirty-Three

Hannah grinned as she hung up the phone. Two weeks had passed since Angelo's visit, and the listings had not stopped rolling in. Every day she got more homes to sell, to the point she was having to offer some to Taylor and Reuben. And they weren't small homes. They were big, expensive, make-months'-worth-of-income-in-one-commission kind of homes.

Christmas had come and gone. It had been a quiet holiday with her still recovering from everything that had happened. In a few weeks it would be her birthday, so they'd decided to do a bigger celebration then. His family had even invited her over for dinner. She couldn't wait to celebrate with a real family for the first time in…God, forever. It had always just been her and Nico when she was young.

Even though they hadn't celebrated Christmas, Erik had still given her a gift in the form of a car. Yes. A freaking car! Her eyes had almost fallen out of her damn head when he'd taken her outside and shown her. And not some cheap, second-hand car. A brand-new Genesis G70. He'd claimed it was a safety thing.

A knock sounded on the door of her office, pulling her out

of her thoughts. She looked up to see her boss leaning a shoulder against the frame. "How are you doing?"

"It's nonstop," she said, the excitement no doubt evident on her face. "It's great."

"Good. Remember, if it becomes too much, just ask for help."

Reuben had been great since everything had gone down with James, Marco, and Angelo. Offering her days off, insisting she take it easy, and shouldering the workload when she needed help. "Thank you. I got more inquiries today, so I'll probably direct a few more your and Taylor's way."

"Got it. Also, I've put out an ad for a replacement for James." Pain laced his quiet words. She knew he tried to hide it for her sake, but the two men had been friends. He'd trusted James. And a part of her thought he felt guilty, like he should have seen what was going on.

"Sounds great, Reuben."

He nodded. "Okay. I'm going to grab a coffee. Want anything?"

"No, thanks. Erik will be here any minute with lunch." And hopefully a coffee too. She was dying for some caffeine.

"Say hi to him for me."

He'd just stepped out when the text dinged on her phone.

Erik: Leaving Black Bean now. Rita threw in some pancakes and Norman forced an iced latte into my hand. That's in addition to the lavender oat latte I already have. Hope you're ready.

Oh, she was ready for all of that. Hell, she was salivating just reading it.

Hannah: Get your ass here now, Hunter.

Word had spread around town pretty quickly that she'd been attacked in her own home and almost drowned. Erik's family had come over to check on her, and she didn't think she'd ever received a hug as hard as Jennifer Hunter's embrace that night. They'd slipped her into their family so easily, and there wasn't a day that passed that she wasn't grateful. She hadn't had a family for so long, it felt foreign. The good kind of foreign. The kind you grabbed onto with two hands because you didn't want it to slip away.

She swallowed at the memory of telling Brigid and Henry what had happened with Marco. She'd never seen their eyes so wide.

Then, after the shock, she'd seen something else in Brigid's eyes…fear. No doubt fear for James and what would happen to him. They'd been together for over four years. Of course she was worried.

Hannah hadn't heard anything about James, and if she was honest, she hoped she didn't. He'd either continue running or he'd be caught, and that was on him.

With a sigh, she turned to her computer and responded to a couple more emails. When she rose and moved to her filing cabinet, slotting in some papers, an arm slid around her waist.

She gasped—then recognized the scent. Familiar and woodsy and home. Yeah, he'd begun to smell like home.

She leaned back into him. "I didn't hear you come in."

The sound Erik made was somewhere between a hum and a growl. "You should have kept the buzzer system." He kissed her neck, and a tremble ran down her spine.

She turned and met those beautiful eyes. "We don't need it now that the danger's gone."

Another sound reverberated from his chest. "Safety is always needed."

She looked down at the carrier of coffees and bag in his hand. "Oh God. That all smells incredible."

His mouth went to her neck. "*You* smell incredible."

When he began to nip and tease her skin, she groaned and grabbed onto his shoulders. "Erik…"

"Mm."

His teeth grazed her neck, causing goose bumps to rise over her flesh.

"We can't," she gasped out. "Reuben's just gone out for a quick coffee, and Taylor's at a client meeting. They could both be back any second."

This time, he groaned.

She laughed. "When we get home, you can kiss me all you want, wherever you want."

Another nip. "Fine. But then I get you all night."

Fire danced in her belly. God, now she was desperate for the day to be over.

When he stepped away, her hands twitched to pull him back. To say screw it and risk her job for a moment with him… then she remembered the coffee.

Erik lowered the drinks to the table, then the bag. "I got some turkey sandwiches and the pancakes from Rita."

Her stomach growled, and she would have been embarrassed if she wasn't so dang hungry. "Turkey sandwiches with a side of pancakes are just what I need." She looked into the bag. "Hang on, there are no napkins. I'll grab some from the kitchen."

She moved into the small office kitchen. She was just about to step back into the hall when the front door opened.

She stopped before reaching her office, the blood draining from her face.

James.

Oh God, he looked awful. His face was black and blue with bruises. His clothes were torn and dirty, like he'd been in them for days, and…was that blood on his shirt? Specks of it were sprinkled across his clothes.

One hand was behind his back, but the other was wrapped in bandages, with more dried blood seeping through. His fingers almost looked like…stumps.

"James…are you—"

He pulled his other hand out to reveal a gun—a gun that he pointed directly at her chest.

Her world stopped, every sound fading to silence around her as a low buzzing took its place.

"You sent Brigid to talk to me, didn't you?" he growled. "Then you reported back to Bonetti."

Suddenly, Erik was in front of her, his hand shoving her back. "What the hell are you doing here?"

James stepped toward the hall, gun still aimed, the piercing intensity in his eyes never wavering. "I just needed some goddamn money! You were doing so fucking well. Getting all the best listings. So I made a deal with Ezra to badmouth you to clients. They went to him, and he gave me a percentage of every commission."

Her lips parted, shock rendering her still.

"But it wasn't enough," James bit out. "The percentage was too low, and you were still getting clients that *I* should have gotten. I even sent a man to your house to fucking end you so I could have the few homes you had left!"

Her heart thrashed in her chest, and Erik's entire body tensed.

"That was you?" she whispered.

"Desperation will turn even the best of men, Hannah." He stepped closer. "When you were talking about losing Angelo's account, a better idea came to me."

"You framed me." Saying that out loud still hurt, even after she'd had time to come to terms with it. "You didn't care what Angelo did to me, just as long as you got your money."

"You don't realize what you're capable of until the alternative is a price you aren't willing to pay."

"What did they do to you?" she whispered, studying his bloodied hand again. His black and blue face.

James took another step, and Erik shoved her toward her office door. "He found me. Fucking tortured me for days until I gave up the location of the painting—then cut off my goddamn *fingers* as punishment! All because *you* gave them the recording!"

Nausea came alive in her belly. The stumps…those were what remained of his fingers. God, she was going to be sick.

"We did nothing to you," Erik said quietly.

"Wrong! You diverted Angelo's attention to me!" James yelled, little specks of spit shooting from his mouth. "Now he has his fucking painting, and I have even less than before I took it! I can only sit and wait until my dealer finds me and finishes me off!" Another step forward. "But not before you pay for your part in making me a dead man. Both of you."

———

ERIK WORKED HIS JAW. He wanted to kick his own ass for not carrying today.

He pushed Hannah closer to her office. "You need to calm down and lower the weapon."

"Actually, I don't. I'm as good as dead, so I'm taking the fuckers responsible with me."

There were so many damn things Erik wanted to say to that, top of the list being that it was no one's fault but James's that he was in the position he was in. But the guy was no longer stable. There was no reasoning with him.

"I'll pay your drug debt," Erik said quietly.

James's brows pinched. "You're lying."

"No. I'm not. I've got the money, and all I want is Hannah's safety. Lower that gun, and I'll write the check to you right now."

There was no way Erik was actually doing that. The asshole would just spend it on drugs and be back for more. All he needed was the pistol lowered so Erik could disarm him.

For a second, James seemed to consider it. Hope danced in

his eyes, lighting the dark brown depths. His fingers even seemed to loosen on the weapon.

Then the door opened behind him.

James cursed and turned, firing blindly at Reuben.

The second the man was distracted, Erik shoved Hannah into the office and lunged.

James swung the gun back around. Mid-swing, Erik grabbed his arm and kicked him into the wall. The pistol dropped. James attempted to punch Erik, but he dodged the feeble attempt. A second punch. Erik dodged again, then followed up with an elbow to James's face.

James reared back.

Erik punched him two more times in the face. The man stumbled, narrowly missing the third hit. Erik saw the knife half a second before it slashed at his stomach.

He reared back, avoiding the blade.

Sirens sounded from somewhere in the distance. Erik let everything fade but the man in front of him.

James slashed the knife at Erik's abdomen again. He twisted, grabbing James's wrist and spinning him, his back pressed to Erik's front. He forced the knife an inch from James's throat, easily overpowering him.

"Get the fuck off me!" James yelled. He tried to pull away, but Erik pressed the knife firmly to his flesh, not breaking skin but close.

He lowered his voice so his words only reached James's ears. "In a second, the police will be here. They will arrest you for attempted murder. And every part of that is on *you*. Do you understand?"

When James didn't immediately respond, Erik pressed the knife harder to his throat, just breaking the surface.

James growled, his breaths short. "I understand."

Erik shoved him forward, releasing him just as the door flew open. Police rushed in, and the second they had James,

Erik turned to find Hannah had left the office and was running back from the kitchen with a towel in hand, eyes on Reuben. When she reached him, she pressed the towel to his side.

Paramedics came next, and as soon as they took over with Reuben, Erik tugged Hannah up and into his arms.

"There's so much blood!" she gasped, her gaze never leaving her boss.

Erik pressed his palm to her cheek and pulled her face toward him. "There's nothing more you can do. They're looking after him." She opened and closed her mouth a couple times, then suddenly her hands raced over his chest like she was searching for injuries.

"What about you?" she gasped. "Are you okay?"

"I'm okay." He gripped her hips and tugged her closer. His heart beat so fast that he wondered if it would break fucking free. But that wasn't because of the altercation. It was because if he hadn't come here today, it would have been just her and James, and the asshole had been planning to kill her.

His chest compressed to the point he almost couldn't get air. "You need to lock these damn doors," he whispered.

She lay her head on his chest. "Thank God you were here."

Erik wrapped his arms tightly around her, swearing he'd never let go.

Chapter Thirty-Four

Warmth cocooned Hannah, making her want to sink deeper into the bed. No, not just the bed. Into the warm arms of Erik.

God, she loved waking with him at her back.

She rolled around to face him, his arm never leaving her side. His eyes were closed, and his chest rose and fell in even succession.

Beautiful. So beautiful, she wanted to trace every inch of his face. Cast it to memory and never forget it.

He'd been doing a lot of hovering over the last couple weeks. And truth be told, she loved it. Having him close not only made her feel safe but at peace. She'd come to terms with that. That Erik was her sanctuary. Her safe place. And everything she'd been missing up to this point.

She hadn't seen her friends much since the events in her office, and, if she was honest with herself, she was worried about Brigid. Her friend had been more distant than ever since James tried to kill Hannah and Erik. He'd been charged with attempted murder. From what Erik had told her, there was a chance at bail, but it had been set too high for James to afford it.

If she could have a redo, she never would have asked for Brigid's help with the painting. She would have found another way. But if there was anything she knew with absolute certainty, it was that you couldn't turn back time.

With a soft sigh, she shuffled to get out of Erik's arms, but they suddenly tightened, and his eyes popped open.

She frowned. The man didn't look tired at all. "How long have you been awake?"

"Not long enough." He lowered his head and kissed her, and immediately she moaned, her hands sliding up his chest, feet tangling with his. His day-old stubble brushed against her cheek, causing her skin to tingle.

When they finally came up for air, she stared into his hazel eyes, knowing she could so easily get lost in them.

"Happy twenty-fourth birthday, Angel."

Her lips tugged into a smile. "Thank you. I'm excited to spend tonight with your family."

She'd never spent a birthday with anyone resembling a family. Only ever Nico and her friends.

"They're excited too. And so am I." He swiped his thumb over her bare hip, causing a shudder to race down her spine. "Mom's been calling nonstop, demanding to know your favorite foods and present ideas."

"Ideas? Plural? She doesn't need to get me anything."

He laughed, and that sound did things to her insides even she didn't understand. "She knows that, but she loves to spoil people. She tends to go a bit overboard."

She shifted her hand to his jaw, running her thumb over his stubble "Are you sure you don't mind driving over to Bellevue with me this morning? I'm happy to go on my own."

Visiting Nico's grave on her birthday felt right, seeing as when he was alive, he'd spent every birthday with her since she was a kid.

"I want to go with you," Erik rasped softly.

"It's a two-hour drive."

Another swipe of his fingers on her flesh. "Luckily, I like spending time with you."

She knew it was a joke but couldn't even muster a smile. "Thank you. It will be nice having someone with me. Nico didn't have a lot of friends, so I don't think he gets many visitors. I wish you'd been able to meet him."

Would Erik have seen what she had? That Nico was good at heart, despite making some bad decisions?

"I wish I'd gotten to meet him too, Angel." He grazed her cheek. "Can I give you your present now?"

She cocked her head. "I told you. No presents. You already bought me a car for Christmas."

After that, the man didn't need to get her a gift ever again.

He leaned forward. "There was no way you weren't getting a birthday present from me today."

He kissed her before rolling out of bed and moving out of the room. When he returned, there were two wrapped presents in his hands, one smaller and one larger.

She cocked her head. "You got me two?"

"Technically one. The larger present is less a birthday gift and more something I always planned to buy you but wasn't sure if you'd accept. Now that it's a birthday present, you have no choice."

Her brows flickered. "Tricky."

He handed her the larger present, and she slowly unwrapped it. Her mouth dropped open at the boxes inside. It was a Dexcom continuous glucose monitor and an Omnipod insulin pump. There was also a printout of the insurance he'd purchased for the kit.

She shook her head. "No. Erik, I can't accept another expensive gift."

It was nothing compared to the car, but still way too much.

"I'm not taking it back, Hannah. Your health isn't something I'm willing to compromise on."

She swallowed, emotion clogging her throat. It would make her life and tracking her health so much easier. She'd always told herself she couldn't miss what she'd never had, but the truth was, she'd craved these items for the simple fact that they'd make her diabetes easier to manage.

She dropped the boxes and leaned into his chest, wrapping her arms around him. "Thank you, Erik."

Thank you didn't seem like enough. But right now, it was all she had.

He didn't hesitate, pulling her close and pressing a kiss to her head.

She straightened and lifted the second box, almost not wanting to open it. He'd already given her too much.

Inside, she found a small jewelry bag. She opened it and tipped the contents onto her hand—and the second she saw it, her heart thumped.

"An angel," she whispered.

He took it from her palm and gently attached it to her bracelet. "Because you're *my* Angel. Have been since the first day I laid eyes on you."

Tears glistened in her eyes, and she traced her finger across the small charm. Nico had given her his charm on her birthday too. "Thank you. It's beautiful."

The bracelet, which had already been priceless to her, just became that much more important. She leaned over and kissed Erik. A long, slow kiss.

"I actually got something for you too."

His brows slashed together. "It's your birthday, not mine."

"I know. It was actually supposed to be your Christmas present, but with everything that happened, I didn't organize it in time."

She climbed off the bed and moved to a drawer, then

pulled out the gift. She nibbled her bottom lip as he opened it and took out the item.

"A bowl?"

"Well…it's more than that. It's a Japanese art called kintsugi, which basically means joining with gold." She leaned over and traced one of the powdered gold cracks in the porcelain. "They take something broken and restore it. Set all the pieces back together. Then the scars and flaws are celebrated. The gold in the cracks are symbols for light."

She looked up, and there was something she couldn't identify in his gaze. Something hot and intense. "Are you telling me there's beauty in my scars?"

"Beauty. And strength. And a lesson…that what has been broken, can always be repaired."

His eyes turned black. "*You* repaired me."

She shook her head. "No. We repair because we *choose* to repair. We choose to make art with our broken pieces."

The way he looked at her…it made her burn. It made the very air she needed to survive become stuck in her chest.

He set the gift to the side and tugged her into his arms once more. "God, I love you."

"I love you more."

Then he kissed her and set her world ablaze.

Chapter Thirty-Five

Erik kept Hannah's hand firmly in his as he drove to Sunset Hills Memorial Park. They were almost there, and with each passing minute, he felt the soberness in Hannah. This was important to her. Nico was important to her.

"Tell me about him," Erik asked quietly.

Her lips curved into a smile. "A lot of people didn't like him. I think he was kicked out of half a dozen schools growing up. But he was always kind to me. He had a good heart, and most people didn't take the time to try to see that heart."

"But you did." It wasn't a question.

"Yeah. He showed me. First, in the little things he did. Like making sure I was always fed when our foster mother was too sick or tired to prepare food. Watching over me when we went to the same school so no one bullied me. Then with..."

When she stopped, he pressed. "What did he help you with?" He wanted to know every fragment and detail of this woman's life.

"After what happened with my foster father, the one who assaulted me...he was there for me."

His muscles tensed. There was more to that story.

She shook her head, like she was trying to erase the memory. "We shouldn't talk about that today."

Questions crawled up his throat. Questions he needed answers to. He pushed them down, not wanting to press her to speak words she wasn't ready to share yet. But soon, he wanted to know everything.

He tightened his hold on her hand. "What's in the bag?"

The corners of her lips tugged up again. "I always bring a packet of Oreos and milk. We used to sit there and dunk the Oreos while we watched the clouds in our foster mother's backyard. It was our thing. So I bring some and eat them with him while I watch the clouds. I also bring him a new game. He was a mad gamer."

"Did you play with him?"

"Oh yeah. I was awesome."

His lips twitched. "You're telling me we could have been gaming all this time?"

"I don't usually play against guys who aren't Nico. They have fragile egos and don't cope well with loss."

"I don't lose, Angel."

"That's what they all say before I annihilate them."

Why the fuck did that make his dick twitch?

"Hey, can I ask you something?" she asked softly.

His gut twisted at the change in her tone. "Anything."

"I've been thinking a bit about..." She paused.

Another twist. "What is it?"

"Kids."

His throat closed at the thought of having kids with Hannah. At the idea of her stomach swelling with his child. Then at the way the images suddenly became something ugly...

The fear was instant and soul-destroying. It dug its claws into his chest, squeezing his damn heart.

"I just...I know you said you don't want them," she continued. "And I understand why. But do you think you'll ever change your mind?"

"No." The single word was out before he could stop it. And he regretted it instantly because he felt the shift in the air. The heaviness of her disappointment.

His hand tightened on the wheel. "Vicky and I didn't have a great relationship. And the day I planned to end our marriage, she told me she was pregnant before I could get the words out."

He paused, taking a moment to collect the pieces of memories that could darken even the brightest day.

"But the moment that baby started to grow, I loved them. And I vowed to make it work between me and Vick…for them." He swallowed the fucking lump in his throat. "I vowed to protect that child. And I failed. It's something I'll never forgive myself for, Hannah."

Her fingers tightened around his. "It wasn't your fault."

It was. Deep down, the only person he blamed was himself.

"But I understand," she added.

A part of him wondered if she did. He felt like a fucking asshole, making her choose between him and a child. But honestly, there was no part of him that felt capable of taking on the responsibility. The guilt over not protecting his unborn child raged inside him to this day. Yet he wasn't willing to walk away from Hannah so she could find someone who'd give her the family she craved.

Fuck, he was a selfish bastard.

He pulled into the lot and stopped the car. When he turned to look at her, it was to see her smile was too bright and nowhere close to reaching her eyes.

She sucked in a deep breath like she was pulling herself together. "Are you ready to meet the man who's the closest thing to family I ever had?" she asked softly.

He shifted some hair behind her ear, wanting to say more

about the kids thing, but he had no words that would make it better. "Yeah, Angel. I'm ready."

They climbed out, and he walked around the car to interlace his fingers with hers. She led them down a narrow path of graves before stopping in front of one.

Hannah's features softened as she ran her gaze over the small tombstone. "Hey, Nico. I wanted to spend the morning of my birthday with you. I hope that's okay. And I brought someone to introduce you to."

She lowered and lifted a framed photo from where it sat in front of the tomb. Using her sleeve, she scrubbed the dirt and dust off.

The second the two people came into view, Erik's world narrowed to pinpoint focus, darkness hedging his vision. In that moment, the world stopped.

It was a photo of Hannah standing beside a man Erik had seen before.

His gaze flicked back to the tombstone, reading over the name for the first time.

"Nicolas." The word was a whisper on his breath.

Hannah leaned into him. "Yeah. Only I called him Nico. His real name was—"

"Nicolas Spalder." A name Erik had heard before. Studied and cast to memory. Because this man had been a job. A threat.

And Erik had killed him.

Order book two in the Beautiful Pieces trilogy, ERIK'S REDEMPTION, now!

Also by Nyssa Kathryn

Jackson

Declan

Cole

Ryker

BEAUTIFUL PIECES

(series ongoing)

Erik's Salvation

Erik's Redemption

Erik's Refuge

JOIN my newsletter and be the first to find out about sales and new releases!

~https://www.nyssakathryn.com/vip-newsletter~

About the Author

Nyssa Kathryn is a romantic suspense author. She lives in South Australia with her daughter and hubby and takes every chance she can to be plotting and writing. Always an avid reader of romance novels, she considers alpha males and happily-ever-afters to be her jam.

Don't forget to follow Nyssa and never miss another release.

Facebook | Instagram | Amazon | Goodreads